Dark and Deepest Red

Also by

ANNA-MARIE McLEMORE

Blanca & Roja

Wild Beauty

When the Moon Was Ours

The Weight of Feathers

Dark and Deepest Red

ANNA-MARIE McLEMORE

Feiwel and Friends
New York

A FEIWEL AND FRIENDS BOOK

An imprint of Macmillan Publishing Group, LLC
120 Broadway, New York, NY 10271

DARK AND DEEPEST RED. Copyright © 2020 by Anna-Marie McLemore. All rights
reserved. Printed in the United States of America.

Our books may be purchased in bulk for promotional, educational, or business
use. Please contact your local bookseller or the Macmillan Corporate and
Premium Sales Department at (800) 221-7945 ext. 5442 or by email at
MacmillanSpecialMarkets@macmillan.com.

Library of Congress Control Number: 2019940845

ISBN 978-1-250-16274-8 (hardcover) / ISBN 978-1-250-16273-1 (ebook)

Book design by Liz Dresner

Feiwel and Friends logo designed by Filomena Tuosto

First edition, 2020

10 9 8 7 6 5 4 3 2 1

fiercereads.com

To my father, who taught me to love books in the first place

Cuando el camino es largo, hasta las zapatillas aprietan.
When the road is long, even slippers are tight.

—PERUVIAN PROVERB

Chacun sent le mieux où le soulier le blesse.
No one knows better where the shoe pinches than
she who wears it.

—FRENCH PROVERB

Dance in red shoes, but make sure they're the ones
you've made by hand.

—CLARISSA PINKOLA ESTÉS,
Women Who Run with the Wolves

Rosella

My mother told me once that being an Oliva meant measuring our lives in lengths of red thread. And probably, that was true.

But growing up in Briar Meadow meant I measured mine by the glimmer that appeared over the reservoir every year.

That was what they called the strangeness that settled onto our town for a week each October, a glimmer. Both for the wavering light that hovered above the water, and because it seemed like the right word for the flicker of magic that came with it.

One year, the glimmer stirred the air between neighbors who hated each other. Families who'd become enemies over fence lines and tree roots suddenly burst into each other's kitchens, trading long-secret recipes for tomato sauce or spice cookies.

Another year, it was icicles that tasted like rose candies. My mother and I ate them all week, licking them like paletas, and tried to save some in our freezer. When the glimmer left at the end of the week, we found them vanished from between the frozen peas and waffles, and managed to be surprised. (My abuela called us fools for thinking we could hold on to Briar Meadow's magic any longer than the glimmer let us.)

And once, it was the thorns on the trees and bushes around

town. They grew so fast even I could sit still long enough to watch them. The wood twisted into shapes, some simple as a corkscrew curl, others intricate as the figurine of a deer, others as sharp as little knives. Sometimes we woke up to find blood dripping down the points, and we couldn't be sure if someone had pricked their fingers, or if the thorns themselves were bleeding.

And maybe my mother was right about measuring our lives in red thread, because those drops of blood looked, to me, like the beads on the most beautiful shoes my family made. Red shoes, the kind everyone knew us for.

They bought other colors, of course, but it was the red ones that carried the whisper of a magic not so different from the glimmer. Our red shoes bore the hint of something forbidden and a little scandalous. Parents bought them for anxious brides, who then kissed their grooms with enough passion to make the wedding guests blush. Women had pairs made for class reunions, strutting into the tinsel-draped auditorium like queens. Husbands gave them to their wives before trips meant to celebrate twenty- or thirty-year anniversaries, and the couple always came back with their eyes glinting, as though they'd just met.

Well-crafted seams and delicate beading gave my family a trade and a living. But red shoes gave us a name. They made us infamous. They made us brazen.

Until they came for us.

Except that's not quite true.

They didn't come for us.

They came for me.

Strasbourg, 1507

The first time Lala catches Alifair on the land, he is stealing crab apples from a tree that belongs to her and her aunt. Though, as it turns out, he will come to be theirs far more than the tree, or the land, ever will. The crab apple tree, along with all others on the plot, belongs to them no more than the house, each paid for by the month.

When Lala and her aunt first arrived in Strasbourg, they found that the stature and upkeep of the shabby wattle and daub had been much exaggerated by the friend of a friend. Lala stood in the shade of the roof, staring into the house's face. The thatch hung so far past the walls that the whole structure seemed to be frowning.

We are new women here, Tante Dorenia told her. *We bring with us nothing of who we were.*

Nothing of who we were means Tante will not wear the dikhle, the pretty head covering of married women, not just because she is unmarried but because the gadje must find no sign that they are Romnia. It is for the same reason that Lala cannot even be called Lala, the name she has heard since the time she could speak. Now she is Lala only in Tante's house and in her own thoughts. Everywhere else she must be Lavinia, her full name, prim and uncomfortable as a starched dress.

Whenever Lala asks why they left the hills outside Riquewihr, left where they buried her mother and father, Tante says, *What we are, they have made it a crime in our own country. So we will go somewhere no one knows us.*

When Lala weeps for her mother and father, as though she might call them from across the weed-tangled land, Tante whispers, *We will always love them. We will mourn them. But we will not speak of them. We will hold them in our hearts but not on our tongues, yes? We will keep an altar for them and let their souls rest, will we not?*

To all this, Tante is quick to add, *We will not lose ourselves here. Because there is work we will do here. Not only for our vitsa, but for others.*

The day Alifair appears, Lala spots him first. She shrieks a moment before realizing the moving figure in the branches is not a young wolf or a hawk but a boy. Older than Lala's five years but still a child.

Tante runs out from the house, wiping her onion-damp hands on her apron and telling Lala to stop carrying on every time she sees a badger, that truly they won't hurt her if she doesn't bother them.

Tante stands beneath the tree.

"Don't look at him," Lala whispers, trying not to stare herself.

"Oh?" Tante asks. "And why not?"

"They'll think we're trying to steal him." Lala keeps her whisper low, even if Tante won't match it.

Lala may be small, but she's old enough to listen. She knows how many gadje mothers and fathers suspect Romnia of being witches who have nothing better to do than steal their children.

Tante tilts her head to look at Lala. "And who exactly will think that?"

With a prickling of guilt, Lala realizes there is a reason Tante does not ask if the boy is lost, or if anyone is missing him. It is clear from his dirt-stained clothes and hungry look that he is on his own.

The boy's eyes shine out from the crab apple branches, more feral than frightened, like a cat caught in a lantern's light.

Lala barely knows anything of their neighbors, or of this place her aunt has brought her. But it seems enough like Riquewihr that she knows what would happen to this boy, or what already has. Farmers' wives chasing him off. Merchants beating him to make sure he never comes back.

Tante sets her hands on her hips, tilts her face up to the tree, and asks the boy, "And what are you good for?"

Not a taunt.

A true question.

Without hesitating, the boy comes down from the crab apple tree. He has hardly set his bare, dirt-grayed feet to the ground when he climbs the great oak next.

Lala watches at Tante's skirt. She winces as the boy ascends into the clouds of wasps that fill the space between boughs.

He plunges his arms into those swarms and grabs handfuls of oak galls, not once being stung.

He climbs down, jumping from the lowest branch.

Soon, Lala and Tante will learn that this boy knows how to keep secrets. Theirs, and his own. As young as he is, he knows how to fold away the things the world would punish him for.

He holds the oak galls out to Tante Dorenia.

Tante looks between the boy and the tree.

"Now that," she says, "is worth something."

Emil

Emil sat at the top of the stairs, letting his parents believe he was asleep.

"It's harmless, Yvette," his father said.

They must have been in the kitchen. It was always easier to hear them when they were in the kitchen than the living room. The sound bounced off the hard floor and counters instead of disappearing into the sofa and rug.

"His teacher used the word *alarming*," his mother said. "Our son somehow managed to *alarm* his grammar school. You want us to ignore that?"

Emil listened harder, his back tensing.

Something about the way his parents said *grammar school* made him feel like he was still in kindergarten.

"All he said was something about us having an ancestor table on holidays," his father said. "It was everyone else who turned it into summoning ghosts from graveyards."

Now the understanding hit Emil in the stomach. And as soon as it touched him, it turned to shame at how stupid he'd been. Stupid enough to think anyone at school would understand, or want to.

Last year, he'd told Rosella Oliva about his family's altars—the white candle, the dish of water, the food left for the dead, the good cloths they used only for this. She'd taken it as naturally as him telling her the name of a particular butterfly. She'd told him about her own family's altars each November, the photos and candles laid out, the food and flowers brought to those they'd lost.

And that, how easily she'd understood, had made him careless around everyone else. He'd forgotten that most gadje buried their dead and then acted like they were as far away as another galaxy.

"You know how this is," Emil's father said. "You mention something harmless, and suddenly they think you're talking about Satan worship."

"You think I don't know that?" His mother's voice rose, good for listening but bad for Emil's sudden wish not to hear her. "Unfortunately, whatever they turn it into is what everyone else believes."

"Just let it be forgotten," his father said.

"And in the meantime, what?" his mother asked. "We let them say whatever they want about our son?"

"It's not worth arguing with them."

"We can explain."

"And what do you think that will accomplish?" Emil could hear his father stop his pacing in the kitchen. He was still now. "This happened to the Olivas last year, remember? Rosella brought in those pictures of the calaveras, and half a dozen parents decided she was trying to frighten their children with skeletons."

The mention of Rosella made Emil both wince and listen harder.

"And the Olivas talked to the school to clear it up," Emil's mother said. "You're only proving my point."

"I am not, because I wasn't done," his father said. "The Olivas tried to *explain*, and it ended with Rosella having to apologize. *Apologize*, for who she and her family are. And a week later she came home wearing lipstick." His father said this last part with the resigned flourish of giving a story's moral.

"What are you saying?" Emil's mother asked. "One wrong move, then what? Next week our son will be a smoker?"

"We can't ask him to hide everything about himself," his father said. "He didn't do anything wrong."

"When has that ever mattered?"

The words made Emil go still, at the same time the kitchen went quiet.

His mother and father wanted him to be proud. He knew that. They had taught him early the names of their vitsi, so he would know what kind of Romani he was. The words Manouche—his mother's vitsa—and Sinti—his father's—were some of the first he remembered learning.

But he also knew enough, from what his parents told him and what he'd overheard. He knew how much of his family had survived by trying to pass as gadje, and how many who couldn't had spent years getting driven out of places they lived, or worse. When a child went missing, his grandmother had had to move, the weight of a whole town's scorn and the threat of all those suspicions driving her away. No one bothered apologizing when the little girl turned up days later, laughing at the harried adults, having hidden in a friend's attic.

A small meow sounded behind Emil. Gerta, announcing her presence in the hall. The kitten batted at the hem of his pajama pants, like she knew he didn't want to be alone.

During the last glimmer, she'd come out of the woods with the other forest cats, fluffy and green-eyed, with early snow dotting their fur as they decided which houses would be theirs. (Gerta decided that she hated everyone, but hated the Woodlocks the least.)

Emil heard his mother crossing the kitchen. He picked up Gerta and went back toward his room before his mother got to the stairs.

"Where are you going?" his father called after her.

"To check our son's room for cigarettes, of course," she called back.

Emil shut his door as quietly as he could. The exaggeration in his mother's voice made him almost sure she was being sarcastic, but he briefly debated jumping into his bed and pretending to be asleep just in case.

His mother passed his room. Then he knew for sure.

Emil leaned against the door and looked down at Gerta, pawing his shirt. He looked at his own hands, at the shade of brown, in a way that felt unfamiliar, unsettled.

That brown made most of the school look at him differently, him and his friends who were their own shades of brown.

Most of Briar Meadow didn't know what Romani meant, and if they did they thought it was the same as another word, one that stung every time he heard it.

Emil closed his eyes, realizing he'd just decided something.

With his family, he could speak of his Romanipen. Every time his cousins came over, or he and his parents baked hyssop into unsalted bread, gave it life, like blowing on embers.

With everyone else, he had to hold his Romanipen hidden inside him, a map to a country he had to pretend didn't exist. In this house, he could be who he was. Outside, he had to be like everyone else.

He would keep altars with his family. He would help his

mother with the recipes that carried the luck of baxtale xajmata.

But he wouldn't ask to know more. He wouldn't learn any more about their family than his mother and father insisted on. Because if he did, it would spill out of him.

If he did, he would just make the same mistake again.

Strasbourg, 1514

Wer Zigeuner schädigt, frevelt nicht.
   Whoever harms a Gypsy commits no crime.
   It is law that spreads across borders like a blight through fields. And it comes alongside decrees that Roma must leave kingdom after kingdom, city after city.

Zigeuner. The term the gadje use for Lala, and Tante Dorenia, and all like them, bites like the teeth of a gadfly.

It is nearly sunrise when Lala goes in from keeping watch with Alifair.

The wattle-and-daub house has become a place where those fleeing can stop, for the night or for long enough to clear a child's cough or an old woman's fever. Tante tends to the families. Lala bakes bread and makes their vegetable patch and root cellar stretch into pot after pot of soup. Alifair gathers scrap firewood from the forests at night, his sharp eyes watching for anyone who might catch him.

Then, like a flame burning through a map, the law consumes Strasbourg.

Tante thought they might be safer in a free city, not beholden to kingdom laws. But now the magistrate issues an order for the apprehending of any Roma in Strasbourg.

Alifair goes out into the trees, collecting frost-chilled berries for a baby to teethe on.

So many families have already gone, fleeing to the forests and mountains to escape laws that will forever be against them. But those who have remained, Lala and Tante and Alifair quietly aid. The hollow-eyed men, the frightened mothers, the families desperate to leave before the arrests, crowd into the wattle and daub. The breath of more bodies than ever before fills the house.

Alifair comes back and hands Lala the iced-over beads of the frozen berries. With a small nod, he leaves again. Tonight a few are moving on from Strasbourg, and Alifair helps the vardos to a far road in the last of the dark.

She watches him go, his form against the dark trees.

With each family they see safely off, Lala feels her own heart growing stronger. Her spirit defies the gadje who would arrest these men and women and their children. Her own Romanipen puts deeper roots into her soul.

Even though it means being so close to all she is not allowed to have. Rromanès, a language she has never been taught. Aprons and layered skirts with more red and age-softened lace than Tante will ever let her risk. Particular ways of braiding hair. The careful embroidery of clovers and horseshoes, roses and certain leaves, the sun and the moon. Things they cannot chance the gadje recognizing.

Lala slips inside, quiet as a cat. She says a prayer of thanks to Sara la Kali that neither the little ones nor their mothers stir. Her steps fade beneath the sound of breathing and soft snoring.

She is so silent, it seems, that the only two voices in the house continue, unaware she can hear their low words. There is not yet enough light through the beams to reveal her.

Lala easily places the first voice. Tante's.

"She is my niece," Tante says, her words firm but her tone polite, deferring. "I know well enough to know what's good for her, I should think."

"And what's good for her is denying her own name," the other voice, a man's, says. The words do not rise in a way suggesting a question. They would seem an accusation if the tone didn't sound so magnanimous, as though it is up to him to give Tante permission.

That voice sends a shiver between Lala's shoulder blades.

It belongs to a man who is older, but holds himself so straight that his back seems that of a young man's.

He has done nothing to explain the shiver, apart from the fact that whenever he looks at Lala or Alifair, he has the pinched smile of someone tolerating a troublesome child. He calls her *Lavinia* in a way that seems pointed, as though to remind her what she misses by so rarely hearing her familiar name.

She wishes she had the nerve to tell him she already knows.

Lala pauses in the dark, listening, hoping they do not hear her.

"And the boy?" the man asks.

Tante sighs. "What of him?" she says, with more exhaustion than annoyance.

"Gadje already think we take their children," the man says, and though it seems the beginning of a thought, he does not go on.

"He has no one to ask after him," Tante says plainly.

The man lets out a brief sound, a curt hum, that at first seems considering but then dismissive.

It is not the first time such disapproval has been made clear to Lala's aunt. If it is not over Alifair's presence in this house, it is something else, mild scorn at the fact that Tante will invite

Roma across her threshold, but will not meet them in the open.

Some pity Lala and Tante for passing among gadje, sure they are losing a little of their souls each day.

Some consider it unforgivable.

The sunrise barely finds its way in. Tante and the man are still only silhouettes.

"She's in love with him," the man says. "You must know that."

Heat blooms in Lala's cheeks as she waits for Tante to ask *Who?*

But after a moment of quiet, Tante only says, "And he hasn't touched her."

The heat in Lala's face grows as she realizes how obvious it must be. How plainly it must show in the way she looks at this boy who first appeared in the crab apple tree.

It is worse than that. She first tried to kiss Alifair last year, and he stopped her in a way that was even more devastating for being so gentle, setting his palms on her upper arms, widening the distance between them.

She has never felt more sharply the slight distance between their ages. They were children together, looking for the shapes of horses in storm clouds, but now that slight distance has put him on one side of a border and left her on the other.

Lala holds her breath, urging Tante to keep the silence, hoping she will not be pressed into breaking it.

Tante knows better than to try to convince this man of Alifair's Romanipen. Alifair was born a gadjo, but from so deep in the Schwarzwald that he came to Lala and Tante already understanding the breath and life of trees. The rest—the auspicious nature of certain foods, the different points of a stream used for washing—he learned.

The children of these families take to him quickly, waiting for him to play the next song on his Blockflöte. But the mothers eye him warily, grateful for how he does not talk to them unless they talk to him first.

The older man's voice cuts through the silence. Tante has outlasted him, and though it is a small victory, it is so clear Lala could sing.

"You let the boy stay here," the man says, "he'll have a baby on her by next year."

Lala hears the catch in Tante's throat, and knows she is trying not to laugh over how much this man thinks he knows.

Alifair has worked so hard to hide that he was given a girl's name at birth, and has to conceal the fact of his body to be considered as the boy he is. He has done this work, learning to bind himself beneath his shirts, settling his voice as low as the other boys', and he has done it so well that even this man doesn't suspect.

They all bear the secrets of their own bodies. Lala and Tante, their blood. Alifair, a form he must hide, one that would make others declare him a woman if he didn't.

Tante collects herself quickly. "We'll see, I suppose."

"Well," the man adds, with a wave of his hand that shows against the coming light. "You have your own opinions of these things."

Lala wishes she could glare at the man, for this slight over Tante remaining unmarried. Women have clucked their tongues at Tante's choice, but somehow this feels sharper, as though it will leave a mark.

Lala's protests grow heavy on her tongue. She slips from the wattle-and-daub house so she will not speak without meaning to.

The sky catches flame, orange and pink blazing through the deep blue.

A silhouette stands alongside the crab apple tree, both forms cut against the bright color.

One of the women. Lala didn't realize anyone else was awake.

Lala draws near enough to see the woman's dress, the yellow apron over the black skirt. The delicate cloth of a worn but well-cared-for dikhle covers her head.

The woman is placing her hands on the bark of the crab apple tree.

"What are you doing?" Lala asks, and then gasps at her own rudeness. It is no better than interrupting a priest who kneels in prayer.

But the woman offers her a smile, shown by the growing light. Not a tolerating smile. One as true as the color in the sky.

"Lowering a fever," she says simply, as though she assumes Lala will understand.

Something behind Lala catches the woman's attention. She looks past Lala, into the growing light.

Lala turns around.

Halfway between the tree and the lane stand Geruscha and Henne, two girls in plain clothes and unadorned hair who live even farther outside the city walls than this house. They have taken to Lala and Alifair so easily, and seem to like them so beyond reason, that it unsettles Lala. Henne brings over vegetables from her mother's garden. Geruscha endlessly admires the scraps of blue cloth Tante Dorenia sometimes gives her.

Geruscha and Henne pause, bread in their hands.

They know they have interrupted something.

Lala's heart falls.

As though Lala and Tante did not have enough gadje watching them.

Now Geruscha and Henne have seen Lala with this woman, this woman in her dikhle, with skin the same brown as Lala's, both of them standing at the crab apple tree as though it is a dear friend.

Geruscha and Henne leave the bread, and back toward the lane.

But it is already done. Lala knows that, even before they vanish against the brightening sky.

It doesn't happen all at once, the way the families stop coming. But they do stop coming, judging the risk too great, either to Tante Dorenia or to themselves.

Lala never finds the nerve to tell Tante why. She leaves her aunt a thousand reasons she could assume—her being an unmarried woman, her taking in a gadjo boy, and raising him with Romanipen at that.

Lala knows it lessens their risk, no longer having families here, or women setting careful hands on their trees.

But Lala cannot help hating Geruscha and Henne for taking it from her.

Rosella

The first time I saw them, the most beautiful pair of red shoes my family ever made, began with a nightmare. It was the year the glimmer left blood on the rosebushes, and I dreamed of nothing but red staining the petals and twists of thorns.

I was still small enough that when I had nightmares, I went looking for someone else in the house. So I crept downstairs, avoiding all the spots that creaked.

That night, my mother and father had taken our rust-reddened car out of town, meeting with the shops that would carry the work of my family's hands. They left me with my grandmother and grandfather, who let me have little sips from the coffee they drank as they worked.

I snuck toward the workroom, listening for the sound of my grandparents' voices.

But there was another voice besides my abuela's soft chatter and my abuelo's low laugh. A man's voice.

People came from all over for Oliva shoes, made by my parents or—if they were really willing to pay—the stiffened but skilled hands of my grandfather. They came to our corner of Briar Meadow, where the houses thinned out, the way my father said stars spread farther at the edges of the universe. Families brought daughters to be fitted for satin heels or velvet ballet flats. They thrilled at the shoes' beauty, and the stories that they made girls hold themselves prouder and taller, or made their hearts lucky, or gave them grace that stayed even after they slipped them off.

I stopped at the cracked door.

A tall, blond man was talking to—no, not to, *at*—my grandfather.

"You expect my daughter to wear *these*?" He shook a pair of red shoes at my grandfather. They were as deep as cranberries, covered in vines of red-on-red embroidery.

Anyone who owned a pair of our red shoes handled them as gently as antique ballet slippers, each pair packed away into attic trunks and under-bed boxes, stuffed with paper to keep their shape.

But the man shook this pair so hard I worried the beads would tremble away. He wielded the red shoes, the workroom lamplight catching the glass beads.

The tight-woven satin looked adorned with tiny drops of blood, and I shivered with some echo of my dream.

"*Red?*" The man spat out the word. "For a debutante ball?"

My grandfather did not cower. But he didn't meet the man's eye either.

My grandmother stepped between them.

"Your daughter asked for red," my abuela said, her face hard.

"She would never," the man bellowed. "She would never ask for a color that made a mockery of the whole event."

"Well," my abuela said, turning through her receipt file and refusing to match the man's volume, "it seems she would, and she did."

The man ignored my grandmother, setting his eyes onto

my grandfather. He stood half a head above my abuelo, lording every inch over him.

A hollow opened in my stomach.

The man slammed the shoes down.

The slight rattle of glass beads made me wince. I felt it on the back of my nightgown.

Then the man's gaze shifted. He studied the shoes, the fine stitching and beading. He couldn't even hide how he admired them.

It was a look I'd seen before, when someone wanted a pair my grandfather was making for someone else, the moment of admiring turning into wanting.

But there was something sharp in this man's eyes. Possessive.

"We'll expect white ones by the end of the week," the man said.

My grandfather nodded, showing neither fear nor defiance.

The hollow in my stomach turned hot. A week? For a pair from scratch? With my grandfather's other commissions, he'd be up every night until his fingers bled.

"And we'll accept these"—the man plucked the shoes off the table and stuffed them back into their tissue-lined box—"as an apology for the delay."

Anger roiled in my stomach and rose up into my chest.

The man would take those red shoes, those beautiful red shoes, and demand white ones (how would my grandfather make full-beaded white shoes in a week without his fingers bleeding on the pale satin?) and he wouldn't even pay for them.

My grandmother took a step forward. "Oh, no, we would never ask you to do that." Even from behind the door I could catch the mocking in her voice. "We would never expect you to bear the sight of something so offensive to you. Here." She snatched the shoes from the box. "I'll save you the bother of carrying them home."

She slipped a pair of scissors off a work table and, quick as a magic trick, cut the red shoes into pieces.

I had to bite my own hand to keep from gasping.

The pieces fell like confetti between the man's horrified face and my abuela's proud glare.

My eyes flicked from the gleam of my grandmother's scissors to my grandfather's face. I braced for the pain that would twist his expression. Every cut, every whine of the scissors' hinges, must have put a crack in his heart.

But wonder opened my grandfather's eyes as wide as I'd ever seen them. No pain. Only awe, like he'd just fallen deeper in love with my grandmother.

At the sound of the blond man shifting his weight, I ran back upstairs, dodging the creaky places in the wood.

I breathed hard in the dark, and I waited.

After the man was gone, after I heard the shuffling-around noises of my grandparents shutting off lights and going to bed, I snuck back down to the workroom.

I had spent whole afternoons in this room, watching my grandfather's dark, weathered hands shape the heel of a shoe, or my father guide cloth through the sewing machine. I studied my mother's calloused fingers stitching patterns and constellations, and my grandmother hunching over her desk, making careful accounts in heavy books that seemed a hundred years old.

I had wanted to be part of my family's craft since I first filled my palms with glass beads and felt like I was holding the stars. My parents could keep me busy with hours of threading needles and sewing tiny stitches, the things my father said were the first skills he learned.

Even without turning on a light, the workroom seemed stuffed with magic. Dyed satin and velvet spilled from the shelves. Tiny buttons sparkled in their glass jars. The length of beads my mother left on stretches of silver cord glittered like salt crystals. Every-color thread confettied the surfaces. When my mother asked me to help clean up, I pretended I was a bird, gathering up scraps to build a bright nest.

But now I picked up the confetti of candy-red satin and apple-red velvet and blood-red beads.

I wrapped them in crumpled tissue paper, my heart ringing with what I now knew.

I would never let this happen again.

When I grew up, I would never let my family, or myself, be where my grandparents had just been, having to cut our own work into pieces so someone else wouldn't steal it.

I would never let this happen again.

And I kept those pieces as a reminder. I would find a way to make sure we never had to destroy something of ourselves just to stop other people from taking it.

Strasbourg, 1518

In the dark, all she has are her hands.

She wants to light a candle so badly she feels the ache of it in her fingers. With nothing but the faintest breath of moon outside, the darkness is so thick that Lala's dress, her hair, her skin feel woven from night. But the sound of iron striking flint would wake her aunt as surely as a thief breaking the cellar door.

Lala pulls back the rushes, wild marjoram woven into the plaited mats to lessen the stale smell, and she unearths a wooden box.

If Tante Dorenia knew what Lala was doing, her glare would be enough to open the ground beneath her. Lala is sixteen now, a woman, old enough to know better than to take such risks.

Lala brushes off the lid, so no dirt will fall inside. It would seem a useless effort to anyone watching, anyone who could see her in the dark, since the box only holds more of the same. A scant handful of earth.

But this earth is worth every field in Alsace.

The sound of weight on the road—a crunching of rock, the give of the ground—startles Lala. Her eyes skim the parchment windows.

Her hands pause in the heart of the wooden box. The thrumming of blood at her throat grows hot. She cannot help the sense of having already been found out.

This box of earth is a sign of all they have hidden. To be caught would mean the loss of their home, their small trade of ink and dye, and far more. Perhaps no one would understand what Lala meant to do with this handful of earth, but that would be all the more dangerous. They would count the hiding of it beneath a rush floor as a sign of unknowable witchcraft.

It is the same reason Lala and Tante put away their secret altar, folding their best length of blue cloth, hiding the candles and dishes. If the magistrate's men were ever of a mind to search houses, they could use it as evidence of whatever crime they liked.

The sound outside fades.

Lala's heart quiets.

Nothing but an oxcart following the ruts in the road.

Lala's fingers skim the inside of the box, the pale wood earth-darkened.

The soft creak of the ladder sounds above her.

"I have it," she whispers as she hears Alifair transfer his weight to the floor.

He insists on going with her, and she is neither proud enough nor stupid enough to refuse. He already knows her secrets and Tante's as well as they know his.

They go out into the night, and the farther they get from the house, the more that handful of ground turns heavy in Lala's skirt. Its weight feels greater as she bends to pick the tiny wildflowers that flash in the dark.

She would have wished to do this in daylight, ribbons of sun gilding the earth from her mother's and father's graves. But with light, there would be the chance of questions, rumors.

What we are, Tante reminds her, *they have made it a crime, wherever we go.*

As though Lala could forget.

Lala follows Alifair, cutting only through land he knows. The flax fields, high with green-gold. The soft marshland. A sheep pasture owned by a man whose wife trades onions for Tante's extra radishes. An orchard that hasn't borne fruit since last winter's frosts.

Alifair has always seen better in the dark than Lala. She imagines he learned growing up deep in the Black Forest, beech trees wreathing it in perpetual dusk. He crouches to pick meadow roses Lala can barely see. Their petals collect what little light there is, as though the moon is showing them to Alifair.

His sharp vision is something she has learned about him not only in the fields near their home, but in the minutes they've stolen in shadow. Last year, he started looking at her in a way that made her wonder if she should try kissing him again. When she did, the winter night was so dark that she made a mess of it, her lips meeting his jawline instead of his mouth, so it seemed more an odd greeting than a try at kissing him. But then his lips caught hers in a way so hard and decisive it showed his certainty about both her and the dark.

The damp grasses prickle Lala's ankles. She lets the feeling chase off the memory of that kiss, the way his mouth took hold of hers.

The green ground offers a clean, sharp perfume alongside the stream. The ribbon of water catches the moon in time with its murmurs.

Lala draws the earth from beneath her underskirt. Alifair hands her the roses and then keeps a respectful distance.

This is the last of it, the ground she has kept, the packed earth she imagines still smelling of the lavender in her mother's hair, and the knife her father kept in his boot, and the bitter salt of the fever that took them both. Every year, in the month that stole them, Lala has brought out a handful from the box, to loosen the world's hold on their spirits.

A few years ago, in a thoughtful moment brought on by the coming of autumn, Tante Dorenia told her about how they once did this for all their dead. And Lala couldn't sleep until she had resolved how to do it for Maman and Papa. Tradition would have called for it once, on the day of their burial. But it had been so long since her mother's and father's deaths, she worried it would take more than the one time.

She bends toward the stream and opens her hands. The flowers tumble away first, their sugar lacing the air. Then the earth twirls from her fingers.

She releases a long breath.

Now they will rest. Now her mother's and father's souls will be free from this ground, this life, from their own dream-troubled, salt-soaked deaths.

Lala prays over the flickering water, over the river stones grown cold in the evening.

As she opens her eyes, a flicker of motion draws her head up.

At first, she cannot catch it. She sees nothing but the dark trees and the distant road, worn down by carts and horses' hooves.

But then Lala catches the streak of movement, the shape cut between the black trees.

The figure—a woman, Lala can tell by the kick of her apron

and skirts—flails and writhes. She runs a few steps and then thrashes out in a way that looks caught between skipping and running.

Lala squints into the dark, trying to make out whether this woman is fleeing wolves or thieves.

Alifair inclines forward, and Lala knows by his posture that he means to help.

She lays a hand on his arm.

"No one can know we're here," she whispers.

"Then hide and I will help her."

"You can't. If anyone . . ."

She loses the end of the thought, both her and Alifair realizing, in the same moment, that the woman is not fleeing.

The woman throws her hands toward the moon, spinning in feverish motion.

"Is she . . ." Now it is Alifair who cannot complete his own thought.

Lala nods, half in confirmation and half in wonder. "Dancing."

Emil

The turquoise of copper chloride. The bright blue of copper sulfate. The cherry-Coke red of cobalt chloride. Sometimes the things Emil took from the lab seemed more like paint pigments than chemicals.

He tapped the powders into glass vials. By now, he'd done this often enough that he knew how much he'd need for the week that school would be closed. And by now, Dr. Ellern had drilled him and his friends on avoiding contamination between compounds, so he could've done it half-asleep.

Emil locked the door behind him. Tonight he'd hand the key back to Aidan. Among the four of them allowed into the lab closet, they'd voted him keeper of the single key they shared. Aidan was so organized that he alphabetized his family's breakfast cereals, and he never lost anything, unless you counted titration bets with Luke.

The back of Emil's neck bristled with the sense that someone was in the hall other than Victor, his and his friends' favorite school janitor. (After Ben Jacobs tried to stuff Eddie into a cabinet in the music room, Victor had helped Luke overwax the floor in front of Ben's locker. They resined the spot before anyone could draw any conclusion but that Ben had, wildly and spectacularly, tripped over his own feet.)

The sound of shifting ice came from the machine around the corner.

Emil took slow steps down the hall.

The noises stopped a second before Rosella Oliva appeared.

Emil jumped, almost dropping the copper chloride.

Rosella looked at his hands.

Emil got his grip back. "I'm not stealing," he said, halting over each word.

It was a reflex, one sharpened by years of classmates looking at him sideways and their parents pretending not to. By the number of times he felt compelled to clarify *Yes, this is my locker.*

By how easily gadje turned the word *Romani* into the word *gypsy,* with all the suspicions they tacked onto those two syllables.

"I know," Rosella said, in a way that was level and soft, like she both knew it was true and didn't blame him for thinking he had to say it. She probably understood the impulse better than just about anyone else in Briar Meadow. For one November show-and-tell, she'd brought in that painting of skeletons dancing and throwing marigolds into a fountain, and it had only taken until lunch for the whispers to start about her trying to talk to the dead.

Rosella adjusted the coffee can in her arms. "I know you're one of Ellern's chosen students." She held up the coffee can, condensation dampening the metal. "I'm just here for ice."

"Ice?" Emil asked.

"Yeah, it's the best. It's all fluffy and crunchy."

"You"—he looked at the coffee can—"actually eat that?"

"What?" she asked. "It makes the best Diet Coke fizz."

"That's the department ice machine. Do you have any idea how many trace chemicals end up in there?"

"This is a high school lab, not CERN. I think it's fine."

CERN? If he wasn't already a little in love with Rosella Oliva, that would've done it.

"Okay," he said. "But don't blame me when you glow in the dark by the time we graduate."

Their eyes met again, and he thought he felt some shared memory pass between them. How they used to see how long they could get lizards to sit on the backs of their hands before either they or the lizards flinched. Or when Rosella brought Gerta a stuffed mouse she'd made just to see her tear it to fabric shreds and quilt batting within a few minutes (she found this far more hilarious than upsetting).

Or the first time he told her about Sara la Kali, and she told him about la Virgen de Guadalupe, these dark, sacred figures who both allowed reverence toward that which was so often despised.

It could have been any of these things, but it also could've been nothing. Emil didn't want to ask. He didn't want to get it wrong.

Rosella and Emil had been friends once, in the way girls and boys were only ever friends before middle school. She had spent so much time at his house, she'd heard his mother's fairy tales more than he had, asking for them after he'd long grown bored. The ones she liked best were ones about dancing, or cursed or enchanted shoes. Go figure. She was an Oliva.

She loved all those stories, even the bloody ones. The little mermaid on land, feeling like there were knives beneath her feet as she danced. Cinderella's glass slippers cracking under her. A girl in red shoes that made her dance until she died.

Rosella looked at his hands again, and Emil wondered if she could see them going clammy against the glass vials.

"So what are you doing with . . . whatever you're not stealing?" she asked.

"Flame tests mostly," Emil said.

"You keep a Bunsen burner in your room?"

"I have a sort-of lab that lives in my mother's gardening shed?" he said, and it turned out as a question. He set the vials in his backpack. "You can come over and see it sometime if you want."

He cringed, instantly.

If there was a worse way to ask out a girl, he couldn't think of it.

"Maybe," she said. "If I'm not too busy eating all the ice in this machine."

She said it in a way that was such a confusing mix of familiarity and flirting that it made him dizzy. He'd barely shrugged it off by the time he got home.

The second he was through the door, his father shoved a piece of paper in his hand.

Emil stared at the printout of a photo, a square of frayed blue cloth on a wooden table. "What am I looking at?"

"What are you looking at?" his father asked. Almost exclaimed. "Do you listen to anything I say?"

"No, not really."

His father frowned and knocked the spine of an academic journal into Emil's forearm. "That"—he jabbed a finger into the paper—"is the exact kind of woad blue *your* ancestors dyed in the sixteenth century."

Emil stared at his father. "That's wonderful."

"How are you my son? You have no appreciation for history."

"History." Emil shrugged off his backpack. "As in, it already happened. There's only so far you can get if you're always looking back."

"Thanks a lot," his father said.

Emil sighed. "I didn't mean it that way."

His parents, both history professors, had a marriage that seemed half-built on finding the same things interesting. They'd met during a conference panel, and as far as Emil could tell, that was the academia equivalent of a fairy tale.

"I just meant it's what you and Maman love," Emil said. "And you're good at it. But I don't, and I'm not."

His father gave a smile that was equal parts fond and wry. It always made him look like a grandfather, older than his sprinklings of gray hair warranted. "Yes, yes, you and your chemicals."

Emil breathed out. *You and your chemicals*. At least they were even. Emil's father had about as much interest in Emil's favorite subjects as Emil had in his. His father's desk perpetually held old records, two-tone pictures, age-yellowed papers kept in plastic sheets, wood-cut prints of old churches. Some were pages fallen out of long-misplaced family Bibles, the names in ornate, back-slanted script. Some were copies his mother had made on her last trip to le Bas-Rhin. Tourists went to France for Paris and Nice. His mother went for les Archives Départementales, with its centuries-old documents in barely legible Middle French and High German.

"You know." His father's eyes drifted toward the floor. "You can't go where you want to go without knowing where you've been."

Emil's back tensed.

The burning of ancestors' vardos. Words stricken from their vocabulary. Being forced from villages, or fleeing in the dark fold of midnight, because there was so often a relative who could feel the threat coming before anyone else, like smelling snow in the air. Fighting back with iron shards and pipes and whatever there was to be found when there was no warning, and there were the old and the small to protect.

What he'd put up with in Briar Meadow—the ignorant questions, the word *gypsy* said in a way that felt like it was sticking to his skin, the pointed looks whenever something went missing—it was so small compared to what those before him had endured. But that made him more, not less, ashamed of it. He couldn't help thinking of it as some kind of failing on his part.

Outside of this house, he couldn't be who he was. He'd known that since the day his parents got that call home. But the more he knew about his family, the harder it was to leave his Romanipen behind every morning.

"I know where we've been," Emil said. He started up the stairs, saying, more to himself than his father, "and I kind of wish I didn't."

Strasbourg, 1518

At daybreak, Lala burns the wooden box, turning to ash the last of her parents' belongings.

She watches the wood crumble, the shade of the oak trees dulling the flames' gold. She offers a prayer of thanks to Sara la Kali, She who watches over Lala and Tante and all like them.

Once the embers have gone as dark as her hair, Lala draws away from the wattle fence.

Alifair is up in the oak trees. He never flinches, not even when wasps crawl along his wrists.

He slips a hand between their buzzing clouds to reach the darkest oak galls. They whir around him but never sting, even as he steals the growths they have laid their eggs inside.

Ever since the day Alifair first appeared in their crab apple tree, this has seemed as much a kind of magic as Tante knowing how long to keep linen in the woad dye. The wasps do not mind him, for some reason as unknown as where he came from. Both his French and his German carry a slight accent, like two kinds of grain mixing in a sieve, so no one can guess which side of the Zorn or the Rhein he was born on.

When she catches his eye, they share a nod, a signal they know as well as each other's hands.

Within minutes, he is down from the tree, she has set aside the bay in her apron, and they meet behind the cellar door.

Lala pulls him to the stone wall. He throws his hands to it, bracing as she presses her palms into his back. His mouth tastes like the lovage he chews after each meal, like parsley but sweeter.

Lala has never asked him whether that first kiss was because they had both gotten older, or because he had grown less skittish about his own body, a body that once tethered him to the girl's name he was given when he was born.

Now Lala knows not only the facts of his body but the landscape of it. She knows where there is more and less of him. She knows where he is both muscled and soft, full-hipped and full-chested, strong in the shoulders and back. The strips of binding cloth beneath his shirt give him the appearance of a heavier man, rather than one laden with a girl's name at birth.

Lala hears footsteps coming in from the lane, and goes still.

"I should go," Lala says, almost moaning it, eyes still shut.

"Later," he whispers, the word coming as a breath against her neck.

Lala squints from the cellar into the light, looking for a stout form—Geruscha—and a second figure with a tight-woven bun, the seldom-talking Henne.

For months, Lala held her breath over the two of them, fearful that any day the magistrate's men would come to Tante's door on the report of these two girls. But their efforts at friendship have only persisted, despite the frosted politeness Lala offers them (cold, so as not to encourage them, but cordial, so as not to offend these two girls who saw her with the woman in the dikhle).

Lala shields her eyes from the sun's glare.

The approaching figure does not turn toward the back garden, but takes the crabgrass-roughened path to the door.

Not Geruscha. Not Henne.

A man.

Lala distinguishes the colors of his garb, white and black.

Her heart quickens.

The robe and cape of a Dominican friar, one trained to root out witchcraft.

Alifair is alongside her, his approach quiet as a moth's.

They listen at the weather-warped door.

They hear the friar's voice, his greeting to Tante Dorenia. His words, however polite, cannot veil the contempt in his tone, his disdain for the fact that Tante is a businesswoman, never married, trading in the richest black and deepest blue.

Lala cannot catch all the words, but hears enough to make out a name, a phrase, a stretch of time.

Delphine.

She has been missing.

Two nights and a day.

Delphine.

The woman whose silhouette Lala and Alifair glimpsed just beyond the trees.

The woman they saw dancing.

Lala feels Alifair's shadow incline forward.

"Alifair," she says.

"We saw her," he whispers. "What if we can be of help?"

She takes hold of his arm. "And don't you think he will wonder what cause we had to be out in the thick of night?"

"I won't tell him about that," he says. "And I'll leave you out of it. No one will even know you were there."

As though that is any comfort. One word to the magistrate

that Alifair was the last to see Delphine, and to see her dancing like some wild spirit at that, and they'll blame him for it. He'll be brought to the scaffold or the stake before he finishes his testimony. The rumors that he appeared out of the woods like some fairy's child will not help.

Lala grips his arm tighter. "Please."

Alifair looks at her, his eyes turning to flint, his jaw hardening.

He shrugs off her hold, and nods.

Lala knows him well enough to recognize this not as agreeing, but as relenting.

He is simply giving in.

Rosella

In Briar Meadow, our small, loosely gathered set of houses bounded in by woods and highway, the glimmers were as much a part of our calendar as the seasons. But I was the only one always dreading another year of blood on rosebushes, and all the slashed cloth and scattered beads that might come with it.

It never came.

Not when I was eight, when daughters who'd given their mothers nothing but silence for months suddenly wanted to spill their hearts out over late-night freezer cake. Not when I was eleven, when congregation members who, according to their choir director, "couldn't carry a tune in a bucket" sang like angels. Not even two years ago, when the glimmer brought Mexican coywolves out of the woods; cute as puppies, they had an annoying talent for getting into houses—even ones where all the doors and windows were locked—and chewing on the nicest shoes they could find.

By the time I turned sixteen, I had almost forgotten to dread the glimmer, so I wasn't even thinking about it when the red shoes started appearing around town. They showed up on sofas and bedroom floors. Instead of resting in attic trunks, or on the high shelves where they'd been stored, they appeared in the open, as though airing themselves out. They were found propped up in corners, heels against baseboards, toes resting on carpet. Or in cupboards, with broom bristles grazing their delicate beading. Mothers stumbled over them in hallways, pausing to yell to their daughters to pick up their things before realizing the red shoes on the floor had been wrapped away in tissue paper for years.

They emerged from linen cabinets and coat closets. They showed up in dining rooms, and slender women who'd sworn off bread years ago ate slices of black forest cake like they were drinking in a new perfume. When red shoes appeared at the senior community out by the pear orchard, eighty-year-olds who'd once been high school sweethearts ran off together.

Aubrey Wyeth, famous for being afraid to drive, found a brick-red pair once belonging to her older sister, in the middle of the street. The neighbors all saw her get into her mother's four door and speed away from that cluster of houses, identical and neat as folded shirts.

Sylvie Everley found a pair resting on her bed, soles down on her great-grandmother's patchwork quilt. The color of the satin, just between red and burgundy, was the near-purple of her mother's favorite wine. The beading made her think of how the light from the dining room chandelier reflected in a glass. The next morning she took a second look at a flush-cheeked boy she sometimes partnered with on the debate team. He'd been trying for weeks to work up the nerve to talk to her. That afternoon they were kissing behind the library.

For all the rumors that Oliva shoes brought grace and luck, it had always been our red ones that carried the spark of secret kisses, of brazen hearts, of eating bread with more butter than flour. And this year, all my friends were wearing them. Their red shoes crunched over the leaf mulch, flashing with the bright magic that had taken hold of them all.

All of them, except me.

I was an Oliva. My family had made all these red shoes, and somehow I was the only one of my friends not wearing them. I had learned to blow-dry my hair straight (sometimes just so Sylvie could curl it again), put on eyeliner in the side mirror of Graham's car (pencil only; I was still working on liquid), eat lemon slices dusted with packets of artificial sweetener (the only thing Piper ever ate before a dance). All the things that made me almost, almost the same kind of girl as Piper Tamsin and Sylvie Everley.

And this would be the thing to remind them that I was nothing like them. It would call attention to my brown skin and brown-black hair. It would remind them that whenever I bought something new, I wore it twice the first week, while they all had so many tags-on things in their closets that they forgot about them.

This would be what set me aside from them, that a pair of red shoes enchanted with this year's glimmer had yet to appear on my windowsill or by my bed.

But when I got home from getting the crunchy, fluffy ice my mother and I loved, pieces of beaded red satin and velvet lay on the floor of my room.

Without bending for a closer look, I recognized them.

The cut-up scraps I'd saved eleven years ago. The last I had of my grandparents' work, both of them dying within months of each other when I was seven.

I let out a breathless laugh, both at the memory and the beauty of the stitching.

For eleven years, I had kept them in the back of my closet,

wrapped in mushroom-colored tissue paper, and now they had swept out like a whirl of bright leaves. It felt like both a blessing from my abuelo and a pointed remark from my abuela.

This was how I could honor the beautiful pair of shoes my grandmother had cut into confetti.

I had learned since that night that if I never wanted families like the Tamsins or the Everleys to make me give up a piece of myself I had made by hand, the best way was to become like their daughters. I had done it for years, and I would do it again. Like their daughters, I would wear red shoes this fall.

But I would do it the way my abuelo and abuela would have wanted.

I had grown up among leather awls and dyed thread. At three, I played with empty wooden spools instead of blocks. At eight, I knew how to measure a shoe's side seam, and at ten, how to run a drawstring through a slipper's casing without bunching it.

I picked up the scraps of beaded cloth.

I was an Oliva. If I wanted the kind of shoes my friends were wearing—shoes that might spark love, or inspire the making of midnight polvorones—of course I would have to sew them myself.

Strasbourg, 1518

"Try it for yourself." Melisende holds out a dish of pale yellow coins. Small rounds of butter.

Lala stares at the dish. She has never seen anyone eat butter on its own, not even the wealthiest Strasbourgeois. Is this a test, to see if she will do it? Will they laugh if she places one on her tongue?

Being liked by these girls has shielded Lala from Strasbourg's inquiring glances. But it comes at the cost of them thinking her strange and intriguing, with her rough palms, her confusion about delicate manners, and the fantastic rumors Tante has started to explain their brown skin.

She looks to Enneleyn, the first of the burgher's daughters who ever offered her friendship, and the one whose lead Lala follows whenever she is unsure.

All Enneleyn says is, "You must be joking."

"It works," Agnesona insists, taking one and rubbing it into her cheek.

Then Lala understands.

There is no end to Melisende and Agnesona's schemes to render their hair more gleaming, their complexions more luminous, their forms more radiant. Two girls, considered the most beautiful in the city except Enneleyn, and they work without rest for it. Last week they dabbed on brimstone ground with oil of turpentine for red spots.

Their limbs are delicate as carved alabaster, their fingers slender and uncalloused. It is the look of having been raised within the city walls, in the wealthier quarters. They let the sun on their faces so little they must pinch their cheeks for the slightest blush. If not for the brilliant red of their curls, the sisters would seem almost colorless, while Enneleyn, with her cloth-of-gold hair, has lips as pink as stained glass.

It took months for Lala to learn not to stare at Enneleyn, trying to guess how she might become such a girl, so adored it would make her and Tante a little safer.

Melisende turns her face toward the window. The grease gleams on her cheekbone. "Look."

Lala would sooner pocket a coin of butter than smear it onto her skin.

"Has she shown you the one she will not even share with me?" Agnesona snatches a jar from a low table.

"Give that back!" Melisende shouts.

But Enneleyn has already taken the jar, filled with a deep amber liquid that holds a point of light at its center.

Enneleyn lifts the jar. "What is it?"

"It's birch sap." Melisende tries to snatch it back.

Enneleyn holds it out of reach.

"With a pearl in it," Agnesona says, laughing. "See how the sap is dissolving it."

"Lavinia, look." Enneleyn tilts the jar toward Lala, showing how the sap eats at the creamy sheen.

These girls, with their Veronese raisins to brighten their complexions, the Tuscan oil they comb through their hair, their dust-rose gowns for Carnival. These girls from whom Lala hides her hands so they will not see the stains and calluses wrought by work. These girls, who only showed interest in Lala when rumors Tante started took hold. Tante planted the bulb, the first whispers that she and Lala were the cast-off issue of Italian noblemen. And it bloomed, quietly explaining the brown of their skin. It flowered so well that no one remembers that Tante herself started it.

It has had the unexpected advantage of making Lala interesting to girls such as Melisende and Agnesona. They would never bother with her otherwise, no more than they would bother with Geruscha and Henne.

They would also never guess that Lala now keeps the secret of a missing woman.

As Agnesona slips the jar from Enneleyn's hands, Lala's stomach pinches hard as a knot in thread.

She and Alifair saw Delphine in the fields outside the city, and have said nothing.

Because Lala insisted they say nothing.

And now Alifair's guilt kicks at him. She can hear it at night, in the creaking of his bed, how he turns over and cannot sleep.

Her thoughts begin to spin, wondering over the safest place to confess. Perhaps the priest at Saint-Pierre-le-Vieux, the one who doesn't fleece his flock for all they can tithe.

"Give it!" Melisende grabs at the jar again.

"So, Lavinia." Agnesona gives the overdone air of pretending not to notice her sister. "How is your changeling? High summer must be his favorite time of year."

Lala swallows a sigh. "Don't call him that."

"Come now." Agnesona lifts a suggestive eyebrow. "If I were the love of a fairy prince, I'd tell everyone."

Her tone is more mocking than whimsical, especially on the word *prince*.

"Not this again," Enneleyn says.

"What?" Agnesona asks. "No one knows where he came from, and he's prettier than the other boys."

Lala's stomach buckles, wondering if *prettier* means Agnesona suspects he was proclaimed a girl at birth.

"Sounds like a forest nixie, if you ask me." Agnesona quirks her lips.

"Are you so desperate for gossip that you must dredge these shallows?" Enneleyn grabs the jar and hands it back to Melisende, settling the dispute with the quiet authority of an older sister.

A scream rises up from the lane. It slices through the bustle, quieting the shopkeepers who call out to customers.

Before Lala can even move, she imagines the scene.

Delphine, barely alive, running home with the wounds of wolves' teeth spilling blood from her limbs.

Enneleyn throws the shutters wider.

The four of them crowd at the window.

A young woman—Isentrud, Lala recalls her name—kneels at her doorstep, recoiling from a mass of blood and flesh staining the cobble.

"What . . ." It is the only word Lala can produce before trailing off.

"A sheep's afterbirth," Enneleyn says, almost mournfully.

"They've left it at her father's door to shame her," Agnesona says, less mournfully.

Lala turns away before the sight of it lifts the acid from her stomach.

"Now everyone will know she's lain with Guarin," Melisende says.

"As though everyone didn't know that," Agnesona says.

Enneleyn rounds on them both. "Can't you two think of anything better to do with your mincing mouths than make an awful thing worse?"

She storms from the room, the windows gilding her hair and gown.

The sisters lower their eyes.

Lala watches the corner of Enneleyn's skirt vanish.

If her lips were still before, now they feel sealed in place. The blood, the wailing woman, it is all a reminder of what Lala had almost forgotten.

In Strasbourg, the only way to survive your own crimes is for no one to know of them.

Emil

Other towns scheduled school breaks around national holidays. In Briar Meadow, school let out for a few days in the middle of fall.

Years ago, according to Emil's mother, it was supposed to be a time for children to help their parents sweep the strange magic out of their houses. They helped get the halos of dandelion fluff wind-borne, to point the out-of-season birds south, to wash the dresses that slipped out of closets and ended up in the mud, like they were making their own snow angels.

And maybe it was true, fifty years ago. Now the only sign of all that was friends dragging friends outside on the first freezing night of the season.

"Let's just go see it," Luke had said.

"Big deal," Aidan had said. "It happens every year."

"You must be a real joy to be around during the holidays."

Emil never thought much about the glimmer over the reservoir. Sure, it looked a little like a Milky Way, small and bright and low, a cirrus cloud made of cosmic dust. But it would be there all week. He'd see it from a distance every time he went anywhere at night, at least until it dimmed and faded.

But raising any objection to Luke's and Eddie's enthusiasm wasn't worth the effort. Path of least resistance, like current through a circuit. So Emil had thrown on his jacket and gone out to the reservoir.

Where his friends proceeded to ignore the sweep of light below the clouds and talk about the physics of a drop experiment.

"It won't reduce the impulse enough," Eddie said.

"Like you have a better idea," Luke said.

"Actually, I do." Eddie unfurled a blueprint from his back pocket.

"That"—Aidan slapped at the paper—"will break if you breathe on it wrong."

"Why, exactly, did we come all the way out here to do this?" Emil asked.

"Hey, Woodlock," Aidan said, "tell them I'm right."

"Oh no." Emil backed up, showing them his palms. "I'm not taking sides here. I learned my lesson with the magnetic fields."

"Wise choice," said a girl's voice, one he placed just as he turned toward it.

"When Sylvie and Aubrey get into it about skirt length, I stay half a mile away," Rosella said.

With rising dread, Emil realized his friends had quieted.

They were all staring at her.

"Sorry," Rosella said. "Am I taking him away from whatever great scientific breakthrough you all are working toward?"

They all shook their heads slightly, snapping back to the moment. It was so similar that despite the far range in their coloring and build, it made them look like brothers.

"Not at all," Eddie said.

"Get out of here, Woodlock," Luke said.

"Yeah, we don't need you," Aidan said.

Emil tried not to cringe, at least not visibly enough that Rosella would see it. His friends may have meant well, shoving him in the direction of a girl they knew he'd liked for years. But if lack of subtlety was a recognized art, they'd all have museum exhibits in their honor.

"Sorry if I scared you earlier," Rosella said, walking a few steps from the fallen tree his friends had spread the blueprint over.

He went with her. "You didn't."

Rosella tripped over a rock or a root.

Emil caught her forearm. "You okay?"

Her hand stayed on him.

The back of his neck went hot. She seemed nervous now, when she hadn't earlier. Instead of making him less nervous, that somehow made it worse, like how jumpy he felt was rubbing off.

A few trees away, two silhouettes leapt from the dark.

Rosella's hand drew back from Emil and flew to her sweater.

Emil couldn't quite place the laughter, but the sound of it was familiar, boys he'd heard laughing behind him in class, boys who considered scaring girls the best way to impress them.

Piper Tamsin and Graham Davies pitched themselves into the dark, sending up twin choruses of, "Chris, you ass! Get back here!"

The boys fled, their laughter ringing through the night.

"Yeah, you better run," Piper yelled after them, and the sound echoed off the clouds.

Emil watched them. "My money's on Piper and Graham."

"It should be," Rosella said. "Don't be fooled by the manicures."

She buttoned the last buttons on her coat and studied the glimmer reflected in the water. It looked silver and shiny as mercury or antimony.

"Why did we stop swimming out here?" she asked.

"You mean other than our fathers' identical safety lectures?" He put on his best Julien Woodlock voice. "'Do you know how cold the water gets down there?'" he quoted.

"'Worse for every foot you go down,'" Rosella jumped in with her closest mimic to her own father.

Emil laughed.

"Seriously, did they rehearse those?" Rosella asked. "It was like they were reading off a script."

Emil and Rosella had stopped going to the reservoir years ago, and it was hard to know if that was part of what had led to them not being friends anymore, or if it was something lost to the fact that they weren't friends anymore. They had never stopped greeting each other in the halls, or inserting dragon and unicorn stuffed animals among the nativity display at church (they had yet to be caught). But the relentless teasing of classmates who singsonged that they were boyfriend and girlfriend had worn them down a little more each year. And realizing how much he liked her—*liked* her, in that way his classmates taunted them both about—had made him less inclined to hold on to her, not more. It was half not wanting them to be right, and half not wanting to find out if it was one-sided.

This whole time, Emil had thought he'd need some kind of nerve, flinty and unhesitating, to talk to Rosella for more than a few sentences. But now it seemed like all it took was falling back into the memory of being nine or ten together, knifing their bodies into the freezing reservoir.

Rosella stopped at a high point on the rocks. Far voices rose off the scattered knots of people they knew, mixing with the smell of cheap beer and cigarettes and the sugary mint gum meant to cover both.

She stared at the ribbon of light above the reservoir. It wavered and flickered, like stars reflected in a still pond. Both the clouds above and the water below mirrored it.

"I never really thought of you as someone who came out for this," she said.

He shrugged, looking where she looked. "I'm not."

He felt the slow turn of her face toward his, like the clouds unveiling the moon.

"Emil?" she said.

"Yeah?" he said, wondering what question she was holding in her mouth.

Being this close to her brought him back to the chill of the water on their skin years ago, the light cutting down through the depth, how it felt like the darkness underneath them was infinite. And how that was both terrifying and thrilling.

The way she stared at him now made him wonder if she was there with him, in the reservoir in July, the thick blanket of dark water letting them pretend that any way they touched was accidental.

The air felt sharp enough to grow frost flowers. And something about the glimmer above them turned his overthinking brain off just enough.

Emil slid his hand onto the back of her neck, a gesture small enough that it could have been the start of anything. He would wait, stay still, until she told him what.

Years ago, they would both go down so far that there was no light, because neither of them wanted to be the first to move back toward the surface. That was everything down there, deciding your own distance from the sun, letting it go and then finding it again. Fingertips brushing each other's skin in ways you could pretend never happened once you came up for air.

It was dark enough now to pretend none of this was happening either.

Except now Rosella kissed him. Hard, in a way so lacking in hesitation that it would go with him into his dreams.

His first out-of-nowhere thought was that his glasses got in the way less than he'd always thought they would. But it burned out and faded as she ran the fingers of one hand through his hair, and pressed the other against his back.

Maybe the glimmer came every year. But something this year caught on the air. It was bitter as smoke, and sweet as the raw crystals of honey. It was a current arcing between them. It was the moment that turned a solution from one color to the next, amber to red, fast as a blink. It was the slight change in chemistry that let algae blooms grow on the ocean, bright as a tide of gas flames.

And he couldn't be sure, not with his eyes closed, but for a second, he could have sworn he caught the glimmer above them flashing as red as Rosella's shoes.

Strasbourg, 1518

"Help me with this," Tante says, dragging the wooden table.

Lala takes the other side. "What are you doing?" Tante conducts it toward the door like a battering ram at a fortress gate, and Lala has no choice but to trot backward.

"Just until we're done with the chopping," Tante says.

"We prepare vegetables out of doors now?" Lala asks, keeping the table from crashing into the frame. Sometimes the house seems so brittle that a stubborn enough cow could knock it over.

"It's the raw garlic and leeks," Tante says, setting down her side in the grass. "The smell is making me ill."

"You always loved that smell," Lala says.

She brings her aunt a handful of dried cherries, to settle the stomach.

"Do you want parsley?" Lala asks. "To chew on."

"No, I do not want parsley," Tante snaps.

Lala cannot blame her aunt for her foul mood. The summer is so deep and harsh it seems molten, as though the air might spark and catch. It is the kind of blazing July that will not soften until September. The back of Lala's neck is damp where her hair falls against it. A dew of sweat is forever beading Alifair's forehead.

They have almost finished with the onions and carrots when they see the women traveling the lane.

Lala dries her leek-damp hands on her apron and nears the path.

Among what little passing talk she can distinguish— mentions of the canon priests, of heaven and hell, of a blaze of light brought by a falling star outside Ensisheim—one word rises above the others.

Possessed.

The word flares inside Lala's chest. It brings with it the buzzing sense of a warning, the sounds that come a moment before wasps swarm.

And then a name, a name that must haunt Alifair's dreams.

Delphine.

Lala runs to catch up, her guilt like pebbles in her shoes.

"Lavinia," Tante calls down the lane.

But Lala does not stop. None of them stop.

She follows the dirt road until Strasbourg proper rises from the fields and forest. The city walls cast their shadows. The roofs and gables of the wealthy Strasbourgeois top the crowded lanes. The spires of churches pierce the blue, and the single tower of the cathedral soars toward the clouds.

The women in the square move so quickly that Lala cannot count them.

Skirts of wool and linen and hemp fly out from hopping legs. Fine embroidered skirts wilt in the heat, as though the very flowers stitched into the cloth are dying away. Coifs and wimples soak through with sweat. They dance, joyless, on bleeding feet and twisted ankles.

Already their hose has torn. Already their shoes are thinning, damp with sweat and the fluid of blisters. The blood of the bare-foot paints the stone.

Mothers turn their daughters' faces away, worried that a glance might afflict them, like the old plagues so easily spread they passed with a look. A few fathers stand their sons to watch, lecturing them about the evils of immoral women.

The relatives of these women, some highborn, some no wealthier than Lala and Tante, make snatching tries at grabbing their loved ones from the fray. But the force of this dance makes the women too quick, their paths too strong. And if they are caught for more than a few moments, they scream as though the hold is burning them.

Lala catches the breath of that word. It carries on the murmuring voices of the crowd.

Possessed.

It seems the only word to explain it, how a few of the most godly women within the city walls have been afflicted with this strange dance. Cateline, the book binder's wife, who offered milk to a journeyman's infant son; the mother's breasts were dry until a month after she gave birth, and they could not afford to hire a nurse. Frederuna, whose knees bleed from nights of saying paternosters. Berchte and Brida, the sisters who bake bread for those who cannot afford it.

And Delphine.

There she is, spinning at the center.

Delphine, a woman thought strange for how she knots her apron strings when nervous, but a woman seen in mass as often as any wife in Strasbourg.

Possessed.

The word is the sudden prick of a needle on Lala's finger.

Possessed.

It echoes in Lala every time she flinches, wondering if Strasbourg's wives are truly flicking their eyes toward her, or if she is only imagining so.

Possessed.

Even Lala cannot deny how it looks, as though these women have demons within them, tormenting them into this frenzy.

Delphine spins fastest of them all, her feet bleeding the most, her face streaked with dirt and salt. She throws her long arms and thin legs, her skirt flying like spilled milk. She leaps and turns, as though her body is letting loose some spirit within her. Her linen cap has soaked through with sweat.

The watching crowd grows by the minute. Merchants cram alongside hawkers, priests with coiffured hair next to tradesmen. Burghers with their jewels and silk gowns sidle near fishmongers if it will give them the best view.

Delphine's husband tries to take hold of her. Her sons try to still her. The strongest men to be found, masons and blacksmiths, lend their help trying to pen her in.

But with each twist of her body, she escapes. With the force of her movement, she breaks from their grasp. She keeps on with her dance.

They plead with her. They order her to stop.

She keeps on.

Her fervor and passion fall on Lala's skin heavier than the day's heat. Her face shows no joy. No satisfaction at disgracing her husband, nor the celebrating air of some festival dance.

She carries the look of a saint in stained glass. Pained but transcendent. Eyes cast toward heaven. As though her body remains among them but her spirit has flown.

This is the expression gilding her face the moment before

her heart gives. She drops, one hand reaching toward heaven as she falls.

Then she is gone from them all.

Lala can see the life leaving the woman, like a wisp of smoke.

In a hushed moment comes the crowd's understanding. Before their eyes, a woman has danced herself to death.

Screams rise through the watchers, as though the sound is a thing being passed from one tongue to the next. As each onlooker realizes what they have witnessed, the horror tears a gasp from each of their throats.

Those screams, the clipped breaths, turn over in Lala's brain in the hours that follow, as the sun falls toward the blue-green ridges of the Vogesen.

And that night, she lives it all again, as though the scene plays before her.

They will not rest, says the crowd in her dreams.

They will not stop for food or drink, the onlookers whisper.

Their places go empty at mass.

See, they are bewitched.

Lala's dreams tumble toward the moment of Delphine falling, the instant of her soul fleeing toward the sky, leaping silhouettes at her back.

Lala wakes to the moon hanging low.

Bewitched. That word leaves even more of a chill on Lala's sleep-damp back than the word *possessed*.

She finds Alifair working by the light of a single candle. The glow lights his face, showing him tense and haunted.

She wonders if he too dreams of a flailing woman whose form scatters into ten more, like light thrown through water drops. Or perhaps he dreams of Delphine lowered into the earth, the funeral shroud offered to the Church, the green-pine smell of rosemary wreaths sharpening the air.

Alifair presses a dye-darkened pestle into an oak gall, and the shell cracks, the inside crumbling like meringue. The darkened center sticks to the pestle like crystallized honey.

Lala and Tante have tried grinding other things for pigment. Alder and blackberry. Walnuts and meadowsweet. Peach stones and vine. But each makes an ink more gray, not the deep purple or black as rich as an autumn night.

And none of them break as the oak gall, into a hundred pieces with a hard first shove of the pestle.

Lala tries to put her arms around Alifair, to stroke a hand down his back.

"Please don't," he says, mixing a jar of water and rusted nails. "You'll distract me."

He usually says such words with flirtation. They both know one lapse in attention can ruin a batch of iron gall ink. A bit too much rust, too little acid, and the ink will turn green rather than purple-black.

But now the words come with a regretful edge.

After a long quiet, after grinding a few more oak galls, Alifair says, "Henne told me thirteen dance now, maybe more."

It is more. Lala already knows.

Alifair pours the solution over the ink base, measuring the way Tante does, this delicate art of balancing tannins and astringents. "We should have said something."

"We couldn't," Lala whispers. "You know that."

He leaves the mixture to soak. "Tell that to Delphine's children."

Rosella

ed shoes. One pair of red shoes I'd sewn back together, and this fall had become more than the bright, almost-lemon smell of rain on leaves. It became more than that spice I could never quite place, as though the trees got their color from being dusted in chili powder.

This fall had become kissing Emil Woodlock, who I had never thought of kissing before tonight. I walked home from the reservoir with the taste of his mouth on mine, and the feeling of the red shoes sparking something into me.

I got so lost in thinking of all this, in licking my own lips to see how long I could feel him there, that I stumbled and pitched forward, like I'd slipped on the rain-glossed leaves.

I tried to get my balance back.

Instead, I slid into the feeling of being dragged from where I stood, like the red shoes were moving without me moving them.

I pressed my feet into the ground.

But the red shoes drove my steps.

They prodded me forward.

The force of them pinched and tore, taking my breath so I couldn't scream.

In a sudden rush, they dragged me past trees and stones, my

feet tripping over roots. They whirled me through the night, their pull as strong as fingers on my ankles.

They were making me dance.

No matter how hard I tried to keep still, I danced.

Even when I threw my body to the ground, the shoes made my feet kick out from me. When I knelt, trying to keep the soles of my feet from touching the undergrowth, the shoes twisted me around. They made me dance on the air as though it were solid as ice.

This was not the delicate turn of the music box ballerinas Sylvie and Piper had when they were little.

This was not the soft mischief the red shoes had been sprinkling over Briar Meadow.

This was a dance as hard and violent as a possession. It had all the fury of vengeance. I felt it in the jerking force with which the shoes led my body.

I reached for them, trying to pull them off.

They wouldn't let go of me.

I tried to slide a finger between my heel and the cloth of my right shoe.

It didn't catch. My finger couldn't find its way into the space. It glanced off the velvet at the back of the slipper.

I grabbed the shoe by the sole.

It didn't give.

I tried to pull the left shoe off my heel.

It stayed.

I tried knocking the back of one foot with the toe of the other. They would not come off.

I tried prying them away. They wouldn't budge. I tried to jam my fingers between the arch and the lining. But there was no give, no space, not even between the side of my foot and the shoe's soft inner wall.

The red shoes would not come off.

I clutched at the ground, digging my fingers into the hardening earth.

But the shoes kept me moving, dragging me by my ankles.

They danced me through the trees, pulling me over roots that bruised my shins and fallen branches that snagged my jeans. They danced me to where the trees thinned again, up to the edge of the county road.

The desperate hope bloomed in me that maybe the woods were doing this. Maybe the second my feet touched the pavement, the shoes would let me go.

But they dragged me toward the centerline, red following the double yellow. They flitted over the asphalt, gleaming with oil sheen.

The first glimpse of headlights broke the darkness.

I looked down at the shoes, willing them to dance me back into the trees.

The headlights grew, turning from far-off lamps into twin moons.

Not a car.

A semi, the kind that came through hauling produce.

My heartbeat grew hard in my throat.

I tried to resist the shoes' pull, but in this moment, my feet weren't mine. They fought my effort as much as I fought the red shoes.

The shoes danced me away from the centerline and into the truck's path. They whirled and spun me until my hair was a veil over my face.

I slipped into the space between terror and resignation, between screaming and bracing, shutting my eyes.

It was only then, with me screaming into the oncoming headlights and the blare of the horn, that the shoes turned me out of the way.

They pulled me from the truck's path, twirling me back into the trees.

Then they went quiet.

They went still, and I fell.

They left me there, crumpled on the undergrowth, fighting to get my breath back, my lungs as lit up as the burning leaves I could smell in the air.

Strasbourg, 1518

"In the name of our Lord, we beseech you," the priests say, as strong men herd the dancing women onto the carts.

Lala watches, her throat tight as a rope.

Even with the carts penned in on the sides, the women writhe and turn. Some cannot be brought on at all, twisting from even the strongest grasp.

At the crier's last count, there were thirty-four. Days of dancing have tumbled blond and copper hair from cornets and rams-horns. Brown and black hair has shaken from its braids. Dirt and blood stain the hemp cloth of shifts, the dyed linen of surcoats, the silk of bliauds.

The ringing of bells for Delphine, the announcement of her death, still tinges the air.

"You will be cured, my daughters," another priest tells the living dancers. "By Saint Vitus, you will find your rest and your salvation."

Saint Vitus? Lala wonders. The cave of Saint Vitus is in Saverne, at least two days' walk from Strasbourg. How well will they make the journey when they can barely keep the women on the carts?

The watching crowd fiddles with their hands, restless in the heat.

Whenever they move, flashes of color show in their palms. Then they close their fingers, and the color vanishes.

Without turning her head, Lala casts her eyes to the side.

They clutch handfuls of bright purple, rich as a queen's gown.

Another look sharpens the green stalks and violet petals. It comes with the chill of realizing how many eyes are on her, how many Strasbourgeois whisper.

Wood betony.

They all hold wood betony, the flowering herb for protection against the devil and the witches he sends into the world.

Lala's throat grows dry as a sunbaked stone.

Witchcraft. It has taken only days for the suspicion to bubble from Strasbourg's houses.

Geruscha shoves alongside Lala, Henne following after.

How plain they look compared to Enneleyn, with the soft brown and dull green of their dresses, their hair tied back in simple chignons. And how plain Lala must seem to Melisende and Agnesona, with her skin that holds brown even in winter, her black hair as coarse as a new harvest of straw, her body that carries its weight low.

Geruscha presses a handful of wood betony into Lala's palm.

"To ward off the devil," she says.

"And his demons." Henne adds a sprig of angelica to Lala's hand, and crosses herself.

Geruscha and Henne, it seems, fail to notice how many clutch their own sprigs tighter at the sight of Lala. Are they oblivious to all things on this earth? The snubs from the burghers' daughters? The scorn rippling toward Lala?

Do they even know what they both witnessed at the crab apple tree four years ago?

Lala listens to the current of whispers.

Some say it is the people's sin that brought this plague. The immorality of loose hair and kissing behind shops has let in the devil, they insist. Or they blame the sky. "The earth has moved across the stars in opposition to the head of Medusa," an astronomer pronounces, showing his maps of the heavens, "and into the twentieth degree of the Virgin."

The crowd breathes and moves like an animal. It shifts at its edges as dancing women who cannot be persuaded onto carts approach. It draws back from their pained, distant expressions as much as from their fevered movement.

Lala can smell their sweat, sharp and sour, and the blood their feet leave on the stones. By the way some dance, the physicians can tell they have broken ribs and loins, cracked bones in their toes, twisted ankles that will take months to mend. And still, they dance on, in clogs, or in boots, or barefoot.

Enneleyn slips alongside Lala, looking neat as the white and gold stars embroidered on her dress. As always, the mere sight of her makes Lala feel disarrayed. She feels the sudden impulse to brush her own hair and straighten her skirts.

Melisende and Agnesona follow behind her. Veil and wimple cover the sisters' heads, as though they are married women.

They are so proud of their hair that to witness them hiding it seems as odd as a cat wearing breeches.

"Is there some new fashion I don't know about?" Lala asks Enneleyn.

"You haven't heard?" Enneleyn says. "Within the city walls, all those with red hair must cover it, married or not."

"Why?" Lala asks.

"The dancers go into fits at the sight of red. They cannot

stand to see the color of Christ's blood." Now Enneleyn whispers. "It's the devil's way of keeping the women from being brought back to the Lord. If they see it"—she glances right and left to be sure no one is listening—"they become violent against their own bodies and others. They scream that they are drowning in a red sea of blood. So the council forbids any shade of red for all but the priests. Cloth, jewels, even hair."

Over the noise of the square, the beating of the women's feet against the stones, comes a new pronouncement. Not from the priests, but decided by the magistrate and his commission, the ammeister and stettmeister, the councils of men who command this city, men who wear their wealth and family names as comfortably as dyed tunics or Swiss leather boots.

From so deep in the crowd, Lala cannot catch all of the crier's words. She wants to reach into the air and snatch them from above her head, but finds only a few at a time.

The council has sought the wisdom of the physicians' guild . . .

. . . a natural affliction, born from overheated blood . . .

Lala cannot help sighing with relief.

It is an explanation free of witches or the devil.

. . . excess heat in the body, which must be released . . .

Lala glances between Enneleyn and Geruscha, who never exchange more than a curt greeting. Their polite but chilled distance should make Lala feel even more favored, but it only reminds her what she is to the burghers' daughters. A curiosity. Perhaps the daughter of some distant nobleman. These girls with smooth, pale fingers wear cloth that she and Alifair dye, and their fathers write in Tante Dorenia's best ink.

At least Enneleyn shows more effort than Melisende and

Agnesona. She at least greets Geruscha and Henne, while the sisters' lips curl into twin sneers as though they might dirty the hems of their skirts.

How quickly Lala would lose their affection if they knew what she and Tante hide.

. . . the only cure will be for them to dance day and night until the affliction passes . . .

The words *cure* and *affliction* snap Lala's attention back to the crier.

"There will be"—at last comes the loud crescendo of the announcement—"a great dance."

A murmur of excitement fills the crowd.

"The trouble is dancing," Lala says to Enneleyn, "and the cure is more dancing?"

Before Enneleyn can answer, a tall man's shadow draws their eyes.

The sergeant named Sewastian pauses before them.

Melisende and Agnesona flicker their eyelashes at him. Sewastian is a handsome man, younger than his hard face would suggest, with a carved jawline and eyes as blue as day-flowers. Ever since he became a widower, the city's maids have wondered who he might marry next. Melisende has told Lala, no less than three times, that his long nose speaks of virility.

Sewastian looks among them, as though he cannot tell them apart. As though they do not look as different as any six girls in Strasbourg. Geruscha, with her pretty but serious features and rush-colored hair. Henne, with her tan forehead and her chignon so tight it seems to pull at her face. Melisende and Agnesona, who, with their covered heads, have only pale green eyes to give color to their faces. Enneleyn, with her linen-flax hair.

And Lala, in all her shades of brown.

"Lavinia Blau," Sewastian says.

Her own name lands with a stone's weight.

Lala swallows, and steps forward.

Emil

It was stranger than the year bats hovered over backyards, fluttering alongside hummingbirds in the half dark before sunrise and after sunset. Stranger than the year that points of light, like the embers off a sparkler, drifted around houses where babies would soon be born.

Tonight, Rosella Oliva had kissed him. It was as much unexpected magic as anything that ever came to Briar Meadow.

He could feel the oddness of the season in the night air. It held the bitter tang of ashes, and the clean cold of the sky. The bright eye of the almost-full moon winked between clouds, like it knew he could still taste her lip gloss on his mouth.

That was what he wanted to hold with him as he fell asleep.

Instead, he dreamed of a time centuries earlier. He dreamed of the corner of Alsace, where his family lived five hundred years ago. The stone bridges and towers, the shuttered windows overlooking the canals, the city walls that shortened the daylight hours.

And the fever his father had told him about a long time ago, the plague of uncontrollable dancing, stranger than anything that had ever happened in Briar Meadow. In his dreams, he could hear their steps striking the stone. He could smell the dust they were kicking up, and the blood on their heels.

He could catch the smallest glimpse of a dark-haired, brown-skinned girl, and the salt-sting of her horror as she watched it all.

When he woke, sitting up fast and breathing hard, the feeling didn't leave him. Ancestors whose names he didn't know seemed to rise and fill the dark. Their calls sounded like the far-off shriek of the wind. Their fear came so sharp he thought they were dragging him back across five hundred years.

He slowed his breath.

Yes, he still had his Romanipen. That meant knowing his family's dead a little better than most gadje knew theirs. But ever since that day he'd listened on the stairs, he'd stayed clear of his parents trying to tell him about their family's history. If it got into him, it could spill out of him again, like those things he never should have said at school.

He couldn't tell what he didn't know. And he didn't know their names, the name of this girl, because he hadn't let his father tell him.

Strasbourg, 1518

The bailiff is a man more imposing in posture than body, but the sight of him still makes Lala's neck tighten.

"It is no secret that this town has fallen under a sort of madness," he says, gesturing at a plain wooden chair.

As she lowers herself, her spirit feels as though it is drifting from her body.

The room is small, sun streaming in from a single window, high and narrow.

In the center stands a table upon which a hundred men and women have probably signed confessions they could not even read.

"Whenever such afflictions reveal themselves," the bailiff says, "there are always rumors."

Lala shuts her eyes, bracing for the charge of witchcraft, for the entrance of the friar who will extract her confession.

The bailiff walks back and forth, his fine, heavy boots sounding his steps. When he stops, he looks at her and says, "There are those who whisper that you are not true Strasbourgeois. And neither is your aunt."

Lala's stomach turns over.

It is not just her.

It is Tante Dorenia with her.

Lala cannot help it; she turns over her hands on her lap, her fingers still blue-green from the woad dye.

Richest blue from those yellow and green plants. Perfect black from the oak galls. To Strasbourg's finest merchants, such color must seem a kind of alchemy. Magic in fine blue and ink black.

And in the hands of two women, it will be called witchcraft.

"The magistrate," the bailiff says, "has no wish for this matter to continue, but only to see it resolved."

At the word *magistrate*, Lala's heart feels brittle as an icicle.

She will be blamed for la fièvre. She will be drowned, or hanged, or burned. She cannot stop herself from imagining the chill of the water, the tightening of the rope, the vicious teeth of the flames.

And Tante. The thought of her bibio being dragged to the stake or gallows leaves her breathless.

She opens her mouth to confess, to keep Tante Dorenia out of it, when the bailiff speaks again.

"As you know," he says, "it has been some time since we have forbidden die Zigeuner within our city walls."

Lala's heart stops, pivots, turns.

The words bring the echo of a common law, not just here but throughout Alsace and far past the Vogesen. The one that chased her and Tante from Riquewihr, and so many other families from their homes.

Wer Zigeuner schädigt, frevelt nicht.

Whoever harms a Gypsy commits no crime.

These few words remind Lala of what she has known her whole life: that gadje will get away with killing their men and burning their houses. And the law provides generous room for it.

This is why there is no friar. She has been brought in on a

matter of city ordinance, one the men of the Church must consider beneath them.

"So you understand our concern with the speculation that you and your aunt . . ." The bailiff trails off, motioning with his hand for her to complete the thought on her own.

Lala nods, because it is all she can do.

And because it is not a lie.

She does understand.

Lala's heart spins faster, like the limbs of the stricken women.

This is how she will be blamed, her and Tante. They will be like the Jews blamed for the plague a century ago, hundreds slaughtered in this very city, all on an unproved suspicion that they put sickness into the wells. And again, four years ago, so many thrown into jail because someone had to be blamed for the bitter winter.

Lala stills her breath. Who has pointed to her and Tante's black hair and their dark eyes and their skin that stays a warm color in winter? She searches the pit of her stomach for any suspicion that it might be Geruscha and Henne. But their strange efforts at friendship persist, and more and more she thinks they do not understand what they saw. So who else? Guilds who do not want Tante Dorenia's competition? Men who think women should not be in the business of ink and dye at all?

"Mademoiselle Blau." The bailiff casts his winter-blue eyes at her. "Are you a woman of die Zigeuner?"

Lala drags herself from her own fear, calling up the words her aunt told her to say if anything like this ever happened. Tante Dorenia taught them to her until she could repeat them back without flinching.

Except that Lala has already failed, because Tante Dorenia taught her never to need them.

Lala's eyes water, her own eyelashes prickling her. She thinks of the fines, the cropping of hair, and far worse, that so many before them have endured.

Now, to save Tante and herself, she must deny her mother and her father, the dead in the ground, her own blood and her aunt's.

It is the thought of leading Tante away from that imagined execution that steadies her tongue.

"No," Lala says.

"And your mother and your father?" the bailiff asks.

Lala crosses herself, out of reverence for the dead, but it brings the benefit of seeming like a gesture of shock.

She replaces her parents' vitsi, Manouche and Sinti, with the words her aunt gave her.

"A Frenchman and a German woman," Lala says, because the bailiff will assume two Roma could not also be French and German.

The bailiff nods, satisfied with a job done.

She has said it.

She has denied her mother, whose heart held the most beautiful fairy tales. She would enthrall children with stories about a čhavo and a princess who glowed gold as the sun, or a young Rom completing an impossible task given by a wicked king or queen. Lala was not old enough to remember them, and whatever small threads live in her, she has now surrendered.

She has denied her father, who spent his short life mastering the davul-zurna. A man with a musician's heart, he was such a contrast to his serious, business-minded sister, Dorenia. What would he say of his own daughter now?

"And you will swear an oath to this, yes?" the bailiff asks.

He asks as though it is nothing, no more than the oaths sworn for the Schwörtag every year.

Her lips part to protest, but no words come.

An oath, one that denies herself and her mother and father.

She is caught, a moth ensnared in the sticky lace of a web she did not notice. She has flown straight into it.

She knows, in this moment, three things.

The first is that she will never tell Tante what has happened in this room. The shame would crush Lala where she stands. Tante taught her the words she has spoken—*a Frenchman and a German woman*—so she would know how to save herself. But Tante taught her more not to need them, not to be brought into this room in the first place.

Second, she will bake hyssop into unsalted bread to atone for the words she is about to speak. She will take it onto her tongue, and perhaps the penitence will stop her heart from growing so heavy it breaks her ribs.

The third is that she cannot touch Alifair again.

She will put an even wider distance between her and Alifair than he did when they were younger. Now that the magistrate has cast an eye toward Lala, any suspicion could catch him too. If she is not careful—more careful than she has been—the very things she loves about him, that which make him someone who could learn Romanipen, will destroy him.

Lala readies her tongue to speak, and is sure she can already taste the bite of hyssop leaves.

Mother and Father, she prays, *forgive me. Forgive me. I must live, and I must save the woman who has treated me as her own.*

The hidden altar Lala and Tante made them feels so paltry now. The best cloth they had, the white candle and dish of water, the food brought as earnestly as Lala would have brought her mother flowers she picked; it seems so small compared to what Lala must now do.

Mother and Father, forgive me.

The words become a chant through her bones, through the blood she must forswear.

"Yes," she forces out, making herself meet the bailiff's eyes. "Of course."

Rosella

I flew past my parents' room, both of them asleep, thinking I was staying over at Piper's.

I went into the bathroom and soaped up my ankles. I splashed them to bubble up the soap, wondering if maybe I could slip the shoes off like a too-tight ring.

But the shoes dried as fast as if I'd left them out in full sun, and still did not move.

I did the same thing in the shower. I let the spray soak my hair and clothes and all of me as I worked to get the shoes damp and pliable. I fluffed up lace sheets of soap bubbles to loosen them from my arches.

The satin only slicked and then dried. My feet did not squish inside the lining. There wasn't even space between the cloth and my skin to let water in. The seal was tight as wax over wood. I couldn't even feel my feet inside the shoes.

I turned off the water, fevered and out of breath.

I dried off, and found everything sharp within reach. Scissors. A letter opener. A kitchen knife with a good enough grip that I wouldn't slip and accidentally impale myself.

I took each to my family's beautiful work.

My hands went at them. My hair, tangled and wet, streamed

in my face as I dragged each sharp point through the beaded patterns.

The blades only left soft imprints on the cloth. And in seconds, even they faded.

I went at the shoes harder, driving the sharp points into the cloth, pulling them across the beading.

They did not give.

The scissors, the letter opener, the knife left no cut in the fabric.

I kept at them until I wore myself out, my heartbeat and breath so hard and fast I fell to the bathroom floor, the red shoes dragging me down. They felt heavy as iron. They had such weight, and fighting them took so much of me, that they pulled sleep over me like heavy curtain.

These shoes would not be pried off, or torn away, or even slashed.

They had sealed to me, like they had become part of my skin.

Strasbourg, 1518

*L*ala walks into the light. She senses the stain of her own words, a weight on her skin. But in the same moment she feels how she has been stripped bare of something that once kept her to the earth. It is as though, all her life, she was held together with a little bit of the stars, and now that part of her has been spooled away. It has been drawn back into the sky. And now what remains of her is crumbling to ash.

The sun and the noise leave her dizzy and unmoored. The clatter and rasp of a wooden stage going up at la Place Broglie is so loud she feels the bones in her head are coming apart.

A rounded thing, warm and soft but with a hard core, strikes Lala's skirt.

She reels back, and it tumbles to the ground.

A pear, bruised and sun rotted. It has gone mushy enough to leave a wet, sticky trail on her skirt.

For a moment, Lala wonders if it has fallen from a cart.

Until she notices the woman staring at her.

The miller's wife. The mother of a girl who dances. She stands with her hands dropped to her sides, her fingers wet from the rotted fruit.

A spoiled apple strikes Lala's hip. She does not see where it came from.

She faces the stares of the close-gathered crowd. The preparing of the stage for the great dance carries on, but those not hurried along in the bustle pause to watch. The fishermen bringing up pike perch and bream from the water. The currier fitting boots. The apothecary taking money for a tincture he insists will guard against the fever. Even the ladies in their striped skirts, attendants pausing at their heels.

Lies that satisfied the bailiff will do nothing in the face of the Strasbourgeois. Any rumor about her and Tante and some lesser Italian prince will crumble to dust. This is a city that slaughtered starving peasants for revolting against their usurers, and Jews for nothing but their faith.

They say that for all things in heaven, God has created a corresponding match on earth. They say there are as many points of light in the sky as fish in the sea. Lala can only imagine what the Strasbourgeois consider her celestial mirror to be. Some dark star. A glint in a constellation that, as it moves across the crystalline spheres, brings misfortune and deadly magic.

This is a city where the story they choose to believe about you depends on how well they think of you, and that story can shift as suddenly as the wink of those stars.

Just as a limp courgette strikes Lala's leg, a tall, fair-headed girl pushes through the crowd.

"There you are!" Enneleyn cries, in a voice so pointed Lala knows it is for show. "Do you know how long I've gone on looking for you?"

For a moment, Lala blinks at Enneleyn, unsure if her friend means to distract the crowd from its scorn. Or, if she is really so oblivious as to not know where Lala has been, why she stands in the murk and mire of this disdain, thick as spring mud.

Which of the two is no simpler to guess than a throw of dice.

To a girl used to silk and pearl pins, all the world must wear a shined gloss, like a delicate frost on a yule morning. How easy it would be for such a daughter to overlook anything ugly befalling a girl like Lala. But then, it was Enneleyn who recounted the full story of the color red, of its banning within the city walls. How often men must speak freely before her watching eyes, how empty they must consider her pretty head, when in truth she is always listening.

The crowd murmurs back to their business, caught by Strasbourg's most beautiful daughter.

Enneleyn takes Lala by the arm. "I've thought of the perfect dress for you to borrow." She leans closer, and whispers, "If we believed everything every fishwife ever said of us, we'd never leave our beds."

Lala lets Enneleyn pull her along, trying to ignore the glances thrown her way.

If it is not rotted vegetables, it will be pine cones and acorns next.

Then, if she does not do exactly as she should, kindling.

So, on the night of the great dance, the one meant to cure the fever, Lala presents herself to Enneleyn, to Melisende and Agnesona. She offers herself, so they will make her into the sort of girl more likely to be tossed admiring glances than spoiled fruit.

The sisters fuss over her hair.

"Is Sewastian so handsome up close?" Melisende asks.

"Did he say anything about us?" Agnesona asks.

"I cannot believe you had him all to yourself," Melisende says, as though Lala met the man in the loft of a barn instead of him escorting her to her own questioning. "I could die of jealousy. My father won't let me alone with a man until I'm a wife."

"Are his eyes so blue indoors?" Agnesona asks. "I bet they were deep as the sea."

Before Lala can remind them that she has never beheld the sea, only the canals and the Rhein, Enneleyn sweeps between them.

Enneleyn throws dresses across the bed and onto chairs. She casts an herb-green gown onto her bed, its weight rippling the red and white roses embroidered into the brocade. She tosses aside one in the golden tones of dried wheat and mustard seed, stitched with leafed vines and red grapes.

Lala's heart bends in sympathy to whichever of her family's maids will have to put them all away, seeing to the wrinkles. But she offers these girls nothing but a grateful smile. If she does not keep herself in the good graces of Strasbourg's favorite daughters, what little guard she and Tante have left will thin even further.

It is already threadbare enough.

Enneleyn holds a wine-colored kirtle between them and gives it a wistful look.

"It really is too bad," she says. "I would lend you this one but"—she sighs—"some priest will declare it too red."

She throws it atop the others.

Something in Lala turns, and for a moment she despises Enneleyn, in a way as small but heavy as how she hated Geruscha and Henne four years ago.

She turns the hate over in her hands. It is not about Enneleyn being spoiled, or pale, or adored.

Just as she hated Geruscha and Henne for seeing a part of herself she wanted to hide, she hates Enneleyn for not seeing it.

Melisende offers Lala a bit of her lip potion, each of them dipping their ring fingers in.

"And will you dance with your fairy prince tonight?" Melisende asks.

Lala smooths the lip potion over her mouth, pretending not to hear the question. She tenses her heart against the thought of Alifair, how she must ignore him tonight especially, when all will be watching.

Enneleyn tucks an amber-adorned hairpin just behind Lala's ear. "When we are through with you, you will have your pick of a dozen young men."

Lala's guilt is heavy as damp wool. Her silence, her allowing these girls to think she is looking for a new love, feels soaked in disloyalty. But the closer she stays to Alifair, the worse peril he will face.

Agnesona tries her pale powders on Lala, even though they are far too light, and only make Lala appear sick.

Her skin and Dorenia's is no browner than it has always been, and not much darker than that of the men who work in the fields. Beneath the July sun, Alifair's back deepens even through his shirt and tunic. If it is something in her features—her dark eyes, the shape of her nose and lips—has she not looked this way all her life?

Something has made them all glance at her again. Something has made the word *Zigeuner* spread within the city walls. And deep within her stomach, Lala fears it resembles a growing crowd of women spinning over the cobblestones. It has the same shape as the word *witchcraft*, the hint of it dangerous as a coiled adder.

She lets Agnesona add blush to her cheeks, made from pigment and rosewater; Agnesona frowns when it takes layer upon layer to show on the brown of Lala's skin.

That frown makes Lala's neck tighten. Is Agnesona taking a more careful look at her? Is she reconsidering whether Lala's particular shade of brown can truly be explained by Italian blood?

Is she thinking the word *Zigeuner*?

Lala's heartbeat feels as though it will drum through her throat.

"God in heaven," Melisende says, snatching the pigment. "Don't make her look a whore."

Lala tries to smile, but her face fights the effort.

The sisters each tie on new kerchiefs bought from a traveling merchant, the cloth embroidered with birds and flowers and trimmed in gold thread. Their particolored dresses make them seem lovely mirrors of each other, the left side of Melisende's cotehardie the same green as Agnesona's right, and the right half a dawn orange, matching Agnesona's left.

Their world, and Enneleyn's, is one of leaf-green pottery glaze, of drinking glasses blown in gray black. These girls' fathers are the reason Strasbourg boasts its own gold coins. And those coins, minted next to the Pfalz, now travel the continent, their gleaming backs declaring the glory of the men who called them into being.

Wealth, to these girls, is a language as familiar as beauty.

If letting these girls dress her will make her seem soft and blameless, she will let them as willingly as though she is their doll. If their rosewater and tinctures will gild her enough to make her look like one of them, she will offer her cheeks and wrists, and accept all the paling powder in Strasbourg.

The brown of her skin has drawn the suspicion of a city. Maybe these girls, with their complexions that seem poured from spring cream, can veil her from it.

Emil

Emil threw on jeans and a sweatshirt. When he couldn't sleep, he usually went out to the old shed that had become his sort-of lab. An hour focusing on something that hard, looking at a flame through cobalt glass or sketching the jagged rainbow of bismuth crystals, was usually enough to wear out his brain.

Outside, he found his mother tugging an old sheet over the vegetable garden.

Emil took one corner and bunched it under the pumpkin vines.

"What?" his mother asked. "No wisecracks?"

Emil's guilt stung. He'd barely concealed his skepticism at his mother covering the pumpkins and melons, shielding them from the moon. His great-aunt had told stories about the full moon felling herbs from their stems, withering violets to the ground, splitting open melons and pumpkins so that, in the morning, blood streaked their rinds.

It wasn't that Emil didn't believe these stories. He did. Sort of. He believed that melons could break open and flowers could fall away from their stems overnight. He believed there was blight or infection, sudden frost or tiny parasites no one could see. He believed that whatever it was, a sheet holding back the light of the full moon probably wouldn't stop it. And that held true whether it was chemistry or bibaxt, misfortune finding its way into their garden.

His mother unfurled another sheet. This was one of the few traditions their family held to. Flour and water in a bowl on the windowsill. The fortuitous meaning of certain days. Lemon and pepper and cabbage. He had never quite figured out the pattern of what they held on to and what got lost, what stayed, and what got cleared away, like his mother reordering her desk every Sunday night.

Emil helped with one side of the new sheet.

"What's gotten into you?" his mother asked, snapping the corner over the Moon and Stars watermelons.

He ignored the question and tapped a knuckle on the deep violet rind. "These are gonna freeze before they're ready."

"All the more reason to cover them," his mother said. "And that was not a rhetorical question. What's going on with you? You usually roll your eyes over this so hard I'm afraid you'll lose them in the back of your head."

He couldn't argue. But tonight there was some kind of turning in the air, a stirring. It was the smoky smell even though no one nearby was burning leaves. It was the shadows lengthening so quickly. It was the jack-o'-lanterns leering out from their porches, soft pumpkin mouths looking ready to make some snide remark. (And around here, you never knew if they might. Mrs. Carrington swore it had happened a few years before Emil was born, the carved pumpkins spouting Poe and Dickinson at one another.)

"Bonne nuit," his mother said, setting a hand to his shoulder on her way inside. "Don't stay up too late."

"I won't."

He went for neatening up his lab bench, because he'd been putting it off, and there were few tasks more boring than that. After fifteen minutes, he'd be half-asleep.

He pulled the overhead string in the shed. The single bulb threw light over the forgotten garden tools that shared space with his secondhand bench and the rusted paint cans that he kept at a healthy distance from his burner.

Emil went hard at the beakers and flasks, something he always put off when the weather got cold because the sink out here didn't get hot water. It took a combination of patience, prayer, and banging on the pipe to get it started. It would only run for a few minutes before he had to do the whole thing again. It always encouraged rushing, as evidenced by the lace of salt residue he was now scrubbing off the glassware.

He moved on to relabeling vials and bottles, fixing the tops and spouts where the plastic had split.

A tuning-fork hum vibrated the air, like the far-off charge before a storm.

Emil's hands stilled.

The feeling of someone touching his shoulder sent a rope of cold down his back.

"Maman?" he said, more a hope than a guess. He could hear the tension in his own voice, the shock of the unfamiliar.

He turned around, losing the sense of both his body and his hands. He lost them so completely that it took a few seconds for him to register the sound and wet feeling of mislaying his grip on a bottle, and acid splashing out over the bench and his hands.

Strasbourg, 1518

Tante brushes away any talk of attending the great dance. Folly, she calls it. Superstition.

But Lala wouldn't be surprised to catch her covering the melons in the garden, the rinds ice blue and not yet ripe, so that they won't bleed in the light of the next full moon.

Tante shows no sign of knowing the oath Lala swore. But even looking at her still brings the taste of the hyssop in Lala's mouth.

Enneleyn leads Lala toward the dance. Her hair flows against the pale satin of her gown, green as early June flax. With each step, the noise grows.

The animals have been moved out to graze, and the whinnying of mares and braying of mules is replaced by shouts and music. The grain markets and two guildhalls have been cleared for the dancers. Hired guards block off the streets, and pen in the afflicted. The raw grain smell of barley water thickens the air, the drink recommended to any afflicted who will take it.

The scene is bright and loud as a carnival, the sight matching the high music. Many wear dyed stockings, adorned buckles, shirts trimmed with lace. The ruffled edges of scalloped sleeves hang wide to show silk linings. Striped and checked cloth flashes one shade, then the next. Men strut about in pointed shoes, or in codpieces of bright color and comical size.

Those with bells dangling from their belts add to the music, their bodies living tambourines. Some dress as devils or beasts, masks over their eyes. Some whom Lala knows to be wealthy burghers wear ripped clothes, playing at being peasants.

Both the stricken and well dance so hard that sweat drenches their bodies. The unafflicted whirl as if spinning around a bonfire.

With one lapse in attention, Lala loses Enneleyn.

She searches for Enneleyn's gown, for the white and yellow lilies embroidered onto the field of green, the thread the same shades as the striped lining.

"Enneleyn?" she calls, feeling as lost as a younger sister.

The sound vanishes under the guiterres and citterns, the vielles à roue and lutes. The music is a tangle of fifes and fiddles, the twinkling of flutes mixed with the hard chimes of tambourines.

Lala stands at the edge of the fray, amid the smell of spilled wine, the storm of limbs, the sound of drum and horn.

The afflicted pass through the crowd so perfectly that, at first, Lala can't pick them out. The sisters of stricken dancers leap alongside them. Men twirl women with so much abandon it seems there is no fever at all, only this great dance. Strong men have been hired not just to haul the drink, but to dance alongside the women, to keep them going.

The only sign of worry is the mothers of the younger girls, chasing after them with brown bread and thinned wine. Each time one collapses, two or three women rush to where she has fallen with water or ale.

All have put on their finest. The ladies who can afford taffeta and damask flaunt their gleam. The burghers wear black underdyed with blue to keep the color fast. Even the poorer Strasbourgeois wear their best hemp and wool, newly dyed with plants and lichen. The color, Lala can tell, has been done cheaply, without mordants or underdye, and will fade within weeks. But for tonight, these skirts and tunics paint the air green and yellow. A few farmers' daughters even wear lighter shades of woad blue; Tante offers her less intensely hued lots at softer prices, especially to families she likes.

Lala collides with a tall, well-built young man, feeling his solid form before she sees his face. He is both slender and muscled, in a way built more for admiring than work. His slashed sleeves reveal a near-purple fabric beneath.

Lala lifts her eyes, trying to comprehend the strange costume this burgher's son has chosen.

Another moment makes his dress sickeningly clear.

He has darkened his face and hair with roots and donned a turban of coiled silk, like the young men declaring they are Turks at Carnival.

It makes her want to slap them all in their painted faces.

She looks away, pretending to study the other dancers. She can pick out the afflicted only by the way they leap a little higher and spin out of time from the music.

"Do you like it?" he asks.

She moves her eyes back to his, the green a shade darker than Enneleyn's dress.

"My costume," he says. "I would think you would enjoy it. It's so much like you."

Now her voice comes. "Pardon?"

He skims his eyes along her hair and dress. "Exotic."

He nearly purrs the word, and it bucks in her stomach.

Exotic. The word such men use when they want to make dark-eyed women into their mistresses, or rare pale deer into their pets. A word that carries both their thrill and the sense that they are entitled to all that interests them.

Exotic. What Melisende and Agnesona probably say of her and the stories about her being the bastard daughter of some southern Italian nobleman.

Exotic. The word that makes Lala pull out of this man's hold.

The burgher's son grabs her arm. "I thought you wanted to get acquainted." He gives her a smile that is both bright with his wealth and slack from how much he has had to drink. "You did throw yourself toward me, after all."

Lala shoves him back.

His grip tightens, and Lala can feel the bruises it will leave.

The burgher's son pulls her close. "Do not think a borrowed dress makes you highborn."

Lala feels her heartbeat at her throat. She wills Enneleyn to appear, to make some joke about how young men are such brutes, to shame this one away with her smile.

Lala has never been so proud or foolish as to refuse help. Not from Enneleyn. Not from Tante.

Not from Alifair.

But the appearance of Alifair now, with his hair lightened by the summer and his skin tanned by it, makes her nearly as wary as the hold of the burgher's son.

Lala arrived at the great dance with burghers' daughters, instead of with Alifair, precisely to keep his name from scandal. And now here he is, shoving the burgher's son off Lala.

"Stop," Lala yells, careful not to say Alifair's name, in case the burgher's son does not know it. She does not want to give him an easier path to complaining about a rude apprentice.

But Alifair pushes the burgher's son back harder, his grip breaking off Lala.

The burgher's son raises an arm to backhand Alifair.

Alifair does not flinch.

Lala leans forward, ready to grab the threatening arm.

But the far sound of yelling stills the three of them.

Past the stationed guards, Lala catches sight of the carts, sent to Saverne, and now back. She glimpses the last moment of the afflicted resting on the carts, and then the fever drawing them in again.

It takes hold of them. The noise of the great dance—the drums, the fifes, the tambourines—has them spilling forward.

The priests plead with them, begging them to heed the blessing of Saint Vitus. Or so Lala guesses; the saint's name is all she can catch of their shouting.

Lala stands on her toes, trying to recognize the women.

Cateline, the book binder's wife.

Frederuna, the barber surgeon's sister.

And the miller's younger daughter, the afflicted one, leaping from the cart and toward the great dance.

The music rises to a great shriek of strings and drums, frightening the horses. They rear and startle back. Their terror is so fine-edged Lala can feel it in the air, their nervous reaction not just to the noise but to the trouble that builds in this city and the sky above.

It is into their path that the miller's daughter crosses before anyone can grab hold of her.

No, worse than into their path.

If she were going into their path, she would miss them, their alarm throwing them backward.

Lala tries to call out to her, warning her. But the noise of the instruments swallows her voice.

The miller's daughter, in as much confused terror as the horses, ends up between them and the cart.

Another strike of noises rattles the horses further, and one kicks backward.

The force catches the miller's daughter in the chest, and the life in her ceases, as quickly as her dance.

Rosella

My body felt wrung out, my ankles stretched and sore. But I shoved myself out of bed and into jeans and my coat. I needed to know if any of my friends had some twist of dangerous magic in their own red shoes.

I found them at the drugstore trying out lipsticks. Aubrey and Graham were drawing on each other's arms with the testers, laughing and shrieking as they went back and forth between evading each other and retaliating.

"These would look perfect on you," Piper said by way of greeting, and drew comet trails of plum eyeliner and gold shimmer on the back of my hand.

"Piper," I said.

She set her green eyes on me. By now I had learned not to wither under that stare, or at the sight of her birthday-cake-golden hair that seemed impossibly shiny.

"Is anything"—I glanced at the cinnamon-candy-red pair she wore on her feet—"weird happening with your shoes?"

"Other than me getting along with Mrs. Tamsin?" she asked.

I tried to smile. Even in Piper's most affectionate moments, her mother was always *Mrs. Tamsin* or *the lady of the house*. Never *Mom* or even *Mother.*

"Do they"—I grasped for the words—"you know, come off okay?"

"Are we about to have another conversation about arch support?" Piper ruffled my hair, already messier than hers. Always messier than hers. "Because I've heard this lecture from Sylvie."

Aubrey craned her neck around the aisle, her red hair brushing the endcap. "What are you two whispering about?"

"She made out with Emil last night," Sylvie said, holding a nail polish bottle up to the fluorescents.

Graham snapped her head toward me. "You made out with Hot Pocket?"

"I'm sorry, what?" I said.

"Hot Pocket," Graham said. "He's the hottest of the pocket-protector guys."

"He does not wear a pocket protector," I said.

"It's implied."

"And also," I said, "worst nickname ever."

"Um, no." Aubrey tried a tester lipstick in the mounted mirror. "WD-40? That was the worst."

"Oh, you earned that one, and you know it," Graham said. "You squeak whenever you get excited about something."

Aubrey swiped moss-green eyeshadow onto Graham's arm. Graham got her back with mustard-blossom yellow.

The overhead lights caught both their red shoes, and they laughed in a way that made me realize, all at once, that they'd be kissing by the end of the week, if they weren't already.

"Are they . . ." I whispered to Piper.

"Oh, yeah," Piper mouthed at me. She bent down a little to whisper, the way she and Graham always did with girls as short as me and Aubrey. "Took them long enough, right?" She straightened up and tucked a stray lock of hair behind her ear, her fingernails flashing purple polish. "What were you talking about before?"

"The shoes," I said. "Have they"—I hesitated—"done anything to you?"

"They're doing things to everyone." Piper tried a shimmer powder on her cheekbone. "You should know that better than anyone after last night." She grinned.

"I mean," I tried again. "Does it seem like there's anything wrong with them?"

Her stare caught me, like the shock of finding my mother's glass measuring cup hot. *Hot glass looks like cold glass*, our science teachers were forever warning us.

"Why?" Piper eyed my shoes. "Should it?"

The distance opened between me and these girls I called my friends. Yes, Sylvie had gotten me to stop buying flower-patterned underwear in packs of five at this very drugstore. Yes, Graham had stared enough at me sprinkling chili powder on oranges that I didn't do it at lunch anymore. Yes, Aubrey had taught me how to take off wine-dark lipstick a minute before getting home. And yes, Piper had made me into a girl who would take a swallow of vanilla extract on a dare, laughing no matter how much it tasted like lighter fluid smelled.

But if anyone knew what the red shoes had done to me the night before, everyone would blame me, not the odd magic lacing the air in town every year. It would be my body, brown and unknowable, that they would consider at fault.

In Briar Meadow, everyone probably thought they were above anything as old-fashioned as suspicions of witchcraft. Here, our magic was small and contained, held within a single week each year. It followed rules set by the light above the reservoir. It stirred us, maybe even unsettled us sometimes, but it didn't have teeth. And if it was found to have grown teeth, it would be my fault. They would blame me, the suspicions the same even if they considered themselves too forward-thinking to call it *witchcraft*.

My own skin, my own body, would be the thing that had turned the red shoes vicious. My brown hands stitching them together, that would be what had sharpened them into something deadly.

The rise of Graham and Aubrey's shared laugh reminded me. Everyone else in red shoes was falling in love, or setting butter and sugar on their tongues.

But my red shoes, the ones I had made by hand, had taken me by my ankles.

If anyone knew, they wouldn't just blame me. They would blame my family. The stain of it could spoil every pair of shoes they made, not just the red ones.

If my mother wouldn't even tell people that we went to curanderas for fevers or nightmares, I knew better than to tell anyone this.

"Look." Piper took my arm and tried a blush on my wrist. "You are making this way too complicated. Do you like Woodlock or not?"

"Well, yeah, but that's not—"

"Then stop overanalyzing." She frowned at the carnation pink and shook her head, a declaration as final as a signature. "Who cares if you needed a really fabulous pair of shoes to give you a push?"

Her choice of words made pain flash through my arches.

But I took the out she was offering.

"You're right."

"Of course I am," Piper said.

If I wanted to get myself out of these shoes—without tearing down everything I had done to become one of Briar Meadow's adored daughters, without wrecking my family's business—I was on my own.

Strasbourg, 1518

Lala and Alifair dry the woad in the sun, pressing the leaves into boules de cocagnes the size and shape of late-season apples, then pounding them into powder. To so many, it's a weed, but in skilled hands, the leaves of this yellow-flowering plant produce such brilliant blue it seems a sorcerer's trick.

They wait for Tante Dorenia to start the dyeing. They don't dare try on their own.

"You never know what blue the powder will give," Tante reminds them. "You are both too young to have the touch for it yet." It takes a different skill, she says, to dye a blue for show than to dye a bottom color for black, or to overdye weld yellow to make green.

At her command, they lower the presoaked garments into the vat.

"Mind the bubbles," Tante says. "Or you'll never get an even color."

The bubbles are always on Lala's side. Alifair's hands are too steady.

Alifair keeps the greatest distance from her he can and still hold the cloth. He reads Lala as well as he reads the turning of leaves before rain. He seems to know she wants him to stay away from her, but the fact that he does not know why, and cannot know why, leaves Lala's heart as heavy as a hailstone.

None of them speaks of Delphine, or the few others who have fallen down dead from this ceaseless dance. Or the miller's daughter, whose life went out of her the moment she took the weight of the horse's hoof.

They lie in the cathedral crypt, priests blessing their worn-out bodies and the souls that once dwelled in them.

Tante marks how long to dye the cloth by the length of Hail Marys and paternosters. She knows just how much muttered penance is needed for each shade of blue.

The wet cloth grows heavy in Lala's hands. She can feel Alifair trying to take more of its weight.

Just as Lala's arms tremble, Tante says, "Now bring it up."

The fabric lifts out yellow as the woad's flowers. Lala and Alifair haul it to the line and flop it over, heavy as a great fish.

Lala blots her hands and forearms on her blue-stained apron, and the three of them stand back. To Lala, this part has always been worth the pulping and the alum fermenting and the grinding. As the air and sun hit the wet cloth, it turns, from that yellow to leaf green, and then to the blue of woad dye. This moment, waiting to see where the shade will settle, has always held the thrill and fear of months.

But there's no joy in it now, not when Alifair will not even meet her eye. Not when the miller's son mourns his youngest sister with a cry so haunting it still pierces the air.

And not when the council's great dance has left the city with more afflicted, not fewer. More dancers than ever crowd the squares; the crier's announcements can hardly keep up with their numbers. They whirl in the full sun of morning, in the hot, unaired guilds and within the crush of the market walls.

The fifes and horns, the tambourines and drums, only lured more to the terrifying dance, their loved ones watching with pained cries.

All that is left from the council's great cure is a mess. Refuse from the market and guildhalls scatters the streets. Boots trample ribbons fallen from girls' hair. Blood from the dancers' feet mixes with spilled wine.

And an edict from the authorities, that all occasions of dancing in the open should cease until autumn, as though they can command such a thing. Dancing at weddings may be done only with stringed instruments, they say, but leave each to his own conscience to use neither tambourine nor drum.

None of the instruments that most frightened the horses, and sounded the death of the miller's youngest daughter.

It is too small an effort, far too late.

As they dye and hang the last sheet, Lala's eyes catch on the road, on figures too far to recognize.

Lala slowly picks out one leaping form from the next.

The figures twirl and throw their arms toward the sun.

They dance.

With deepening horror, Lala watches them draw nearer, and finds features she recognizes. The papermaker's niece, with her hair the color of wheat stalks. The long limbs of the eel fisher's daughter.

The cartographer's young second wife, with her embroidered skirt meant to show off her husband's wealth. But neither the fine thread nor his coffers have spared her from this.

And following after, their mothers and sisters, reaching out their arms, calling for them, pleading with them to resist the devils within them and with the devils themselves to let them go.

When they cannot catch them, they stand on the road, weeping into their hands.

The dancers jump higher. They strike the ground hard enough to kick up dust. They trample wildflowers on their way, releasing the smell of summer nectar.

The scene bears the haze of a nightmare.

Lala blinks, but the figures stay. Girls Lala grew up alongside now spin toward town.

She runs after them, trying to grasp their arms.

If she cannot keep Strasbourg from looking toward her to cast blame, she must stop the dance itself.

"No," she yells, as helpless and desperate as if they were cows escaped through a fence. "Be still."

She would fall to the ground and beg Sara la Kali, even beg the dancers themselves, if she thought it would halt them. Instead, she runs, trying to catch hold of them. But a moment after her fingers meet an arm or shoulder, it slips away. They are too fast, their limbs too sweat-slicked to hold.

Geruscha and Henne stand by the side of the road, hands clasped. They lightly shake their heads, either in horror at the scene or in warning to Lala, that there is no stopping it.

The afflicted girls keep on, dancing toward town.

"Stop!" Now Lala is screaming. "All of you!"

Their faces show no response. They seem not to hear her at all. Even if they wanted to stop, they are helpless against la fièvre.

They seem made to do it. Compelled, either by something outside them, or so deep in their bodies it is written into their marrow.

Worst among their distant faces, halfway between pained and serene, is one Lala recognizes with a start.

The older of the miller's daughters.

The one surviving after this fever took her younger sister.

Her older brother, the one whose mourning cry still echoes in the air, runs after her. "No!" he shouts after her. "Do not follow your sister into death!"

But at the sight of Lala, he halts.

He stands, and his glare seems enough to singe her skirt.

Lala remembers herself, and twists from under his stare. She starts again with chasing them all. The tanner's sister. A knot of ploughmen's daughters.

And the miller's one surviving daughter. The single living sister of the young man whose gaze now feels as though it is searing her dress.

"Stop!" Lala screams. "Be still!"

But they do not stop. The fever is worlds stronger than any voice or hand in Strasbourg.

Emil

Emil had known that the next time he saw Rosella would, probably, be an inescapable kind of awkward.

But the night before had worn him down so much that he forgot to dread it until the second it happened.

"Hi," he said, and he hated how wary he sounded.

"Hi," she said, seeming even more apprehensive than he was.

Well, this was off to a solid start.

Her eyes ticked toward his hands.

He couldn't help looking down. Even following the same wash procedure he always did, the brown of his knuckles had reddened and paled in a way he couldn't pass off as coming from the cold air.

Rosella pressed her back teeth together. "What happened?"

"Nothing."

"Nothing," she repeated.

"It's just acid."

"*Just* acid?" she asked. "What were you doing?"

"It's not as bad as it looks." He put his hands in his pockets.

"Emil," she said, digging through her purse. "That's a burn. Come here."

She pulled him over to one of the benches that dotted the center of town, the wood split by months of sun and cold.

When she took her other hand out of her purse, her fingers gripped a tiny glass jar. The label had been ripped off, like it had held something else before.

When she unscrewed the cap, it smelled green and wet, like rain-soaked grass.

"This'll hurt for a minute but then it should help," she said.

"You keep that in your purse?" Emil asked.

"I'm a future abuela," she deadpanned. "I keep everything in my purse."

He laughed, and the memory of her family, the Oliva house, came back. His own mother and father could only agree on neutrals. Gray and deep beige and ink black. But the Olivas' house always seemed like it held every color at once. A sofa the red of cranberries. Big fluffy yellow and orange flowers. A blue-green blanket tossed over a grass-bright chair. The dark green carpet that Rosella's father loved and her mother hated.

Their house was the smell of salt and cinnamon and epazote. It was the windowsill where Rosella and her mother set tiny vases of silver-dollar eucalyptus, which everyone else in this town hated like a weed but that they loved like a favorite flower.

Rosella's fingers slid over Emil's hands and wrists. His breath caught, and felt jagged, like cloth snagging.

"Sorry," she said, mistaking it for pain.

He let her wrong impression stand.

"For what it's worth," Emil said, trying not to let the shiver down his neck get into his voice, "this is pretty tame."

"Compared to what?" Rosella asked.

He pushed up his sleeve and showed her the back of his

arm where a patch of hair had been singed away and still hadn't grown back. "Bunsen burner. Magnesium oxide experiment."

Rosella cringed. "I've got one uglier than that." She rolled up her sleeve and showed a paler slash on the brown of her forearm. "Hot glue, last holiday season."

Emil winced. He held up his left hand, showing her the patch of tightened, shinier skin that crossed two fingers. "Reconstituting stearic acid. Tube clamp slipped."

She pulled down the neck of her sweater. A thin scar notched across her collarbone. "Leather awl, two years ago."

Emil sucked air in through his teeth. "What the hell were you doing, hugging it?"

She laughed.

He had made her laugh.

He would probably never have the kind of charm his mother had, the kind that softened everything. She could critique how someone was arranging strawberries haphazardly in a tart or setting an oven at the wrong temperature, and it would sound like a compliment. She would take knives out of friends' hands or stop them in the middle of salting meat. *No, no, ma chérie, you must do it this way.* And always she made it sound less like she was correcting them and more like she was sharing some family secret. *You don't do that,* his mother said when people turned on the stove too early and then shut it off again. *You don't heat up a pan and then cool it down and then start it back up again. The oil, the metal, they are ready the first time.*

It wasn't a talent Emil had inherited. The same as how he'd missed whatever gene made his mother and father the kind of academics everyone wanted at dinner parties, the kind whose historical facts drunk people loved—*did you know there was a kind of marriage between men in medieval France? Affrèrement!*

Emil would probably turn out to be the kind of academic written off as pedantic by everyone except his cat.

But he could do this. He could, sometimes, when he was lucky, make Rosella Oliva laugh, even while he was trying not to think of kissing that scar on her collarbone.

Graham Davies passed by on the sidewalk. "Hey, Hot Pocket."

She was down the block so fast Emil couldn't even tell which one of them she'd been talking to.

Rosella looked like she wanted to hide behind the hardware store's sidewalk sign.

Emil opened his mouth, hesitated, tried again. "Do I even want to know?"

Rosella answered before he was done asking. "Absolutely not."

Strasbourg, 1518

There is satisfaction in feeling something crumble beneath her hands. Lala puts her arm and her anger into it, the grinding of oak galls.

When the oak galls are ground, there is still rage in her hands, so she kneads hot-water dough for the gougère.

"You are fortunate." Tante Dorenia stands alongside.

"Oh?" Lala asks. "And why is that?"

Tante inspects the rhythm of Lala's palms. "Because in your great-great-great-grandmother's day, la gougère was prepared in a sheep's stomach."

Lala kneads on, not in the mood for Tante's history tutoring.

"Lala," Tante says. "Why does the hare run to the forest?"

Lala tries to smile.

Garude lava, the kind of riddles Lala's father, Tante's own brother, so loved.

"Because the forest will not run to the hare," Lala says.

"And who is the brother who runs after his brother but can never catch him?"

The thought of the miller's son glaring rises in Lala's throat like bile.

She turns over the dough, still warm on her hands. "Is that all you can think of? Riddles?" The rage that kneading the dough calmed now flares. "Why did you bring us here?"

"Because this was where we could afford to live," Tante says.

"Not this house." Lala looks up from her kneading. "Why Strasbourg?"

"Because it is a free city, not beholden to laws either French or German," Tante says, her voice trimmed down to a whisper. "Because we needed a place large enough to let us disappear and large enough for us to sell our blue. Because I knew there were families we could help here."

Yes, Lala wants to say. *And look how long it was before the gadje took even that.*

"But why here?" Lala asks. "Why a place where they walk the streets with such hate in their hearts?"

"There is hate in all hearts." Tante takes Lala by her sleeve. "I should think you would know that by now."

"And in your heart?" Lala asks. "What do you have for me and Alifair?"

Tante's gaze sharpens. Not in anger. More like Lala has caught her attention.

"I heard you," Lala says. "Four years ago. With the elder."

Tante looks not even a little surprised.

"The only defense you had for Alifair is that he hadn't touched me," Lala says. "So what is your defense of us now?" Her voice grows defiant. She knows she sounds younger but she cannot stop it. "What is it you think of us now?"

"I think it is against Romanipen," Tante says. "And I think you know that."

"So is your remaining unmarried."

Tante's stare grows hard edges. "And I have not judged you, or him. So don't you dare stand in judgment of me."

Lala feels herself both shrinking and returning the glare.

With a sigh, Tante's face softens. "I have only feared for the lives you will have. They are difficult enough each on your own. But together"—she pauses, closes and opens her mouth, as though collecting her words—"what is it you want me to tell you? What fairy story do you wish to believe? That you two being together would lessen your burden? That you both carrying something you must hide would make this life easier for you? That is not the way the world works. If it were, there wouldn't be so many of us who feel we have no choice but to marry gadje."

"Why is it that you have choices more than the rest of us?" Lala asks. "You do what you like." It is times such as this that Lala feels how small the years between them are, the gap more between an older and younger sister than between a mother and daughter. "You never have to draw yourself back or hide anything."

"I am with child," Tante says.

The words cut off any Lala has left. They drift away as quietly as woad seeds on the wind.

So much of the strangeness comes in the sudden remembering that her bibio has a whole life of which she knows nothing. She does not know whom Tante admires and whom she despises, not beyond what Tante tells her. Lala has been too caught in the weave of her own worry.

"Who?" is all the answer Lala can manage.

"Onfroi," Tante says.

It takes Lala a moment to place the name.

"The flax farmer?" she asks. She has rarely thought of the man by his Christian name. "But . . . he is so old."

"Everyone looks old when you're sixteen," Tante says, as though she herself is eighty. She is young enough and beautiful enough that boys Lala's age leer at her.

"Did you want to?" Lala asks, and even as she says the words she hears how clumsy they are. She does not know how to ask any other way.

"Yes," Tante says. "I did."

Lala falls into relief and then wonderment. The man is quiet and plain as a pail of milk, so what could Tante have seen in him? Does she watch him scattering the flax seed in April, stooking the sheaves in September, and find it graceful as a dance? Does he stroke her hair like the pure strands of linen combed from the stalks?

"Then you love him?" Lala asks.

Tante gives a small shrug. "I am fond enough of him. And he is a dear friend."

"But do you love him?"

The roll of Tante's eyes flutters her lashes. "Yes, a love to move the heavens, he and I."

The things Lala comes to understand in a single instant knit themselves together.

Her aunt has lain with a man she perhaps cares for, but does not truly love. Whether it happened once or a dozen times, it has got her a baby. This is why she has taken to her bed so often, a week's worth of mornings. This is why she cannot stand when the air inside grows stagnant and ripe, why she refuses the lift of thyme and marjoram, the fresh sharpness of parsley for the settling of her stomach.

She will not eat greens, because she will not risk the life of her baby.

This is why she would not join everyone else at the city dance, for fear of losing a child. With as many souls as have leapt into their own graves, Tante would not risk dancing to nothing the life inside her.

Lala's fear spins into a desire to pack as many of their things as they can, take Tante's and Alifair's hands, and pull them out of Strasbourg. She would take them to the far meadows of the Alsatian countryside, the forest, or the low, green mountains of the Vogesen. Or deep in the Black Forest where Alifair was born. Anywhere free from dancing plagues and suspicious eyes.

Lala looks for a rise in Tante's stomach. Her skirts and apron are loose enough, and Tante holds herself upright enough, that if she had told Lala nothing, it might have been another month before she noticed the slight curve.

The only further reply Lala can manage is, "When?"

"October, I think," Tante says. "Maybe November."

Autumn. They will welcome this baby into the world amid the amber flurry of beech leaves tumbling from their branches.

If they all survive until then.

Not just Lala and Alifair and Tante, but now the small life inside Tante.

Each time Lala breathes, she discovers there is more to lose.

"Lala," Tante says.

Lala looks up.

"Who is one who goes to town and stays there?" Tante says.

Lala shakes her head, to say she does not know this one.

"A road," her aunt says.

An idea flares within Lala, and catches fire.

Any blame cast toward Lala will stain not only her, but Alifair, and Tante, and now Tante's child. And the dancers cannot be made to stop, so it is the affliction itself that must be stanched.

If it will take a cure to the fever to spare them all from being blamed, Lala will defy the laws of the earth and the heavens to see it end.

She will defy even the dead.

Rosella

I snuck into the workroom, slipping into this world whose colors shifted every time I crossed the threshold. Tonight it was heeled shoes the gold of saffron threads. Slippers that looked made of olive leaves. Beading as delicate as hoarfrost.

If the shoes sealed to my feet were made by my abuelo and taken apart by my abuela, then maybe, somewhere in their things, was something that could help me pry them off.

On a high shelf sat my abuela's sewing box, the top upholstered in worn cloth. I took it down, setting it on the floor and kneeling in front of it. It held the things my parents no longer used, but couldn't even think about throwing out. Needles still holding the last of thread dye lots. A moss-green measuring tape gone brittle with age. Bits of my grandparents' favorite velvets and satins. Old tea tins filled with straight pins.

A seam ripper.

My eyes caught on its point, still gleaming silver even after years untouched.

The workroom door creaked open.

I whirled around.

"What are you doing down there?" my father asked.

With my hands in the sewing box, and the red shoes glinting on my feet, I almost, almost thought of telling him.

But every way I could explain felt like these needles, sharp, and so easily dropped and lost. How would I tell him that I had sewn these beautiful shoes back together, and this was what had come of it, a terrifying fever dream?

And what could my father do for me? I was the one who had done this. I had made Briar Meadow's magic flinty and dangerous. My hands, my body, had turned the gentle enchantment of red shoes to a bitter spell.

The thought of disgracing my family, and their craft, was a deeper ache than the soreness in my tendons. My great-grandparents had worked to get out of the maquiladoras. They had learned this trade in the poison air from the blowdown stacks, from fingertips lost to equipment that never got kept up, palms stained with burning varnish. They had gotten out, and they had turned all of it into their craft.

Everything my family had worked for. If anyone found out about my red shoes, I would ruin it all.

"Nothing." I shut the sewing box. "It's silly."

My father opened the woven top of the basket. "It's not silly." He took one of the beads rattling around in the top tray and looped it onto a length of indigo thread. "I miss them too."

He gave my red shoes a pained glance.

"Especially this year," he said, with a sad smile that cracked my heart in two.

I said nothing, and then I bristled under the lie of my own silence.

I would have to come back for that seam ripper later, in the dark, while my parents slept.

My father tied the bead onto my neck. In the hollow of my collarbone, it looked like a rose hip.

It grew heavy with the weight of lying to my own father, about his own parents.

Strasbourg, 1518

As she approaches la cathédrale in the early dawn, she prays into her hands. Not just into her palms and fingers, but into three blue ribbons cupped in the hollow.

Until she reaches the cave of Saint Vitus, these dyed ribbons, laced with her prayers, are all the protection she can leave for those she loves.

The thought of the forested road to Saverne casts a shiver onto her back. But she must go. The stares of Strasbourg's wives, the piercing gaze of the miller's son, drive her on. If she cannot stop la fièvre de la danse, there is only so long before she, and Alifair, and Tante will be blamed for it.

Tante, with her baby growing inside her.

As Lala steps through the cathedral's heavy door and into the nave, her stomach both hollows with awe and roils in revulsion. The vaulted stone of the ceilings seems to reach heaven itself. The stained glass looks like rainbows woven together. The gilded pulpit gleams with the same gold from which the city mint stamps coins.

Geld und gut. Gold and goods. It is a song that men hold dearer on their tongues than any prayer or communion host. All this, built off the wealth of wine and grains, off the profit of the cannon foundries, and off the backs of those so poor they sell their last seed to pay their taxes.

All this, built on marsh, so soft that wooden piles had to be driven deep into the earth and then tipped with iron just so the ground could support the weight of the stone.

Lala passes the Dreikönigsuhr, the Three Kings Clock of iron and gilded copper. She stares with wonder at the wooden rooster that, at appointed times, spreads his wings and opens his beak to reveal a clockwork tongue. The astrolabe dials and the carillon of bells always seemed like a kind of forbidding magic.

The astrolabe. A reminder that the Strasbourgeois consider each illness to correspond to a configuration in the sky.

Lala has become, to them, some wicked star.

She tucks the ribbons into her pocket. Alongside the waldglas bottle they seem nearly weightless.

A silent prayer to Sara la Kali mixes with the taste of hyssop still on her tongue, the green, bitter tone of protection and penitence.

With a glance over her shoulder, she nears the stone steps that lead down.

She takes a last full breath, as though plunging into water.

But just as she means to throw herself in, a candle and a cassocked form emerges from the shadows.

Her heart and throat tighten as one.

"Lavinia?" the priest asks.

At the familiar voice, Lala catches her breath.

It is a voice she is more used to hearing at l'Église Saint-Pierre-le-Vieux. He is one of the few kind priests left in Strasbourg, one who does not press money from his poorest parishioners so he can dress in furs. One who polishes altar rails himself, telling the acolytes to go home to their families before dark.

And one, it seems, that the canon priests, the ones who wear jeweled rings and sire children by their mistresses, have pressed into guarding the cathedral crypt.

"Are you all right?" he asks.

"I . . ." She means to lie, but in the presence of this man, with his thinning, silvering hair and soft eyes, only half a lie comes. "I came to bless the dead."

He pauses. "It's good of you," he says, hesitating. "But I fear I cannot allow it."

"Please," she says, desperation so deep in her voice it wavers. "I cannot sleep until I have done it."

For just a moment, the light he carries seems to take flight.

The priest places the candle in Lala's hand.

"Recall the Gospel of Matthew," the priest says. "The story of The Demons and the Pigs."

Lala grasps the candle, trying not to let her bristling show. The Demons and the Pigs? Which one is he about to declare her?

"Remember that it was not only demons who were cast out into pigs," the priest says. "It was our very Lord who was then cast out from the whole region."

She tries to grasp the words, but they slip from her hands. He cannot be likening her to Christ more than the demons.

The priest lowers his gaze. "Powerful men may count you as lowly as an animal, Lavinia," he says, "but remember that the Lord counts men hating you as a sign of that which is holy within you."

It is a small gift, only a few words. But the weight of them is enough that Lala can barely hold them. For just a moment, they lift the stain of the rotted fruit, and the bailiff's words, and the oath that still lingers bitter on her tongue.

The priest glances over his shoulder into the dark. "If I were to see you approaching the crypt"—he looks back to her—"I would be obliged to stop you."

She understands only when he turns his back, repeats, "*If* I were to see you," and saunters toward the shadows beneath the Three Kings Clock.

Lala breathes out, and takes this small light with her into the dark.

The stone steps seemed chilled with death. She can feel it through her stockings and shoes. By the time she reaches the last, her toes feel like frozen buds on a hazel branch.

The candle's light shows vaulted stone in smaller proportion than in the sanctuary above. With each step farther in, she expects the smell of rot and death, and it is there, the seeping stench of decay. But every other smell is a surprise. The earth and spice of oakum, myrrh, incense. The bite of white wine and balsam rubbed onto the bodies. The herbs stuffed into their throats.

She does not look at their shrouds, thin enough to show their features. She does not lift the candle enough to light them. Not just because she does not want to see if their eyes have swollen back open. But because she does not want to be one of the many gawking at them in death. These bodies lie on stone for the priests to pray over, for the physicians to speculate over, for any powerful man to gaze upon as though they were strange insects.

She looks only at their feet, and only long enough to take the bloodied shreds of their shoes, the best she can think of to bring to the shrine at Saverne.

Saverne. She must succeed where even priests failed.

Lala only wishes it did not mean facing the bodies of the dead.

Their souls have left them, leaving their corpses as hollow as rinds.

She holds her breath as she pours out a portion of honey wine before the bodies, an offering she hopes will be enough to guard her, to make sure she does not bring the bibaxt of these dead home with her. There is little Tante and Alifair need less than another measure of bad luck.

Lala pauses at the miller's younger daughter. Even before Lala reaches for what remains of her shoes, she glimpses the bruising on the girl's ankles, purpling the pale skin. There is not enough left of her hose to conceal it.

She does it so lightly, her breath tight in her chest, hoping that if she does not stir the air, perhaps she will not disturb the dead.

A pair of large hands takes hold of Lala.

The candle falls. The moment before it darkens, it lights the face of the miller's son.

The torn shoes tumble from Lala's hands.

The miller's son shoves her against the stone wall. "So you've come to torment her further."

"I never did anything to her." Lala gasps the words.

The miller's son holds a wide hand to her throat. "Then why is she dead?"

He is little older than her, younger even than Alifair, but grief has left him as ragged and aged as his father.

He grips Lala's throat so hard she feels the pulse in his hands meeting the one in her neck.

"Your sister," Lala chokes out. "I want to help."

His hands tighten, and pain gathers in her forehead.

"There is no helping her now," he says, pushing into her harder with each word. "And you dare disturb her."

The pressure is great enough that she cannot keep her eyes

open. "Only to see if there might be help for others, including your sister who still lives and dances."

His grip does not relent. "And what is it you would do for her?"

"I want to bless her soul at Saverne," she says with what little breath she has.

"Bless?" he says. "Is that what you call your deeds?"

"I want this to end." She shouts it, as well as she can.

"The priests brought three dozen to Saverne and it cured nothing," he says, fairly spitting the town name at her. "How many high masses? How many turns about the altar? And nothing. What would you do that they could not?"

"Anything I can." She tries to scream it. At first, it comes out so quiet she can barely hear her own words. But the scream blooms within her. It is a desperate will to keep the blame of this fever from landing at the door of those she loves. "Anything I must. Even if it means surrendering my own soul."

Her head feels as though it is fogging over, her thoughts disappearing into mist.

The hands drop her.

"Then go," he says.

She grabs at the wall behind her to keep from falling, coughing to get her breath back.

"Use every dark scheme to save her," he says. "I do not care if you must offer your flesh for demons to tear to pieces."

Lala swallows, twisting beneath this new understanding.

She has done nothing to convince him she is no witch.

All she has done is convince him that she will offer her wicked deeds to spare his sister.

He has taken the promise of her efforts as a vow to cure la fièvre.

"You say you will surrender your own soul." The miller's son shoves the pieces of tattered shoes into her hands. "Save those who still live, or you may have the chance to make good on your word."

The threat wears a veil thinner than a funeral shroud.

If she fails, this man will stand ready to accuse her.

Emil

"You're banning me from my own lab?" Emil asked.

"I am doing no such thing," his mother said. "I am simply insisting that you get some sleep before handling chemicals."

He braced against the memory of the dreams he couldn't shrug off, the girl with the same black hair and brown skin as so many of his relatives, witnessing that strange fever.

"I'm fine," he said.

"I saw your hands, Emil."

On reflex, he slipped them into his pockets.

His mother put a palm to his cheek. "You look terrible."

"And you've clearly been reading the school pamphlets about self-esteem."

"Sleep." His mother held up the key to the old garden shed. "Then you get this back."

"What am I, five?"

"This is not punishment," his mother said, already on her way out of the room. "It's precaution."

Emil sulked into the kitchen.

He had no idea how his mother heard him drinking from a cupped palm at the sink, but she did.

"Use a glass," she said, appearing and setting one down on the counter.

He shut off the tap and wiped his mouth on the back of his hand.

She narrowed her eyes. "You enjoy irritating me, don't you?"

He wiped the back of his hand on his jeans. "Immensely."

"I brought you into this world," she said, sweeping down the hall. "I can end your existence in it."

Emil slumped onto the sofa and called Aidan.

"Sorry," Aidan said, almost in the same breath as answering. "Your mother's recruited me. I'm not supposed to enable your insomnia."

Emil swore silently. He didn't know what was more humiliating: the fact that his mother called his friends or that they went along with pretty much whatever she asked.

"And don't even try Luke," Aidan said. "Or Eddie. He's with Eddie." Awkwardness flooded Aidan's voice. "Luke, I mean. Luke's with Eddie."

"*With* as in . . ."

"Yes, *as in.*"

Emil laughed. No wonder Luke wanted to go out to see the glimmer. "Took them long enough."

"You're one to talk," Aidan said.

"Sorry, you're breaking up."

"Sure I am," Aidan said. "See you when you're allowed out again."

"I am allowed out," Emil said. "I'm just not allowed in my own—"

But Aidan had already hung up.

Emil breathed out.

If his friends were busy—with each other or with being

traitors—and his own mother wouldn't let him at his own lab bench, he was going back out to the reservoir. Whatever restlessness the glimmer had given him, whatever it had sown into his dreams, maybe he could give it back.

Maybe he could refuse it.

Strasbourg, 1518

The sun is just warming the gray of the city's stone lanes when Enneleyn meets Lala.

"Is everything all right?" Enneleyn asks, still knotting the silk belt around her kirtle.

They stay close to the face of her father's home, clinging to its shadow.

Lala presses a blue-dyed ribbon into Enneleyn's hand.

Enneleyn's smile lights. "It's lovely. But why?"

For the turn of a single moment, Lala considers telling her. She nearly speaks the hope that perhaps, if Enneleyn holds this ribbon, whatever cure Lala may manage in Saverne will reach her before the fever can take her.

The thought crumbles and falls, dried as December leaves.

How can Lala tell her the hope she has pinned to this ribbon and two more like it? How could Lala even explain it, the gesture of a ribbon meant to keep the thread between two people?

As kind as Enneleyn has been to her, their friendship suddenly feels hollow in a way that has always been there, but that Lala has tried not to notice.

Enneleyn never offered her friendship to a Romani girl in love with a boy who had to shrug away a girl's name. Enneleyn's affection is for the cast-off daughter of Italian nobility.

Enneleyn's affection is for a girl who does not exist.

Lala settles on saying, "Keep it with you."

Enneleyn meets the gravity of Lala's voice with a laugh, soft as the dew in the window boxes. "Oh, Lavinia."

It is so easy for her to laugh in the midst of this fever. Her life, glazed green as fine tiles, leaves no room for the horror that fills the square.

"Just promise me you will keep it," is all Lala says.

"Wait," Enneleyn says. "Are you leaving?"

Lala drops her eyes to the cobbles.

"But you are coming back," Enneleyn says, her face open and hopeful as a child's. "Aren't you?"

Lala folds Enneleyn's fingers over the blue ribbon. "I promise."

She leaves the second ribbon beneath Tante's pillow, the third between Alifair's straw mattress and the timber bed frame. And then, laden with what she can carry, what will not be missed, she sets off for the rough, forested path through the foothills.

Lala cannot risk the main roads. They are little safer than the woods, and they bring the risk of more suspicious gazes, questions about the brown of her skin, arrest if anyone places her as what she truly is.

After a few hours of traveling rocky ground, the soreness in her feet turns to a deep ache. But there is no helping it. She must stay in shadow, hiding from those who would prey on a girl traveling alone. That means walking the stone-studded earth between trees.

Just for a moment, she cannot help wishing she were a merchant's daughter, with boats to glide along the Rhein and the Zorn. So many perils of the road are lessened by water.

As the afternoon falls into night, the air cools so quickly she thinks it will grow ice. The green gray of the silver firs steals the last light, and Lala pulls her cloak tighter.

There's only once she can remember a summer night having such a forbidding chill.

It was years ago, when she and Alifair were still small. It was high summer, as it is tonight. That part Lala knows, because both woad and flax were in bloom. She had gotten away from Tante, so she could stand in the border between the flax fields and a fallow meadow where woad grew wild.

Tante hated when she just stood, staring at the color. "Nothing good comes from being dream eyed," she would say as she took in the washing from the lines. But whenever Lala could sneak away, she ran to the path between the fields, so narrow that the dirt bore no cart ruts.

She looked out over the land, an ocean of blue to her left, one of yellow to her right, green stems and leaves undergirding each. They seemed painted, the blooms thick and stretching out toward the sky. They seemed the kind of petal lakes that fairies would dance in at night, their small lights hovering over the blue and yellow. It always seemed strange to her, how the woad with its yellow flowers made such blue dye, and how the flax with its sky-colored blossoms made fabric of palest yellow. They seemed to trade colors, like girls exchanging ribbons.

That day, Lala had drawn her cape around her, warming herself against the strange chill of the evening.

The sky darkened all at once, from a blue as rich as the center of the flax flowers to a wet-stone gray.

Lala tilted her face to the sky, hoping for a warm summer rain despite the breath of cold.

The next day, rumor would insist that a frozen goose had fallen out of the sky and taken four days to thaw. On Sunday, the canons would say it was a form of God's wrath on Strasbourg.

But all Lala knew the instant the sky opened was that the clouds were throwing down hailstones the size of late apples. They pummeled trees and vines and the swaying, bending flowers on either side of the path.

And Lala.

They beat down on her, and she huddled to the ground to cover herself. She spread her hands over the back of her head, pinching her own neck because it all seemed as strange and awful as a nightmare.

The hail kept on, striking her shoulders and rounded back. Lala bit her cheek both to keep from crying and to try to wake herself up.

Lala has never known how he knew, at once, where to look for her. But Alifair appeared, quick as the hail itself. He gathered her up off the ice-covered path and brought her home, shielding her on the way. It was the first time she could remember him ever touching her, and her grip, her arms tight around this boy's neck, was the first time she could remember touching him.

At the memory, her skin feels cold as hail. But she walks on. She cannot stop for the night, not yet. And she dares not light a candle so soon, both in case the journey is longer than she expects and in case its flare announces her to brigands roaming the woods.

And the noble sons from nearby estates.

When Lala hears the crunch of footsteps in the undergrowth, it is both of these that she thinks of. The thieves who would lift her skirts to make sure she isn't hiding anything they might steal. And the young heirs on horseback, hunting both women and stags, who would ignore her pockets but lift her skirts anyway.

"I see something," a man's voice says. Not a warning. A hope. A light fills his voice.

He steadies his horse.

Lala's breath turns to a living thing in her throat, a bird caught in an attic.

"Where?" another man asks, bringing his mount to a stop.

The horses' hooves quiet.

Lala's heart grows into a hard knot.

Hunters.

They have the refined, cheerful cadences of highborn men who kill for sport, not food.

She stays still.

But of course they will expect their prey to stay still. A fawn, or yearling bear.

There is no good in announcing herself as a woman. To such men, she would simply become prey of a different kind.

The dark undergrowth seems to move. Forms emerge closer to the ground, sinewy bodies on four legs. The fur at the points of their ears glints silver.

The animals have coats as deep and beautiful as the best ink she has ever made. Their teeth clatter in their jaws, and their eyes glow like alder leaves in full sun.

Their gait sounds in the dark, eyes shining through the trees.

"Wolves," one of the men says. Fear chases the joy from his voice.

The wolves' frightening beauty halts Lala's breath. But the way they come, steady and slow, lets her meet them with the calm of old friends. She is like the old stories Tante has told her about sailors who both love and fear the ocean. These wolves hold the awe and wonder of endless blue waves.

"Go," the other man says, and they drive on their horses. "There's a pack of them."

From the elm and oak darkness, the wolves show themselves, one muscled frame at a time.

And with them, a boy who was born with a map of the woods on his heart, a boy who seemed to appear from the branches of a crab apple tree years ago.

Rosella

Once I heard the click of my parents turning off lamps, I snuck back down to the workroom.

I traced my fingers along the shoes my parents were working on, kept on wooden forms to hold their shapes. A peridot-green set meant for a dance recital. A pair for a wedding, the candlelight satin an exact match to the bride's gown. A third in royal blue, a cross between a dancing shoe and a vintage heel. Two almost-identical pairs, one deep yellow, one the orange of marigolds, were flecked with bright yellow beads that looked like they were glowing, pairs a mother bought her daughters for Diwali.

And red ones. Always a few pairs of red shoes. Especially this year.

I stood on tiptoes on a chair, feeling around for the seam ripper without taking down the sewing box.

This was how I would end this. Like my grandparents, I would tear apart the work of my own hands.

I went at the red shoes, driving the seam ripper into the veins along the vamp and side quarters. I hooked it into any thread loop I could find along the casing and the wings.

With each pull of the seam ripper, I thought I could feel it, the tearing apart of these shoes mapped onto my own body.

I kept on. I went at them harder. I found every seam I'd made myself, every place I'd sewn the red cloth back together, and I dragged the seam ripper through the stitches.

But with the next pull of the metal hook, a shock of new pain struck me, like I was tearing the seams of my own heart. The inside of me was ripping into shreds.

And within that bloom of pain, the shoes sparked back to life.

They felt like hands beneath my feet, pushing me off the ground, turning me, driving me out of the workroom.

I thought they would throw me into the back door, until the wind's own hands seemed to swing it open. The air outside howled and tore at the tree branches.

The red shoes drove me out into the night, and the world blurred into the smell of highway and far-off fields.

They dragged me farther away, my heart tight as a knot of thread.

My hair whipped into my face. By the time I cleared it, the far light over my parents' front steps had disappeared behind me, quiet and quick as a sleight of hand.

The shoes kept going, pulling me over the ground like a child's doll.

I was that music box ballerina, made for twirling.

I was a falling-star streak of blood red.

Strasbourg, 1518

Alifair adds kindling to the fire.

He still does not speak to her, and has not spoken since he appeared, bringing the wolves with him.

She cannot work out whether they followed him, or he followed them. They walked alongside each other in a way that was both vigilant and familiar.

Lala breaks what they have gathered into pieces. "How did you find me?"

"I could guess where you were going."

"And why did you come?"

He prods the fire. "Because whatever you may believe, your aunt and I aren't so stupid as to let you go all the way to Saverne and back on your own."

Even with the sharp edge to his voice, she thinks again of the hail.

He guarded her then, taking the bruises of those falling stones of ice so she wouldn't.

It is her turn to guard him now. The stain of suspicion that dyes the edges of her skirt mars him every time she touches him.

She must put an end to it.

She imagines her heart as a hailstone, fallen from the sky, hard and cold and the size of her own fist.

"I don't love you," she says.

The words are held up by her memory of the bailiff's questions, and the thought of Alifair being brought to that room. What would they ask him, this boy who was paler than Lala and Tante, but who many still think is some unknowable child from the deepest shadows of the Schwarzwald?

Alifair flinches, as though at the memory of a slap.

She keeps that flinch from staying on her skin. She braces her heart into being nothing but handfuls of frost.

"I know," he says.

How easily he believes her should give her relief. But his quick acceptance makes her crueler.

"You are my aunt's apprentice," she says. "That is all you are to me."

He draws in air through barely parted lips.

She knows him enough to know this is one of the ways he steadies himself.

He gets to his feet, taking his knife for more kindling. "Your aunt has been good to me. I do as she says. I followed you for her, not for myself."

And again, they fall into silence.

It is there, in that quiet, that they remain while they sleep, on and beneath the coarse wool blankets. It is there they remain the next day, as they walk the miles beneath the maple and beech.

She has always had the small suspicion that he is a little more German than French. Of course, in Strasbourg, most everyone is some German and some French. Except for the way Alifair pronounces his *As*, his French could pass for the language he has spoken all his life. It is only the small things Lala knows to listen for, the low trilling of the vowels, like the buzz of a hummingbird's wings.

But the way he walks the forest, sure and fearless, makes her all the more certain that he came from the Schwarzwald. He warns her of roots that might trip her. He changes their path when he senses wolves or men on horseback, or when he thinks they might find mushrooms or wild sorrel. He marks their route by the way the wind has molded the soft yellow clouds of smoke bush trees. He hears the whisper of water so early she does not even know what they are following until he leads them to a stream.

It makes her watch him all the more, seeing him in this landscape with which he shares a common language. She studies the way he kneels alongside water, dipping his hand in and bringing it to his mouth.

She cannot love him, not now, not until la fièvre passes. Until it does, any tie to her is a danger to him.

These very things that made her fall in love with him, the things that make him understand her and Tante better than anyone else in Strasbourg, are the things that might damn him.

In Strasbourg, in the crowded lanes within the city walls, he has always been as out of place as Lala and Tante are among gadje. It is up to Lala to make sure no one takes more notice than they already have.

The silence between them thickens in the last miles before Saverne. But when they approach la grotte Saint-Vit, the flinted quiet settles, like the surface of a pond. Near the rock mouth of the chapel, forbidding in the moonlight, it becomes something sacred, and true.

Alifair builds the smallest fire he can that will burn the blood-ied scraps of the dancers' shoes. The flames swallow the tattered fabric.

As they wait for the ashes to cool, they kneel before the painted wood images of the Virgin and Child.

Lala tries to offer well-ordered prayers to Saint Vitus. But within moments, she loses hold of her own thoughts, and her desperate heart cries out to Sara la Kali.

Let this leave us.

Sara la Kali, She who protects, who cures sickness, who turns bibaxt into luck and life. The gadje do not recognize Her as a saint, but they have made up stories that make Her fierce heart and dark form more acceptable to them.

Please. Let this leave us.

Sara la Kali, to whom Lala prays in church, for whom she lights candles in the transepts, letting any who watch think she is worshipping some distant, paler saint.

Her eyes still shut, Lala hears Alifair stirring the ashes. It is a mild rushing sound, him checking for embers. It softens the edges of the quiet.

Please, Lala asks, with the raw hope of a child. *Let this leave us.*

She has never wished more for a statue of Sara la Kali, so she could lay flowers at Her feet, so she could lay before Her the garments of the afflicted and beg Her help.

"What are you burning?" A woman's voice startles Lala out of her prayer.

Alifair stops, his hands pausing.

Lala scrambles to her feet, and Alifair rises from where he crouches, both of them ready.

A woman's face appears from the dark, her pale expression stricken.

Lala stares, but her vision at night has never been as sharp as Alifair's.

Alifair reads the woman quickly. "She's alone," he says, not whispering, but in a low enough voice that the woman will not hear.

The woman is better dressed than Lala would expect of a woman traveling on her own. Not damask or a silk bliaud, but a well-dyed overdress.

"Nothing," Lala says so firmly it sounds an insult. "We only wish to stay warm."

The woman looks almost disappointed. She dips her head, and the auburn of her hair catches fire by moonlight.

What answer did she hope for?

"We've come to pray to Saint Vitus," Alifair says, standing in front of the extinguished fire. "For the healing of a fever."

Lala thanks Sara la Kali that the dancers' shoes have already turned to ash.

The woman steps closer. "Would you pray for my sister?"

"Is she afflicted?" Lala asks.

"Afflicted?" the woman asks.

"With la fièvre de la danse?"

"The what?"

Lala and Alifair blink at each other. So this woman wishes a cure for something else. Who would they pray to? Saint Vitus? Sara la Kali, She who Lala's heart cannot help crying out to? Both?

But the woman looks so hopeful.

Lala's understanding comes as a hard pinch.

Of course the woman was disappointed. She saw their small fire and must have hoped it signaled a ritual that would give her prayers more weight.

"Yes," Lala says. "Of course we will."

Lala kneels and prays, truly, for this sister she does not know. She can feel Alifair and the woman on either side of her, their fervor bristling against her arms.

The woman prays and weeps with such intensity that she falls asleep in la grotte, collapsing as though at midnight needlework.

Alifair draws one of their blankets over her.

Then he silently gathers up the ashes.

We can't, Lala mouths, tilting her head toward the woman who has prayed herself into a dream.

Lala gets close enough to Alifair to whisper, "What if she wakes up and sees what we're doing?"

"We're not doing it here," Alifair says.

"The entire point was coming here." Lala's whispering sharpens.

Alifair's eyes find her in the dark. "Trust me."

His gaze pins her in place, his eyes holding twin moons.

"Come with me," he says.

For a little while, they retrace the path they took to la grotte. But then Alifair leads them deep into the woods.

"Have I ever told you about aspen trees?" he asks, his voice soft as the rustling of the leaves. "Their roots are all connected." He holds a branch out of her way. "As though they grow as one tree."

He holds another branch aside, and the night fills with fluttering green.

A gasp catches in Lala's throat.

Endless heart-shaped leaves dress a copse of trees.

Alifair stands, and she stops alongside him, watching the uncountable leaves.

"They're one body," he says, with the quiet reverence of sharing a secret. "Something can be one tree, and a whole wood."

Lala breathes the chilled air and imagines the ground under their feet, how the boughs and branches open to a wide spread of shared roots.

With the turn of the breeze, she can smell the warmth of Alifair's skin.

She snaps herself away from the thought.

Lala should not encourage this in him, the part of him that lives in these woods, and that made him easy for Tante Dorenia to teach. This boy, who speaks the language of these woods, and whose Romanipen she has never seen more sharply.

She cannot love him as long as every touch of her fingers brings suspicion on him. She cannot love him as long as half of Strasbourg whispers about whether she is Romani, and the other half about whether she is a witch.

Lala remembers the woman she saw against the dawn years ago, standing at the crab apple tree, lowering a fever. For that, Strasbourg would call her a witch twice over. Lala knows so much less than that woman, and it feels nothing short of arrogance to hope she might imitate a drabarni's wisdom. It feels as presumptuous and hopeful as being a little girl trying on her aunt's skirts, putting on that which is beyond her, that which she has never learned.

But Lala and Alifair offer the ashes to the trees, asking them to take this collective fever. In the streaming of ash from their fingers, she prays the afflicted are spinning for the last time. That they are recovering their senses and halting their dance. That they are stumbling along the stone lanes back to their homes.

The air turns again, and a slight warmth seems to lift from the aspen trunks, as though they are breathing not only with each other but with her.

Lala's hope grows sharp, both pain and relief at once, like a full breath of winter air.

She has often heard that all things on earth have their celestial mirror in heaven. But here, in these trees, she finds the divine health that stands contrary to the dancing sickness. In Strasbourg, a shared fever drives so many bodies to exhaustion or death. In the afflicted, a shared life and breath means they perish. But in these trees, that same collective breath makes the trees their most alive. She feels them speaking to each other in their roots and in the whisper of their leaves. She feels them sharing water as though from cupped hands. They give to her palms the sense of being each themselves and part of a greater, shared life. These trees are not only the divine opposite of Strasbourg's fever. They are the glinting mirror of everything Lala does not have, the vitsa she and Tante Dorenia were made to relinquish.

All she has left, the only other trees whose roots she can reach, are her aunt, and this boy. They are why she locks any blight deep inside her own heartwood, so it will never touch them.

Lala breathes in the memory of the woman at the crab apple tree, and her hands act without her thinking.

She reaches for Alifair's and sets them on the aspen's trunk. Her palms lie against the backs of his hands, both of them speaking to these trees as one.

Emil

The moon and the glimmer milked up the surface of the reservoir. Flickers of movement stirred the fog.

The movement was too high and spindly to be a bear or a wolf. A deer, maybe. He kept his approach slow in case he was right. One crackle of branches underfoot, and the deer would bolt.

He came closer, and what he'd thought was a deer's body resolved into human limbs, hands and hips. What he'd thought were antlers were arms.

They drew forward from the fog.

A girl, spinning through the dark, dancing along the rock ledge.

His dreams bled into the scene in front of him. The thread of being awake, all chilled air and silhouette, tangled with the heat and features of his nightmares. They ran together like paint.

The girl's features emerged from the fog. Dark, full hair. Brown skin. And though he couldn't make out the specific features of her face, he caught the gleam of her eyes, the bright flash of terror as she flew.

The girl, the woman, from five centuries earlier. The one who was a little bit his blood.

His father had told him the thinnest details of la fièvre de la danse, the strange dancing plague his ancestors witnessed five hundred years ago, because the thinnest details were all Emil would listen to. Until now, he had never considered that any of them might have gotten caught up in the fever, and danced.

Maybe this girl had. If there was evidence in the disintegrating papers his parents had tracked down, they wouldn't have told Emil, because he'd made clear he didn't want to know.

But here she was, come to life in these woods.

A ghost, wearing jeans.

That last detail would have made him laugh.

Except that she was getting closer to the edge.

In one half second, she looked like she was thinking of throwing herself down to the rocks below. In the next, she looked like she was skipping along the ledge, letting chance decide if she'd go over. And in the next, Emil found a mismatch between her upper body and her legs, like she was fighting the motion of her own feet.

Like the dance itself was compelling her toward the edge.

He went for her without thinking. Only in a small space at the back of his mind did he wonder if he had imagined her, and if she would vanish the moment he touched her.

She wavered at the farthest edge, her arms out like she was trying to balance and stop herself from going over.

Just as her center of gravity seemed to incline toward the reservoir below, he caught her arm.

"Hey." He pulled her away from the edge.

She didn't vanish.

She was a living girl, and she fell into him, her breath hard against his chest.

He drew her back farther, putting space between them and the ledge.

Her breath still came loud as the rustle of voles in the underbrush.

He cringed at the thought of looking at her, this ghost come to life so completely she had a body. Would it be like looking at some sister he didn't have? Like looking at old photos of his mother? Would he recognize his own features in her face?

But she was already looking at him. He could feel her stare on his forehead, hotter than her breath on his collarbone.

Emil lifted his eyes.

The colors he expected were there. The winter-brush-field brown of her skin, made darker in this light. The coarse black of her hair. Her eyes as deep as wet earth.

But the mismatch between the girl he expected and the girl he saw, how she did look familiar but in the wrong way, it shorted out something, like one Christmas bulb going out and the rest going with it.

Emil's brain was too full, too muddled with his dreams and everything in front of him, the confusion of wondering if he was asleep, the fast bridging of five hundred years. He felt those five centuries condensing in him, like the stars that fit a world's worth of heat and light in the volume of a teaspoon.

So when he heard Rosella Oliva's sharp breath in, when he felt their shared startle of recognition, he didn't have enough of himself back to say anything. He lost his grasp on all the things he was trying to keep in his brain. So when she stared at him, eyes so big the white caught the glimmer, and then ran, he couldn't even think fast enough to go after her.

CStrasbourg, 1518

In the morning, the woman—Petrissa—insists on taking them as far as she can toward Strasbourg on her way to Rheinau. She insists in a way that speaks of some small protectiveness toward them. As young as she looked under the moon, daylight shows the creasing at the corners of her eyes, and Lala can guess she either has, or has lost, children near Lala's and Alifair's age.

"My sister," Petrissa says after a few silent miles.

Lala has been so lulled by the oxcart's rhythm, and the way Petrissa murmurs to the animal, that to hear the woman speak to her startles her.

"She has fits," Petrissa says. She does not look at Lala. She keeps her eyes on the wood-shaded path before them. "The priests say she is possessed, but I do not believe it. And as long as I do not believe it, they will not pray for her, not truly."

"So you went to the shrine," Lala says. "To do it yourself."

Petrissa gives what Lala guesses is the best smile she can manage. It is still pitifully small.

"You asked what we were doing with the fire," Lala says. "I fear I did not give you the answer you hoped for."

Now the smile falls. "Each time my sister comes back from

her fits, she remembers less and trembles more. God forgive me, if I thought it would spare her, I would try anything. I would ask the devil himself for his prayers."

Lala should rush to judge this woman. She understands that she should. But the fierce love Lala has known herself—for Alifair, for Tante, for the baby she has not even met, for the families whose voices brushed the beams inside their house—only makes Petrissa's words sound in her own heart.

Lala is grasping for something to say when Alifair jumps down from the cart.

"Stay back," he says, in a whisper so loud it becomes a hiss.

Petrissa halts the ox, murmuring to him like a skittish child and then asking, "What is it?"

"Just stop and stay where you are."

Alifair darts ahead, keeping hidden among the blackthorn.

Lala hears the horses' steps moments before they appear.

And moments before she understands that Alifair has erred.

The horses have not kept to the road.

They ride between the trees, trampling the wild angelica.

Then they stop.

Lala sneaks through the trees until she sees them.

Fine, tall stallions, ridden by two men in velvet-adorned tunics. Embroidery and gold embossing declare their families' crests, and fur-lined mantles drape their shoulders, of no use in the summer but to display their wealth.

These are the sort of men who consider the woods theirs, and who so often have the force of law on their side. They are the kind who could have had Alifair lashed if they'd caught him scavenging fallen branches in winter. They are ones who would see Lala's skin and hair, and pin the word *exotic* to her, a bright flag they would chase for sport.

These are the same kind of men who thought her a deer, and would have little guilt over slaying her and discovering her to be a woman.

Except there are no wolves this time. The daylight has driven them into hiding.

"And look what we have found," one of them says. "A feral boy de la forêt."

"Out here all on your own?" the other asks, in mincing imitation of concern.

"Stay with the ox," Lala whispers to Petrissa.

"Lavinia," Petrissa warns her. "You can't."

"Keep back," Lala tells her, and then runs between the trees.

Alifair catches the sound of her steps before she reaches the clearing, his head turning just enough to meet her eyes through the trees.

He shakes his head, so slightly the men on horseback might not notice.

She does not slow.

His chest falls, his eyes shutting.

Not relief.

The settling resignation of something going even worse than it was.

In a moment more, she is close enough for the two men to see.

How quickly and easily they come down from their horses shows their youth, and their leers show the sense of place they have no doubt learned from their fathers.

They do not care how clearly Lala and Alifair see their faces. They show off their pride and power like the embroidery on their doublets, silver as just-minted groschen.

Nothing Lala and Alifair say against them would ever be believed.

"Mais non, not on your own." With a breath of amusement, the fairer haired of the two steps forward. "She goes with you?" He glances at Alifair. "Let's see how well you share."

Alifair pitches forward after him.

The second man shoves Alifair away.

Lala casts herself at the fair-haired one, but he bats her to the side. With each throw of their fists, the men pen them in, backing them toward a stand of trees.

That fair hair is now askew, matching the rage in the man's eyes. "I've had servants whipped for far less."

The fair-haired man lunges forward, the other raising a fist toward Alifair.

Then, like a celestial body descending from heaven, a dark round comes down on the second man's head.

It is so strange and miraculous, it seems a new moon is swinging downward from the sky.

The man tumbles like a felled tree.

The fair-haired man turns.

The dark moon arcs once more and catches him in the temple.

He falls, revealing the woman who holds the black moon.

An iron pan, the long arm gripped in both her hands.

The woman looks near Petrissa's age, with similar delicate lines around her eyes. But the colors of her are each different. Black hair instead of auburn. Brown skin instead of Petrissa's pale that has gone pink in the sun.

Instead of small, fragile-looking features, hers more closely resemble Tante's.

And Lala's own.

The woman stands with her feet far enough apart to plant

her, still holding the iron pan. She wears a plain blouse with skirts of linen and lace, the sort of clothes that are familiar only because Lala knows she cannot wear them.

The ends of Lala's hair prickle with the sense that there are others in the woods behind her. It is far different than her worry over the men in fine tunics. More a familiar comfort, as when Tante moves around the wattle and daub when she thinks Lala is asleep.

Alifair looks between Lala and the woman. In his face, she sees the first flare of recognition, before she has it herself.

They know her.

Lala remembers her, one of the women Tante helped leave Strasbourg.

Then Lala recalls the colors and layers of her skirts, the yellow and black. She pictures her hands on the crab apple tree, and wonders if the woman can sense the touch of aspen bark on Lala's palms.

The oath Lala swore for the bailiff comes back to her, like a bitter root in her mouth.

Lala wants to say something to acknowledge the unseen threads between this woman and herself.

But all that rears up in her is the sense that they must both survive.

Lala casts her eyes down at the men, their finery even more absurd in the undergrowth. Fallen branches snag the velvet and fur. Their puffed sleeves have bunched as though the air has gone out of them.

Each still breathes, but they will at least wake with headaches to rival their longest nights of drink.

She looks again to the woman.

The woman speaks a few words, in the Rromanès that Lala

never learned. She heard the sounds from the families who stayed in Tante's house, and now they flit past her again. She loses them like the bloom off a dandelion.

Lala says the only words she has on her lips.

"Take their horses," she breathes, her voice sounding as small as a child's.

The woman's eyes dull for a moment, as though her heart has broken a little that they cannot exchange a few words in a common language.

"Go now," Lala says.

Then the light comes back into them, as though the woman realizes that they have.

It is the only one they have left, the small, quiet language of vanquishing over men who can wreck and ruin, and still show their faces in daylight.

Rosella

From the window of my room, I could see a corner of the glimmer, like catching the edge of some glittering cloth.

Spotting the glimmer was its own sport around Briar Meadow. We looked for slices of it between buildings in town. Graham and Aubrey rode their bikes to the tallest hill, watching it loom over them as they sped down. My mother and father and I crowded at this window late at night, counting the seconds between each time the trembling light shifted.

Right now, it wasn't so much the glimmer I was looking for as a flash of color within that wavering light, a heart of red. Something to explain the shoes sealed to my feet, and the dance they dragged me into. A dance that had led me to the centerline of the highway, to the edge of the rocks above the reservoir.

And to turn my back on Emil Woodlock and run, like we were strangers.

I knew it was there, that heart of red. My attention would wander, I would look away for just a second, and that wash of color would flash at the corner of my vision. But whenever I looked back, all I found was that edge of the glimmer, its thick sugaring of stars.

"What is it, mija?" My mother's voice came from the doorway.

I sat up straight. "Just looking."

"Really." She quirked a perfectly penciled eyebrow. "What's wrong?"

I shook my head, shrugged. I meant it as some universal gesture of *I'm fine, nothing to see here*. But even as I did it, I could feel how forced it must have looked.

My mother perched on my bed. "You can tell me."

I wasn't telling her, or my father, anything. It didn't matter what the shoes tried to do to me. My mother and father would tear open the sky, the glimmer itself, to help me, until everyone was so frightened of us that they would never buy another pair of Oliva shoes.

If anyone knew, I would bear the contempt of the whole town, and so would my family. Red shoes would no longer hold the lore of making daughters fall in love and mothers sing from second-story windows. And Briar Meadow would hold it against me, against us, that I had spoiled something about red shoes. I would have ruined the joy of them, for everyone.

"Whatever it is," my mother said, standing up and smoothing a hand over my hair, "it won't last. Nothing this time of year ever does." She paused at the doorway. "You want tea? I'll make tea."

I pushed myself off the windowsill, her words ringing through me. "What did you say?"

"I asked if you wanted tea."

"No, before that."

Her smile was mostly assuring, but tinted with sympathy, as lightly as the way she added cinnamon to coffee. "I know it's probably strange for you, everything this year with our shoes," she said. "It probably feels like everyone's talking about us, but they're really not. They're too busy with their own lives. And even if they weren't, nothing that comes with the glimmer stays. Remember that."

Hope streaked through me, bright and fast as a comet.

Since Emil had pulled me back—and God knew how much he'd seen—I'd burrowed into my own embarrassment, trying to hide under it.

But my mother was right.

Nothing that came with the glimmer ever lasted.

No one had been able to drive off the coywolves. No one had been able to stop things disappearing into the ground a few years ago, house keys and dropped necklaces absorbing into the earth like they were water. But when the light over the reservoir faded, the coywolves left our houses and shoes alone. When that ribbon of light dimmed, the ground gave back the lost things.

I didn't have to find some way to pry the shoes off my feet.

All I had to do was outlast them.

I went to the calendar my mother had tacked up on my wall.

I knew how to learn rules. I had done it with my friends. Ironing my hair. Fluffing peony-pink blush onto my birch-brown cheeks. Letting them shape my eyebrows, even though letting gringas near me with tweezers was sacrilege in my family.

My friends had taught me to carry tote bags or an oversized purse instead of a backpack, how to take off the glitter polish without wrecking my nails, how to put in a tampon, which my mother had thought was self-explanatory (she never needed manuals for kitchen appliances either).

I had learned to lessen the differences between them and me, so it would be a little less noticeable that I was brown where they were pale. I was autumn colors while they were the cream and blush of spring. Jeans and skirts might have tightened around my thighs and butt instead of lying as flat as theirs did, but I could wear the same kind of chandelier earrings they did.

If I could learn all of that, I could learn the rules of the red shoes. I could survive them until Briar Meadow took back its magic like it did every year.

First, stay away from the reservoir, or the glimmer, until the night we knew it would fade.

Second, don't try to pry the shoes, cut them, or tear them off my own feet. As much as I wanted to claw them away, I knew better now. They had danced me out of my own house last night, taking revenge for that seam ripper. I had to leave the red shoes alone. I had to bear them until the end of the week.

I counted the few calendar squares until then, until the day the glimmer faded every year.

If I followed the rules of the red shoes, I would last those few days until they let me go, instead of paying every price that came with someone finding out.

Strasbourg, 1518

"And here is where I leave you." Petrissa halts the ox. "Mind yourselves on the road, and may God lead you safe."

"And you," Alifair says with a dip of his head.

He and Lala climb down from the cart.

Lala grasps Petrissa's hand. "I will pray for your sister," she whispers.

The woman's throat tightens, and Lala knows her nod is as much answer as she has.

Lala and Alifair walk on, Lala's heart held too tight to watch Petrissa and her well-loved ox disappear.

The air around them smells of Alifair, the smell she has always thought of as his. Oak leaves and wood. Dust caught in beams of sunlight. The clean growing smell she imagines as the scent of beech trees, a perfume given to him by the place he was born and that he carries on his skin still.

The summer stretches the light of each day. Even beneath the yew boughs, in the early evening, the gold has not yet cooled to blue. The space between branches glows like the flame on a wick.

Every few steps, she cannot help glancing over to him, his silhouette among the delicate cutouts of leaves and branches. The green brown of his eyes turns gold by the falling sun.

Tell me something about it, she used to ask. *Where you're from.*

Most of the time, he gave her a single detail. *My father could carve a dozen wooden leaves in an afternoon. My mother had eyes like juniper berries. Green and brown and purple all at once.*

Somewhere with aspen trees, he once said.

Alifair, this boy with as much of a life before Strasbourg as Tante and Lala. This boy, with his heart so fearless that there is room for endless mercy. So many in Strasbourg know his kindness. The poor brother and sister he has often brought fish or a basket of apples. An exhausted mother whose children he helps sleep with the music of his pearwood Blockflöte. An old woman he visited every day until she died.

The stir of something proprietary rises up in Lala. She has felt the breath of it before. But now it is a current, bracing and strong as river water, though she knows she has no right to feel it. He had parents once, and a homeland outside of Alsace; he does not belong to their plot yellowed by woad flowers. And it was Tante who took him into their household, turned him from a boy gathering milk thistles from wattle fences, a boy who risked beating and arrest every time he foraged for acorns, into one who knew a trade.

Lala has no claim on him.

"If you're going to look at me, look at me," Alifair says now, his eyes still forward.

A cord of heat runs through Lala's heart.

"I wasn't," she says.

He nods once, his gaze still ahead.

"I know how your friends talk of me," he says. "That I am nothing but your aunt's worker. That I am some changeling who came out of the beech trees. That I am beneath you. I hear all of it. Even though they think I don't." He gives a resigned laugh. "They think their own servants can't hear them."

The heat spreads like a fire catching. How much he has gotten wrong would be funny if it were not a briar around her heart.

"So what were you doing with me?" he asks. "Dulling your boredom until someone else came along?"

That heat bursts open in her.

"My boredom?" She stops. "You think I am bored?"

The rise of her voice quiets him.

"You think I've ever thought you were beneath me?" she asks. "Do you think I wanted to be near anyone but you? Everything I've done has been out of fear for you and Tante. All of it."

"And you think your aunt and I don't know how to look after ourselves?"

"I have already been taken to the bailiff once," Lala says, her voice thinning so quickly she doesn't need to try at a whisper.

Alifair's eyes widen, just for a moment, before he wrests back control of his expression.

"All the talk about me," Lala says. "Did you think it started from nothing?"

"This city invents reasons to blame people," Alifair says. "You know that. Especially anyone like you and your aunt."

So Alifair has been observant enough to know that powerful men cast suspicion on brown-skinned women, but not enough to realize they may cast it on him next.

"All I have wanted is for you both to be safe," Lala says.

"So you push me away yet keep staring at me," he says.

Lala shakes her head, a knot building in her throat. "It's all I can have of you."

He holds his jaw tight. His anger carves and refines him. It brings out angles in his face that both unnerve Lala and that she cannot help finding beautiful. And it is that beauty, the unfamiliar look of him, that roots her to where she stands, in the grassy light between beech and chestnut trees.

"If you want to look at me," he says again, "then go on, look at me."

He shrugs away his tunic.

Lala glances forward and back on the path. "Alifair." They are veiled only by the yews. Madness has taken Strasbourg, not only in la fièvre but in those who think the color red causes it, in her aunt sharing a bed with the flax farmer, in Alifair showing himself to these trees.

Alifair has always been careful. He wears such loose-fitting garments, his shift and shirt hanging from his body, to turn the impression of him into that of a more solid boy, a little stout even, instead of suggesting the true shape of him. His chemise and tunic leave so much room between the hemp and his skin that in winter the cold air finds its way between, his stomach chilled as an axe blade.

Next he removes his shirt, leaving nothing but the cloths bound across his chest. "Do not stare at me unless you are willing to see me."

He stands, steady as a hunter's aim.

"Look at me," he says. "Look at this body. My body. Or stop looking. Deny it, and deny me."

The sight of him, his bare shoulders and arms in the half daylight, stuns her silent. He binds himself down, the effect of which makes him seem broad-chested beneath his clothes. His hips keep the hose up, but without the length of the tunic, it is more obvious, to her at least, how he stuffs extra cloth into the plain fabric of his trousers, to hide what is not there.

Lala's fingers have never wanted more to find their way past that cloth.

"But do not act as though I am some pathetic, lovesick boy while your eyes stay on me," he says, each word with a sharp point. "I will not let you have both anymore. If you do not want me, then deny me. All of me."

She tells her mouth to speak the words. She gives the command again, as though her tongue is a stubborn horse.

But the feeling of wanting rises up in her. It opens in her so wide she can feel it in Alifair's body, a desire spread through them like the shared life inside his aspen trees.

When she kisses him, her mouth warm and wet on his, it is this she thinks of. How she cannot quite tell the feeling of his body beneath her hands from her own body under his palms.

When he kisses her back so hard she stumbles, she thinks of these trees, taking in water together.

"There is nothing I want more than I want you," she says, her lips brushing his with each word. They come more fierce than soft, more angry than tender.

"Then stop thinking of what it will cost me," he says, keeping the same slight distance, the same tone, hard and set as a stone in the earth.

When she touches the fabric between his legs, when she finds him beneath the scrap of extra cloth, their breath catches between their mouths, and she thinks of those aspen leaves all breathing at once.

He takes his hands through her hair, and she thinks of the wind fanning out the leaves.

She has thought so often of him at night, as her hand drifted down her body and between her legs, her shift a thin veil over the patch of coarse hair. She thought so much of being alongside him in the dark as she pressed her fingers into her body, harder, until the ribbon of longing folded in on itself.

Now her hands are on him, and he is naked to the waist, in nothing but his breeches. It is the first time she has gotten to both see his body, the muscles forged by work, and feel its warmth for this long.

They fall onto the shade-cool moss, her legs intertwining with his, and she thinks of the trees' roots beneath the ground, all sharing the space like clasped hands.

And when the way he touches her makes her tip her head back, there is nothing but the shared life threading through both their hearts. It is bright as the red jewels of the berries studding the yew branches above them. It is the breath that stays between them as the sky grows dark and fills with the living sapphires of the stars.

Emil

When he tried to sleep, she was there.

Not Rosella.

His five-centuries-ago relative, with her hair, the same coarse black as his and his cousins', and her skin a tone of brown that ran through him and his whole family. She was there, in the dust-softened cloth of her dyed skirt, among the stone and canal water of Strasbourg. She was there, in this city that smelled like iron and sweat and summer heat, with its sky that seemed sliced in half by la cathédrale's pink-tinted spire. She was there, within the chaos and flurry of all those dancing bodies.

She wasn't dancing.

She was screaming.

The sound broke above the dancing over stone and panicked murmurs and the accusing shouts, like one of his mother's planted bulbs pushing up through hard ground. It came with the salt smell of blood and death. It carried a weight he could almost feel on his own back.

Blame.

This city held her at fault for the dancing plague before them.

Emil startled awake, breathing hard, a question opening in him.

The force of that blame, blame this girl had borne, lay thick on his skin.

He reached for his glasses. Even placing himself in the dark room, with the familiarity of his bed and his desk and his books, it stayed.

The question twisted into its own answer.

There was more to what happened in Strasbourg than some passing story in his family's history.

And whatever it was, it was reaching across five centuries to grab hold of him.

Strasbourg, 1518

*L*ala wakes to realize Alifair is not beside her.

She sits up, shrugging her shoulders to unknot them. Through the raw-beam light, she finds the shape of him, carved against the morning. The sun finds seams in the leaves and gilds the brown of his hair.

She stands beneath the oak he has climbed.

"What are you doing?" she asks, a laugh in her half-asleep voice.

He reaches for a fat oak gall. "Your aunt will like these."

"And I would like to see you come down before you break your neck."

He smiles.

As he does, his hand moves, so slightly that Lala would miss it if not for the change in shadow.

She realizes it is a false move only a moment before the first wasp stings.

Alifair flinches, and that flinch stirs the others.

The wasps that have always seemed to treat him as a brother now turn on him. It is as though they are waking up, another stinging, then a third and fourth.

"Come down," Lala yells, and once he does, she pulls him away from the tree.

The wasps' buzz heats the air.

It is a thread of noise that feels like a warning.

She packs up their things and leads him the distance to home, where she and Tante can apply honey and cider vinegar to his stings, then lavender and calendula. Maybe wild thyme, the same as Tante puts on burns from splattering oil.

And still, the sound of the wasps' buzz seems to follow them.

She leads him toward the berry brambles and courgette plots of their rented land.

Before Tante's threshold, the smell of blood draws her up short.

At first, she recoils from the tangled, bloody mess. At first, she thinks it is an animal's afterbirth, as was left in front of Isentrud's home. The uncleanness of it seems as though it is already touching her skin, reaching out like fingers.

As Lala draws closer, she distinguishes reedy leaves and stalks.

Wood betony, and blood. Someone has taken handfuls of the purple-flowering plant, meant to protect against witches, and soaked them in an animal's blood. The flowers and stalks have taken it up, turning to pulp. It looks like something that came from a living thing's body, not just plant but animal, even human. The gadje who put it there may not have known she would reel back from how marime the spilled blood is, how unclean no matter the source. But it is no less awful for their ignorance.

Thick ropes of horror and disgust braid together with Lala's rage.

She gives them only the space of one breath.

Lala takes Alifair by the shoulders and points him toward the door. "Go inside. Show my aunt your stings."

He blinks at her, more dazed than she has ever seen him.

She tries to smile. "Show her the oak galls you brought her. She will love them." She gives him as gentle a push toward the door as she can.

And then she runs.

Rosella

Emil's house was a language I had almost forgotten, a few words coming back at a time. The French blue of the painted siding. The way his parents insisted I call them by their first names, because when I tried calling either of them Dr. Woodlock, Julien waved a hand and said, "I don't know which of us you're talking to, use our names."

There was the tree I once helped Emil and Julien pick plums off, so Yvette could show me the perfect way she arranged fruit in a clafoutis. And Yvette's petit four daffodils in the side yard, the flowers soft and pink as cotton candy; five falls ago, they all burst into out-of-season bloom in the middle of October.

Then there was the hissing ball of fur Emil insisted on calling a cat.

"Gerta," Emil said in his most calming voice when he came to the door. "Don't hiss at our guests, okay?"

Gerta scampered off.

"She's in one of her moods," Emil said.

"Isn't she always?" I asked.

"Good memory."

Gerta, the cutest, fluffiest, most misogynistic cat in Briar Meadow. She had come out of the woods the year the forest cats appeared, with a ruff of orange-gold fur at her neck and a pissed-off affect that only calmed when Emil, then a little boy, gathered her up and talked to her. Yvette had named her for Maria Margaretha Kirch, who charted the paths of Saturn and Venus in the eighteenth century.

Of course, a cat named for a feminist astronomer had turned out to hate other women. All except Yvette Woodlock herself.

"Do you want to come in?" he asked. "We've gotten her out of the habit of biting. Mostly."

Gerta batted first at the edge of the sofa and then at the hem of my jeans.

"Gerta," Emil said, as though trying to reason with her.

"She's not bothering me," I said.

"Not yet."

As though she understood, the cat arched her back, pricked her ears, and showed her teeth.

"And this is why I don't have a girlfriend." Emil picked her up, and she turned into a purring round. "She does this every time."

"Sure, blame the cat," I said.

He petted Gerta's ears.

"Can I get you anything?" he asked. "Water? Tea? Coffee strong enough that you can chew it?"

My laugh sounded more tired than I meant it to. "I'm okay."

He set the cat down, his shirt now flecked with orange fur. "Be nice, *liebling*." The sound in his voice brought me back to grade school, how he spoke the same as his parents, any German word tinted with a French accent and the other way around.

Yvette Woodlock breezed through the living room. I always saw her and Julien in town, alternating who picked up both of their suits at the dry cleaner's. She was fine boned without seeming birdlike, with black hair that fell in even waves I'd always envied, and thin-framed glasses so much like Emil's I wondered if they'd bought them together. Even in her own home, she wore neat slacks and collared shirts that would have looked stuffy if she didn't have that cloud of French refinement always following her.

At first glance, Yvette and her husband seemed mismatched. Julien, taller and broader than both his wife and his son, had hair a little like old photos of Einstein. Already all white, it grew less neat throughout the day because he put his hands in it whenever he was thinking. He threw papers in fanned messes across his desk, always able to find a particular one despite the chaos. (Emil took after his mother, with her labeled folders and paper clips always fastened straight up and down.)

Each insisted they were the better cook, Yvette tidily recording her recipe for sauerkraut with onions and butter and flat champagne, while Julien thought instructions deadened the soul of the chef.

Now Yvette noticed me.

"Oh," she said, surveying me in a way that was surprised but not unfriendly. "*Ça fait longtemps.*"

I gave Yvette the best smile I had, though I felt it on my own face, weak and watered down.

Yvette Woodlock's gaze was as sharp and unyielding as the fairy tales she used to tell our class. Snow White's queen demanding her heart as proof that she was dead, the hunter cutting out the heart of a deer. The queen made to dance herself to death in iron shoes. Stepsisters cutting off parts of themselves for nothing but a glass slipper and a prince so boring we never learned his name.

Only Yvette Woodlock could tell us fairy stories and have

it seem like she was telling us the truth about how the world worked.

"If my son takes you outside," Yvette said to me on her way out of the room, "wear protective equipment."

"What?" I asked Emil.

"Thanks a lot, Maman," Emil mumbled.

Yvette paused next to her son. "*Ne sois pas un poulet mouillé,*" she said, talking to him but glancing at me.

Emil shut his eyes in the same cringing, forced smile I had given my parents a hundred times.

"Do I want to know?" I asked Emil when Yvette was out of the room.

"Absolutely not," he said.

I started remembering what the Woodlocks' house smelled like, all the different kinds of tea they kept in their kitchen. Black and chamomile, dried berries and cloves, fennel and rose hip.

I wondered if Emil had memories of my house that mirrored mine of his. My mother teaching Emil to make a tortilla at the same time she taught me, when we were six, our hands shaping the masa. How making manriklo with Yvette meant Emil was instantly better at it than I was, and how I never heard the end of it from my mother.

A slash of pain crossed my anklebone. I took a slow breath to keep myself from reacting. The air I drew in brought the smell of everything else I remembered from the Woodlocks' downstairs. Wood and paper. Yvette's favorite rosemary candles. And another smell I'd come to think of as the ink in their books.

"Are you okay?" Emil asked.

"Yeah," I said. "I just stopped by because I wanted to say thank you."

Stopped by. As though Emil's house was on the way from my house to anything in Briar Meadow.

"And I'm sorry for taking off like I did," I said.

"Don't worry about it," he said. "Can I ask what you were doing out there?"

"It's stupid," I said, feeling the pinprick of anticipating my own lie. "I was looking at the glimmer and I just lost my balance."

He gave the kind of half-raised-eyebrow, slow nod I remembered from years ago.

I remembered it meaning he didn't believe me at all. Like when I said the bruise on my knee was from the stairs when really it was from trying to imitate Sylvie's ballet-class pirouettes. Or when I told him I'd missed school because I had a cold when it had been because my cousins got me to eat something that contained the nuts I was allergic to (like hell I was telling Emil about the hives, so many of them that my painkiller-fuzzed brain couldn't count them).

Now Emil moved in a way that made me notice a streak of color, a brushstroke of teal against the brown of his forearm.

"What's that?" I asked.

He looked down. "Oh," he said. "Just flame tests. I'm comparing different kinds of cobalt glass to see which is best at filtering out orange light from sodium ions"—his tone shifted mid-sentence without him pausing—"and I'm gonna stop talking because I'm probably boring you to death."

"No," I said. "I was just gonna ask, what's a flame test again?"

He half closed his eyes. "You're serious? It's one of the few labs even non–pocket protectors remember."

I felt my eyes widening.

"Yeah," he said, stretching out the word. "Graham's not quiet about calling us that."

"Sorry," I said. Graham meant it as a term of endearment. Mostly. But I still couldn't help apologizing for her.

"Do you want to see it?" he asked.

"Your pocket protector?"

"Sorry," he said, leading me toward the back door. "Just brought it in for dry cleaning."

I went out to the old garden shed with him, wondering if he'd been this cute in middle school, last year, last week, and I hadn't noticed. He had always just been Emil, the boy who used to tell me about geode formation while I snored, pointedly and loudly, pretending to be far more bored than I was.

He had a lab bench now. Garden tools leaned in the corners on either side, like they were standing guard.

"You've come a long way from growing crystals in sugar water," I said.

He laughed. "Thanks."

He set up a row of glass vials, each holding a labeled powder. Some white, some blue green or dark red. I watched his hands, his brown fingers that always had a few paper cuts from library reference books.

Emil handed me a pair of goggles. "Insert preamble about not trying this at home."

I put them on. "Got it."

He put on his own and started the burner. With a few clicks of the striker, the petal of hot blue appeared.

He tapped a wooden stick into one of the vials and held it into the flame. It turned green as light through honey locust leaves.

I looked at him. "How'd you do that?"

"Barium," he said. "The ions burn different colors."

The next one turned the flame fall-leaf orange ("calcium,"

he said). The one after purpled it to the winter-dusk color that always made me think of December.

Except now, it made me think of the purple tint to the sky around the glimmer.

"Emil," I said.

"Cesium chloride," he said.

"No," I said, the words hot in my throat. "I was just gonna say, if . . ."

He was looking at me now.

Out by the reservoir, the way I'd grabbed him and kissed him had seemed almost inevitable, like the glimmer had set some charge between us. Static electricity that would stay on our skin unless we touched and sent it into the air. It was logic that had followed from the light in the sky.

But now, with daylight outside and the dark inside the shed, the contrast left me with a kind of delayed embarrassment so intense I was sure he could see it through my skin.

"If what I did the other night," I said, still stumbling, "if I did something you didn't want me to . . ." No matter how many ways I went at it, I could not catch the end of my own sentence.

He looked back at the flame. "I didn't mind."

That should have let me breathe out. Instead, his words just fluttered inside me instead of my own.

I didn't mind, meaning what? *I didn't mind*, meaning he wouldn't mind doing it again? *I didn't mind*, meaning he'd already forgotten about it?

He handed me a stick and a vial of turquoise powder. Our fingers brushed in a way that seemed like it could have been on purpose.

"You'll like this one," he said.

I dipped the wood into the powder and held it into the flame.

It turned to a gradient between green and blue, chlorine-pool green at the tip darkening to iris blue at the base.

My breath caught in my throat.

"Copper sulfate," he said.

I looked from the teal flame to Emil, his face behind the safety plastic and his glasses. I used to know what Emil looked like without glasses, but not anymore. Now the fact of him, this close, seemed more fever dream than the red shoes themselves.

"Emil?" I asked.

He glanced at me. "Yeah?"

"Why did we stop being friends?"

He held a powder to the flame that burned the color of early lilacs. "Because there's always a point when girls stop being friends with boys."

He didn't sound bitter about it. More resigned.

With another coating of powder, he turned the flame mint green.

After a few more colors, and a long time of both of us being quiet, Emil said, "You know, the first time I ever saw the ocean was with my grandfather."

I almost asked, *What does that have to do with anything?* But I kept my tongue still, realizing I wanted to hear him talk, even if I had no idea what he was talking about.

"It was from a bridge, and I saw this buoy in the water," he said, turning the flame pink. "And this buoy, it stayed in place. I knew it was staying in place because it was a buoy, right? But I didn't understand, because it looked like it was moving. It was still, but it left a wake behind it, because it was staying still while all the water around it was moving. It was staying in the same place in a current. That's why it left the wake."

I shook my head. "I don't get it."

"Sometimes you have to stay still." He looked at me, the brown of his eyes as dark as his hair. "You have to work to stay where you are. Sometimes if you want to move things around you, you have to do everything you can to stay still."

"What do you mean?" I asked.

He turned the flame the bright yellow of a field daffodil. "I mean we should've stayed friends."

Our eyes stayed on each other long enough that I felt the heat of it on my shoulders.

I felt caught between kissing him and telling him, two equally impulsive and probably disastrous possibilities.

I didn't mind didn't mean I should try it again. *I didn't mind* could have meant he was writing it off as an aberration, a shift in a gravitational field, the color of a rare bird, a strange result of this year filled with red shoes.

And telling Emil the truth, telling this boy who held science and logic as close as a first language, made even less sense than telling my parents. He wouldn't believe it anyway. He'd probably just think I was stupid and reckless, or susceptible to the suggestion of magic that all red shoes held this year. He'd think I'd fallen under some shared hysteria, or conversion disorder, like the girls we'd read about in history class, the ones who seemed possessed during the Salem witch trials. Briar Meadow's magic probably wouldn't even be real to him if it weren't for Gerta.

When Emil looked at me, my skin felt like glass to him, like he could see everything inside.

"Try this one," he said, and handed me a vial and a stick, our fingers brushing again.

The powder turned the flame as red as cherry candy, as red as blood or berries, and any thought I had of telling Emil the truth burned up with it.

Strasbourg, 1518

Lala's chest sears from running, but she does not stop.

Gall nuts, her aunt taught her, begin in the spring, when a wasp punctures an oak tree to make a home for its eggs in the soft, young buds.

The tree, quite understandably, protests, forming the galls around the holes the wasp has made.

When something living senses the presence of something new and venomous, it closes it off.

The spire of pink sandstone looms high over Strasbourg's tiled roofs and country churches, a crown of blush-hued stone. The light from the morning is still cool, silvering la cathédrale's single tower. The rose window catches the sun, knives of perfect white pointing at the flower in the center, strokes of lapis blue, harvest-warm leaves inlaid among sea colors. The cathedral seems enormous as a mountain but delicate as if it were carved from alabaster. It is the guide by which Lala first learned her way from Tante's house to the city.

Where Lala would expect wings and soft rustling sounds, she hears, instead, voices, and the hard pounding of steps.

Lala rushes through a narrow lane until it opens onto the cathedral square.

Instead of the usual flock of birds, the square holds as many bodies.

Instead of the horned larks with their yellow heads and pristine brown backs, the bodies here leap and flail. They turn and jump.

They dance.

This is more than the familiar sweep of skirts. Cassocks mix with the spin of kirtles. Priests chase after them, canons calling out orders. Some urge them to rest, in the name of our Lord. Others demand their confession. Others still yell at the dancers, or, if they can grab hold of them, scream down their throats. "I order the devil from you. I command the demons to leave you." Some try to grasp the dancers and shake them out of it, but they only whirl away.

Lala's understanding feels like a thumb pressed to her throat.

It is not just cassocks and dresses in the fray.

It is a sprinkling of tunics and hose.

Men.

Lala does as fast a count as she can manage, trying to keep up with their furious movements.

At least twenty men.

Thirty.

More.

There are so many dancers she cannot count them.

Dozens.

More than dozens.

A hundred.

Two hundred.

The stone beneath Lala's feet seems as though it is crumbling.

Lala has faced death to see the end of this fever, Alifair along-side her.

But now it rages all the fiercer, wrathful as a fire across dry fields.

Lala weaves through Strasbourg's streets. She rushes past the dancers who flail and throw themselves about. Past those with red-rimmed eyes. Past the mothers who fear for their children.

Past two weeping girls who tend to a cousin, collapsed from the dance.

Past Melisende and Agnesona, their heads still veiled in fine scarves.

Their eyes follow Lala. They do not greet her.

A noblewoman and her attendants pass between them. Her dyed leather shoes kick up a stripe of color.

Blue.

Lala stands, staring even after the noblewoman passes.

A familiar scrap of fabric.

A ribbon dyed with Tante's woad blue.

A ribbon Lala prayed into, and then gave to a friend.

A ribbon now trampled into Strasbourg's cobblestones.

Enneleyn.

"Lavinia Blau?" The voice comes with a man's broad shadow.

Two sergeants pause before her.

She lifts her face to them, and all she can ask is, "Where is Enneleyn?"

"If you will come with us, Mademoiselle Blau," the elder one says.

"What happened to her?" is still the only question Lala can speak.

"You must come now," the younger one says.

"Where is Enneleyn?" She is shouting it now, all in the square watching.

The sergeants take her arms and lead her away, her eyes clinging to that blue ribbon.

But the question still breaks from her lips. She yells it. "Where is she?"

———

Emil

Even when Rosella was gone, the smell of her stayed in the shed, that powdery, flowery smell he always thought of as belonging to the Olivas' house. He'd learned a long time ago that it was her mother's favorite fabric softener, one that always sat on the windowsill in its yellow bottle like a vase of flowers.

He wanted to hold on to it, that scent, their fingers touching near the burner, the way her expression shifted like the colors of flames. He wanted to know all of it as well as he knew the details of sodium and selenium.

But the question he'd had all day still knocked around in him.

A minute after his father came home, his parents were in the kitchen arguing.

Not fighting.

Arguing.

"Mon cheri," his mother said. "We all know it is yours about the fluctuation of grain pricing according to storage method."

"Mais non, mon trésor," his father said. "It is clearly yours on the evolution of the codpiece."

"That is my most popular and you know it!"

Emil set his thumb and third finger to his temples.

They were back to the long-running debate over which of them had written the most boring paper.

"Your exploration of nitrogen fixing in the arable region of the Vosges Mountains?" his mother said. "You want to talk about watching grass grow."

"Your sixty-page treatise expounding on the ratio of domesticated to wild goats in the Bas-Rhin?" his father asked.

"It was feral goats!"

Emil cleared his throat. Loudly.

They both turned.

His mother studied him. "Tu vas bien?"

Emil looked at his mother, then his father.

Was he really doing this? He'd spent years learning as little as he could about their family. He knew his grandmother's prayers to Sara la Kali, his cousins' heart for certain trees. But he'd kept away from tracing their family back like his mother and father had, learning about the hundreds of years before them. Hadn't it been talk of caring for their dead that had gotten his parents that first call home?

Emil never could turn his back on family he knew by name or face, those he kept in his own memory or who he learned in old photographs. But dredging up something five centuries old? It went against everything he'd taught himself since grade school.

He took a sharp breath like he was going underwater. "What really happened in Strasbourg?"

His mother's stare joined Emil's, both squarely on his father.

"You've made it very clear you don't want to be bored with all this," his father said, in a way that managed to be sad but not bitter. "So why do you ask?"

It had never been a matter of Emil being bored. Was that really what his parents thought?

"I want to know about the dancing plague," Emil said.

His father glanced at his mother.

Then at Emil.

"People died," his father said, the words as unadorned as in an academic paper.

"Died," Emil said. "From dancing?"

"Their hearts gave out," his mother said softly. "They had strokes. They, more or less, died of exhaustion."

Emil braced enough to ask, "Did that happen to anyone we're related to?"

"No," his father said. "Not that we know of."

"Why didn't they stop?" Emil asked. "The dancers, I mean. They had to feel it killing them, so why did they keep going?"

"They couldn't," his mother said. "At least that's how it seemed to everyone watching. There could have been some biological cause, but most likely it was a form of mass hysteria."

"What—" Emil stumbled over the start of a question, not quite knowing where he was going until halfway in. "What stopped it?"

"We don't know that either," his mother said.

"What do they think stopped it?"

His father looked away.

"Papa," Emil said. "What do they think cured it?"

His parents swapped another look.

"Will you two stop trying to signal each other and just tell me?" Emil asked.

His father sighed in a way so heavy Emil felt it in his own chest.

"Emil," his father said. "Two of our relatives weren't just in Strasbourg during the dancing plague."

Emil's heart tightened, and he almost stopped his father, told him he didn't want to know. The air hummed in a way that told the truth a second before his father could.

"They were blamed for it," Emil said, the words falling between him and his parents. "Weren't they?"

The girl, the woman, in his dreams. A fever from five hundred years ago.

The screaming.

Emil hovered between the two awful possibilities, two potential results of Strasbourg needing someone to blame for their dancing plague.

The first, the least, was that those relatives were stripped of their home and livelihoods. Because so often, that was what being Romani meant. It meant being blamed. It meant holding your ground as best you could, because if you gave every inch they asked for, they would drive you off the earth. And sometimes it meant they did anyway.

But that screaming, so deep it felt written into his bones, left him standing with the second possibility.

He made himself ask. He made the words come.

"What happened to them?" he asked.

His father shook his head, as though telling him to turn back. It was the first time Emil wondered if his father knew what he'd been doing this whole time, keeping distance from their family's history so he didn't have to rip it out of himself every time he left the house. And for the first time, Emil wondered if his father maybe thought he was onto something.

"Papa," Emil said. "What happened?"

His father's eyes fell, and in that small flinch, Emil knew.

Emil had never asked how their sixteenth-century relatives had died. He already knew there were a stomach-turning number of ways to die five hundred years ago. He'd seen them in his parents' papers. Childbed fever. Bloody flux. Saint Anthony's fire. Lepry. The ague. Venereal disease. Unexplained fever. "The red plague." The bite of a "wayward sow." Being thrown into a river by "a skittish calf." Drowning in a ditch. Scythes. Falling from things—a tree, a window, a yarn winder's stand. Falling onto or into things—a rock, a well, the horns of a bull.

He had never before considered death from a dancing plague.

And he had never before considered execution, not for those relatives in Strasbourg.

But now, when he shut his eyes, all that history grew its own voices and called up its own ghosts. The scream of that girl, that woman, burned away every possibility except that one.

In the few seconds before his father said, "They were executed," Emil had already run through the possibilities. Even from what little he'd heard of his parents' lectures, he knew enough about criminals hanged in the center of town. Women thought to be adulterers strangled by the tradesmen with the strongest hands. Poor men punished with lashing that led to infection and then fever.

Suspected witches murdered by water or rope or fire.

"How do you know?" Emil asked. "How do we know any of this?"

"Church records," his father said. "Coroners' rolls. Physicians' logs. Transcripts of sermons. Strasbourg city council notes. Firsthand accounts. Transcriptions after the fact."

Emil flinched. It was all so damningly specific, detailed as the footnotes in his mother's articles.

"All of them say that?" Emil asked. "That they were executed?"

"No," his father said. "But we have enough to guess."

"How?" Emil asked.

"Death records," his father said, without hesitation or ceremony. "Their names are spelled a little differently every place you find them, but it's the same women. Lavinia and Dorenia Blau, their ages more than ten years apart, both listed as, *Commended back into the hands of the devil for the blessing and good of the people, who now live free from the demons who once plagued them.*"

Emil tensed. He wondered how many times his father must have read that translation to have committed it to memory.

"'Commended back into the hands of the devil'?" Emil asked. "What does that even mean?"

His father set a hand on the counter and looked away. "What do you think it means?"

Those strange words—*commended back into the hands of the devil*—fit so neatly with what gadje thought of them. It mapped so cleanly against the scorn that landed on his grandmother when that little girl went missing, and the lack of apology when she turned up again.

"You know so little about those who came before us, Emil," his mother said. "Don't let this be all you think of. We are more than what we've survived."

But Emil swore he could smell the dust and stone of Strasbourg, a thin cord through the house.

In those few seconds above the reservoir, the space between centuries had thinned and faded.

In those few seconds, Rosella Oliva had blurred into a girl from five centuries earlier.

He had thought he'd imagined it all, that he'd lost himself somewhere in the haze of not-sleeping. But everything that had happened five hundred years ago was coming back to life, and it was dragging Rosella with it.

Strasbourg, 1518

So many dead, their names rung out in the square, one after the next.

Cateline, the book binder's wife, and the book binder with her.

Enneleyn, the girl called the Lily of Strasbourg.

And the miller's elder daughter.

"The miller's son himself swears he has seen you engaging in witchcraft," the friar says.

The bailiff has left her in the room with this tall, proud man in his robes.

That is the worst sign thus far.

"And that he caught you pilfering artifacts from the dead for your dark magic," the friar says. "Do you deny his charges?"

She must, if there is any chance of surviving this.

"I deny them," she says.

"And you deny even his claim that he saw you fly from the crypt on a pitchfork? That which he was sworn to see with his own eyes?"

Perhaps in any other place, such a charge would make her laugh. But here that laugh comes as nothing but a stalled, disbelieving breath.

"Yes," Lala says, forcing straightness into her back and composure into her voice. "I deny this."

"The finest physicians in the city have testified before the Council of Twenty-One." The friar's voice rises. "They say that there is no reason of body for this madness, that it could only come from the devil himself, and still you deny it?"

She swallows, and it sticks in her throat, dry from saying the same words so many times. She must say the words again, or they will assume the testimony needed to condemn her.

"I deny it," she says.

"You deny the truth that you were seen bewitching a stream?" the friar asks.

Lala's throat grows hard as a knot in rope. The suggestion of tampered-with water was the death of so many Jews, what gave the Strasbourgeois the reason they needed to kill a quarter of them, whole families who had done nothing.

All she can say is, "I deny it."

"Do you deny that you bewitched one of your own friends simply by the grasp of your hand?" the friar asks.

"I never bewitched her," she says.

She shuts her eyes, knowing, in the same instant, how she has erred. She has strayed from the three words—*I deny it*—like wandering from a path in a brambled forest.

"Really." The friar circles. "You visited her in the early morning and not a day later, she is afflicted, and you deny this?"

"I cared about her!" Lala's eyes flit open. She cannot keep herself from raising her voice. "She was my friend! I would never!"

The council and the physicians chose to exclude the canons when they decided on a great dance. They ignored explanation of divine chastisement, or the arrangement of stars.

But now that tambourines and drums have only spread the affliction, they have given in and brought in a friar. Now that the blood of so many boils over, now that not only women but men fall down in the streets, now that they have lost the Lily of Strasbourg, they must blame someone.

"And did you not try to flee the city to escape justice for your crimes?" the friar asks.

"I did not," she says.

"Did you not attempt to capture your aunt's apprentice into your dark service?"

Lala shuts her eyes once more.

"He has nothing to do with me," she says, each word stinging her lips. "He performs only tasks for my aunt."

All she has done, all the effort she has made to guard those she cares for, all will be used to damn her.

And, if she does not take care, him.

"There is talk of this plague passing by sight," the friar says. "Do you know nothing of that, Mademoiselle Blau?"

"I know nothing of it," she says.

"Families attempt to restrain their loved ones from the dance, but they scream and thrash as though demons rip their hearts in two. And you know nothing of this?"

"I know nothing of it."

"Music must now be banned because of how it spreads," the friar says, his voice taunting and proud. "Even the singing of ꞏs for fear that blessed souls will dance toward the altar. Do ꞏo guilt, no fear for your immortal soul?"

ꞏ immortal soul to God," she says, biting back the

ꞏt to you or any man like you.

"The faithful of this city fall down dead, and you think God will receive your soul?" the friar asks.

"I trust my immortal soul to God," she repeats.

"The Dreikönigsuhr has stopped, and three women swear you have done it with witchcraft. Do you deny this?"

Lala's back stiffens. "In the name of our Lord, I deny it."

"You will not confess your pact with the devil?" the friar yells.

Her throat is summer ground now, parched as dust, from her nerves, from thirst, from how long she has been made to speak. Her tongue feels like dried moss in her mouth.

"I have no pact with the devil." Lala chokes on the words.

"And your consorting with demons?"

"I have had nothing to do with demons."

"What of the reports that you have been seen in the woods with werewolves and lupine devils?"

A memory pinches, the recollection of the wolves alongside Alifair, how their claws ticking against stones drove away the men who thought she was prey.

"They are lies," she says.

"And the pitchforks that have gone missing from farms?"

"I know nothing of them."

"Do you not fly on them with your sisterhood of *legion* witches?"

"I do not," Lala says. "I have no such sisters."

"Four hundred souls dance," the friar says. *Their* hearts and their bodies relent and release their spirit *just* yesterday, fifteen more were afflicted. The spotless *heart* now dance as though they are covens of witches. *They* *dance* in church and cannot be dissuaded with holy *water or* *the* sight of the cr

Whose work but the devil's?" His yell is so forceful that his spit catches in Lala's hair.

Lala braces her hands on the wooden seat.

They would not have brought in this friar, not one as young as Sewastian, if he had not been well trained in the *Malleus Maleficarum*, the book that insists all witches be burned.

And because he is young, he is eager to show his skill and his wrath, like a young snake cutting its teeth.

Lala holds her tongue tight in her mouth.

The whole town is gripped by fear and frenzy, and if she says a further wrong word, she will pay for it.

Rosella

All I had to do was follow their rules. All I had to do was survive them for a few more days.

But that night, I slept through the red shoes bucking to life. I slept through them pulling me into the woods, while I dreamed of my body turning to starbursts of blood-red beads.

I dreamed of the night turning into everything my family's shoes looked like. The crushed-jewel embroidery. The heels that seemed crafted out of icicles or poured gold. The dancing slippers that appeared woven from moonlight and stitched with threads of spun sugar.

The red shoes dragged me through brambles and briars that tore at my pajama pants and my legs. They dragged me down the embankment, rocks cutting my ankles as I dreamed of the air turning to water. I ran but the water slowed me, like I was running on the bed of a river, my limbs cutting through the current.

I didn't wake up until my body hit the reservoir, the chill as hard as packed snow.

The dancing stayed in me. It stayed in me even as fighting for the surface took what little breath I had.

It stayed as the red shoes took me under, the cold like handful of knives. The motion of my legs became treading, the only way I could fight.

I had a few seconds of being all the way awake.

But in those few seconds, a scream caught in my throat, not just because the shoes were taking me under, but because they had made me silent in the first place.

The reason I couldn't have told my mother and father about them was not only because it could ruin us, but because I could never confess what I had done. I had turned my grandfather's beautiful work, and my grandmother's defiance, into this. I had failed my family. My hands had failed them. All they had worked for over generations, I had twisted into poison the moment I picked up a needle and thread.

The scream of all this built in my throat, and died without breath to give it sound.

I had barely shaken out of sleep when the lack of air blurred my brain, and the shoes took me under again.

Strasbourg, 1518

The friar circles her. "Perhaps you have been taught by your aunt. A fellow witch?"

Lala closes her eyes again. "No."

Now the friar stands behind her. "Perhaps she has not taught you the way of God, and has invited the devil into your house."

"No," Lala says, the start of a sob weakening the word. Now it sounds almost a plea. Not Tante. Not her baby.

"Do you deny the witchcraft in your very house?" the friar asks. "Have you and your aunt not spent the Sabbath concocting poisons?"

"Never."

"Are you not both among the legion witches?"

"We are not."

"Do you not hold *maleficia* in your hearts?"

"We do not."

The friar sighs. "Must we trouble the Bishop von Hohenstein with this matter? Draw him from his palace?" The man's breath comes hot on the back of her neck, and he lowers his voice. "If so, perhaps we will have to break the joints of both you and your aunt and see if we can uncover the witchcraft in your very bodies."

"No," Lala says, and the words cracks in two. If she speaks

a single word more out of place, she and Tante Dorenia will be declared witches. The magistrates will chatter among themselves to decide their fate. They will ponder hanging them as traitors against the city, or burning them to be sure their wicked hearts have become ash.

Lala lowers her head, sobbing taking her.

They have tortured peasant rebels for wanting nothing more than bags of seed and relief from their usurers. What will they do to women they call witches?

The friar bends lower. "Dozens dead or dying, falling down from exhaustion, their bodies giving out, and you cry only when we threaten yours?"

Lala watches the stones at her feet.

The friar straightens back to standing. "It is, of course, not entirely your fault." He takes a more relaxed posture. "Women are born with weaker minds, more susceptible to demon possession."

Lala does not protest. If him thinking her weak or stupid will save her and Tante, she will let him.

"So let us speak of other things," the friar says.

Lala would breathe, if she did not know this to be a trap. He will make her feel safe, absolved, then trip her into a confession.

"You have other crimes, Lavinia," the friar says to her back. "Let us not pretend you were blameless before."

Lala clenches, bracing for talk of her and Tante being Romnia.

"You have committed sins of the flesh." The friar's voice falls almost to a whisper. "You and your aunt's apprentice have lain together."

Lala stays still enough that she cannot breathe. She waits for the friar to go on, praying that the only sin he will assign her is bedding a man outside of marriage.

"You must know that for you to lie with each other is against the natural law of God," the friar says.

The natural law of God.

Lala feels as though the floor beneath her has broken open and she has fallen into canal water.

"Do not tell me you have never heard from Paul's Letter to the Romans." Now the friar's voice rises. "'For even their women did change the natural use into that which is against nature.'"

The words pin her skirt to the floor. She could not run even if the friar were to throw the door wide.

Others in Strasbourg know that Alifair is the kind of boy who was given a girl's name at birth. They know there is a reason he has never tried to show off his form in the way young men so often try.

Lala should know well enough by now. There are no true secrets in this city, or this world. Not hers. Not Tante's. Not Alifair's.

"'And likewise also the men, leaving the natural use of the woman'"—the friar is nearly yelling now—"'burned in this lust one toward another.'"

Lala shuts her eyes, trying to clear away all before her, the awfulness and the impossibility. Not just this careless damning of men with men and women with women, but how profoundly the friar misunderstands Alifair himself. Lala is a girl. Alifair is a boy. Despite any common features their bodies may possess, to compare them, to call them the same, has always seemed unthinkable.

The friar strolls in front of her. "You are familiar with *Li livres de jostice et de plet*?"

Lala's throat feels as though it holds a stone.

Alifair might have gone his whole life without his name being spoken in this room. Yes, some may have known for years, but they must have decided they did not care, so long as he didn't lure their daughters into the fields. It is the same as how some must have known of Lala's blood but likely thought little of it, provided she did not seduce their sons with whatever dark charms they imagine brown-armed girls possessing.

But now, now that there is something that someone must be blamed for, there comes a miraculous reemergence of memory. These things, known but nearly forgotten, are brought out and aired like shirts from a trunk.

"Ah," the friar says. "So you know the treatise. Then you must also know that we keep similar laws here in Strasbourg."

All this, the threat now crawling toward Alifair, is Lala's fault. If they hadn't looked first to her, they might never have looked to him.

"Then you know the penalty for the offense you and your lover commit?" the friar asks.

Offense. Lala almost kicks up from her chair at the word. In this proud country, so many men pay no price for forcing themselves on women. But for a man to want a man, or for a woman to care for a woman, or for a girl like Lala to love a boy who was given a girl's name at birth, these are all *offenses*.

"And you know," the friar says, "that on the first offense, the offender will lose a limb."

A chill crawls over Lala.

"And on the second, another limb," the friar says.

Lala sets her back teeth.

"And on the third," he says, "offenders are to be burned, and all their goods confiscated."

Lala grips the wooden seat so hard splinters catch in her palms.

"If you do not wish to confess how you have bewitched the souls who dance," the friar says, "perhaps you would care to discuss your other sins. Or those committed by your aunt's apprentice."

No. Alifair's name cannot be spoken in this room. He is a boy who always dips his fingers into the stoups of holy water and crosses himself. He has never thrown sticks at horses or dogs, or mocked his elders behind their backs.

Which boy in Strasbourg should be mentioned in this room less than Alifair?

"What do you think?" the friar asks, as though musing. "Would you both find it a sign of your love to lose the same limb on the same day? To have the same parts of your bodies taken within the same hour of each other? Tell me, is that romance to such perverted souls as yours?"

Lala pulls at the air for breath but cannot find it.

"I . . ." Lala chokes out the sound.

They consider him nothing but a peasant with no known parentage. They will wound him without a thought.

"But should you confess the crimes of your own heart"— the friar steps forward, seeming to have thought of an idea— "perhaps we can be merciful enough to let your aunt's apprentice repent in the dignity of a priest's confidence." His tone is almost encouraging, a promise folded in. "Should you confess yourself, we might leave the matter of Alifair's sin at a private confession."

Lala cannot think of it, the attic emptied of Alifair. It is as much a shock as if a farmer's scythe were to shear away the moon. The thought of him hurt or gone gives her a halting start, as though she is skimming her hands over the floor of a dark room and her palm has just caught a needle.

Tante Dorenia, the woman who has been mother and father to Lala since the season she lost both. Alifair, the boy who played his Blockflöte when she could not sleep, who combed out her hair when Tante lacked the patience.

These two are her family, and she will guard them, against sickness and rumor, against dancing and fever. They have survived plague and pox and sweat, hunger and ice-silvered winters. They have survived tilling their garden plot in seasons when it gave back nothing but thorns and thistles, years when even ploughmen spat those words—*dornen und disteln*—at the very earth, accusing it for being so willfully barren. They have survived, when the motions of the sky, when the very stars, seemed set against them.

She cannot let this be what takes them.

Whatever Lala must do, she will. She will make her heart into a knot of wood, as true and deep and pure as the blackest ink she and Tante have ever made.

She will let it lead her wherever will save Tante and Alifair.

"I have done it." She breathes out the words. "All on my own."

She is losing her life. But the relief of saving Alifair's and Tante Dorenia's and her baby's brings air into her.

The friar looks both satisfied and disappointed, as though he has a hundred more threats he wished to try.

"You confess to these crimes?" he asks.

"I confess to the crime of witchcraft," she says, her voice growing steady with each word. "Any crimes Alifair has committed are ones I have bewitched him into. Any sin I have brought into my aunt's house has been of my own wicked, ungrateful soul."

No matter what becomes of her, Alifair will live, and Tante will live, and he will help her look after her baby.

"I have made a pact with the devil," she says, as her heart whispers, *God forgive me.*

Her soul chants, *God forgive me for speaking these words, God protect those I love, God and all His angels, please guard them.*

"I have bewitched the souls who dance." Lala's tears cling to her cheeks. Already, she feels the breath of the flames they will feed her to.

May God take me into His hands, her heart calls out. *Whatever they will do with me, return me to my mother and my father.*

"I have betrayed the blameless soul of the woman who raised me. I have allowed the devil to tempt me away from the good and holy upbringing she has given me." Lala lifts her voice, forcing it clear and strong. "And I have ensorcelled Alifair, whose soul was blameless before my corruption. I confess to this all. I confess."

Emil

Rosella Oliva was still all the bright points he'd kept with him for years.

The rosy maple moth that had ridden home on her shoulder one afternoon, its fuzzy body and feet and powdered wings, the lemon and raspberry colors she'd later tried to match by mixing crayons.

The daffodils that grew in his mother's yard and that Rosella always loved. The ones with the pink ruffles and darker pink centers. The white-petaled ones with orange middles that Rosella said looked like fried eggs.

The way she asked his mother how she got them to bloom early and late, and when his mother made a joke about cutting out the heart of the town's fairest maiden, Rosella laughed. She actually laughed.

And tonight, when he found her under the water instead of near it, it seemed wrong, like she'd gotten caught on the wrong side of a mirror. The shape of her drifted under the moon-whitened surface. Her limbs floated in the dark, reflecting the glimmer in the sky like raw opal. Her shoes, ones that should have fallen off her, were bright as blood on her feet.

His history had pulled her into this.

When he went in after her, he tried to keep as much breath

in him as he could, bracing so the cold wouldn't take the air he had.

It needled into his body anyway, both the pain of it and the shock of how freezing the reservoir always got in fall.

The water felt like it had a current, dragging her down. Rosella's arms had gone limp as pondweed. Her skin looked pale as the spider bite scar she still had on her upper arm.

None of this even seemed like the same reservoir, or the same girl, he knew. He and Rosella had touched hands in this water not in the cold of fall but in the heat of July and August, when the light warmed a layer near the top. They always went farther down together, finding the stark border between that sun-heated water and where it got cold, and how it was always more sudden, more distinct, than they expected.

Right now, it was all cold, a water version of how he'd always imagined space. Frozen and quiet and punctuated only by stars.

He had a good enough grip on her that when she came back to him, he could feel it, the awareness sparking back through her body. He felt it in how she worked them both toward the surface, like she had come back to life enough to follow the moon.

He pulled her up on the bank, and her coughing rasped in the cold air.

"Are you okay?" he asked, reaching for the glasses he'd left in the wild grass. He got them on in time to see her nodding in answer to what he now registered as an incredibly stupid question.

She held on to him, her wet hands gripping his soaked shirt so hard that threads of water ran down his upper arms. How she did it seemed less like she was looking for comfort and more like she was checking him, making sure he was all there. The way she shivered made him feel the cold in a way that went deeper than the reservoir hitting him.

Her coughing quieted into breathing.

"You're okay," he said, and he hated how much it sounded like a question. "You're okay."

The light overhead warmed.

Rosella tilted her face toward the sky.

A vein of red snaked through the glimmer, fast as a lightning strike.

Rosella tensed, pulling away from Emil.

The glimmer lit her face enough to show her panic as she scrambled to her feet.

"Rosella," he called after her.

But he didn't follow her. He let her go.

⟨Strasbourg, 1518

The sergeant leads her out, no doubt toward a stone cell where she will be held until the method of execution is decided.

The sight of Alifair stills her, even with the men at her back.

She is sure that, in this moment, she imagines him. To know she will never again touch this boy, never again brush her lips against his neck or feel his hands pushing up her skirt, cracks her heart in two. She longs even for the simplest tasks, the ones she hated, but that she would perform for a lifetime if only she could do them with him, and with Tante looking on. Grinding the oak galls. Weeding the vegetable patch. Hanging the heavy, just-dyed fabric over the line, watching it turn from yellow to green to blue.

Alongside him are the friar and a canon priest, each looking proud, accomplished, as though Alifair is a stag they have hunted and caught.

Have they brought him to confess already? And should they not be taking him to the church?

Rage rises up in her, and she wonders if she has been a fool to believe they would take her confession and be lenient with him.

She keeps up her posture, as though her soul has been unburdened by her admission. She hopes she will pass close enough to Alifair to whisper, *Tell them I bewitched you. Tell them I am a daughter of the devil.*

"Come," the canon says to Alifair, urging him on.

Lala's eyes adjust to the light, and she catches the pain in Alifair's face.

"May I speak to her?" he asks.

The bailiff hesitates.

"Please," he says, the word plain. "It will ready my soul for confession."

"One motion of the devil," the priest warns.

Motion of the devil? Alifair stands here, ready to confess to lusts of the heart and sins of the body, and they think the devil is in him?

Alifair steps forward, the sergeant moving toward the door as though he might run, and neither the prim, well-adorned canon nor the friar can be trusted to stop him.

"I am sorry, Mademoiselle Blau," Alifair says in an upright, formal way.

Lala knows at once it is for the benefit of the men listening.

"I am sorry I brought the devil into your house after your aunt so kindly took me in," he says. "You both deserved better gratitude." He glances at the other men, sweeping them into his words. "I am sorry that my wickedness has brought such a fever on Strasbourg, and such pain to you and your aunt."

The sting of the words grows worse the more she grasps them.

"What?" she asks, barely a breath.

Alifair straightens. "And I am sorry that I beviled you into confessing," he declares, loud enough for the men to hear.

In one strike of cold horror, she realizes what he is doing.

"No," she says, the word rasping.

"No," she says again, louder, finding her voice this time.

She grabs his sleeve and pulls him close.

He winces, and only then does she remember the wasp stings.

She adjusts her grip. "You cannot do this."

"Your aunt needs you," he says through clenched teeth to keep the words quiet. "Her child will need you."

The understanding that Alifair knows of the baby stills her, but only for a moment.

"You cannot give yourself up," she says.

"They would have taken me eventually," he says, his face so weary he looks like a life-worn man, instead of a young one just out of being a boy. "They accepted it when I was a child, but I am older now. If they would not pardon La Pucelle d'Orléans, do you think they would pardon me?"

The common name for Jeanne d'Arc presses at Lala's throat. A greater soldier than any other on the battlefield, and they burned her for wearing a man's tunic and hose.

Lala grabs Alifair tighter. "I will deny whatever you say."

He gives her a sad smile. "I led them to a grave digger in Riquewihr. He remembers me taking the earth from your mother and father's graves. He will swear he witnessed me troubling the dead."

Riquewihr.

The stones beneath Lala seem as though they are giving, as though she will be swallowed into the ground.

Alifair had seen Lala's sleeplessness, and she had confessed the fear that her parents' souls were not at rest. She and Tante had not fulfilled the death traditions, fearing to be driven out in the middle of the night, or worse, simply for being Romnia. So Alifair had stolen away in the dark, gone to the hills outside

Riquewihr, taken the earth from their graves. He had brought it back for her to give to the water, one year at a time.

He had done this for her, for the repose of her parents' souls, and now all Lala can imagine is how it must look to these priests. A boy they think immoral, and he has been witnessed meddling with the dead. The priests will fall into accusations of witchcraft as easily as they do into their feather beds.

"You protected me," he whispers. "Let me do the same for you."

"Why?" Lala breathes.

Alifair presses his lips together, dampening his dry mouth. "The day the hail came."

Lala is pulled back into that afternoon that faded into an early evening, the cold and sting of the hailstones on her back, the warmth of Alifair as he picked her up off the path. The memory rises up from under the smell on Alifair's skin, the salt of sweat, the petal and wood of common hazel.

She did not realize he remembered.

"I went out as soon as the sky began to darken," he says, with a smile both small and sad. "I knew where you would be. The way I knew what you would do today."

Her skin feels covered in the hailstones' chill.

"How could you do this?" she asks, the words bursting from her lips so hard they sound angry.

"Lavinia," the canon says. "Contain yourself." He grips her upper arm, pulling her back from Alifair, this boy whose face holds so much pain and so much relief.

"Your anger is a human impulse," the friar says, both of them misplacing the center of her rage.

"Resist your baser instincts," the canon adds.

"Justice will be served," the friar says, as though an hour earlier he was not smirking over having gotten a confession from Lala. "You will leave it to us and to God."

To us and to God.

Of course these men place their own power first.

The sergeants take Alifair, binding his wrists with heavy rope as Lala screams. She screams after him, and the friar and canon continue their urging, still convinced it is her rage at Alifair that gives her such a voice.

She keeps screaming, and they think nothing of it but that she is a woman wailing over the deeds of a demon-filled boy.

She screams, loud enough that she hopes it rattles la cathédrale's single spire.

She wishes it to echo over Alsace, to the Vogesen, and to the Black Forest.

She bids it to Paris and Rome, into the souls of kings and emperors, to every man who makes the law of a land he has never bent to touch.

She commands it to carry across a thousand years.

She wills it to reach the very ears of God, so He will know what men on this earth do in His name.

Rosella

Whatever hope I had that my parents would still be asleep withered when I saw the living room light on.

I crossed my arms against the feeling that all the water on me was turning to ice. I had to brace myself to walk through the front door.

My mother stood just inside.

She took in my soaked clothes. "Where have you been?"

"I'm fine, Mamá," I said, dragging myself and my damp pajama pants toward the stairs.

She eyed the red shoes, the fabric a little darker from being wet. The candy-apple sheen they had in daylight looked deep and slicked as blood.

"Take those off," she said.

Her voice came as forbidding as I'd ever heard it.

"What?" I asked.

"I know all your friends are wearing them," she said. "I know they make you feel like you can do anything you want. But the things you've been doing, they're not you. Sneaking out. And this." She gestured at the water dripping off me.

"Mom," I said. "It's not like that."

"Then what were you doing?" Her voice rose, more panicked

than angry, and that just made me feel worse. "Was it some kind of dare? Something those girls told you to do?"

I couldn't meet her eyes.

"Take them off," she said, sounding as scared as she was stern.

"Mom," I said.

"Take them off." She hit each word.

I withered under her stare, until two breathed words slipped out of me:

"I can't."

An odd expression flashed over my mother's face, an uncomprehending panic.

"What do you mean you can't?" she asked.

I went to the kitchen and grabbed a knife from the block.

My mother followed.

I moved it toward my own feet.

My mother gasped. "Rosella, no."

But I was already dragging it across the fabric.

A seam opened, and my mother breathed in as though she might scream.

Then the seam closed, like a wound healing in seconds.

She stared at me, her fear of my own recklessness shifting toward the red cloth on my feet.

A stricken look tinted her features. All this fear, without her even knowing that they had been making me dance.

I slid the knife back into the block.

Her face hardened.

Not anger.

Resolve.

"We'll call your cousins," she said.

"Mom."

She cast her eyes to the floor. "Every curandera we know."

"Mamá," I said.

"Every one that everyone else knows, we'll ask them all. And all the priests."

"Mamá," I said.

This time, I landed on the word hard enough to stop her.

She and my father would rip apart this town trying to help me. They wouldn't care who found out. By the time they were done, everyone would think of our shoes as more murderous than beautiful.

One cursed pair could gut our family's business. All of it would fall away. The peacock and plums and bronzes that painted our workroom. The indigos and flame yellows and oranges that dyed our lives. I had learned the seasons by what colors we sewed. Pastels for the spring, grays and ice blues for winter. Clusters of beads like lilac blossoms. The moss green that made me think of wood fairies.

We would lose all the months by colors.

It would ruin us.

Everything my great-grandparents had worked for, the years they'd endured in the maquiladoras, the factories where they were paid pennies for each seam, where their blood darkened the metal corners of the equipment, all of it would turn to ashes.

All the whispered magic of Oliva shoes would turn to poison.

"You're the one who said it never lasts," I said. "That it always leaves with the glimmer."

"This is different," my mother said.

"How?" I asked. "All I have to do is wait until it's over. Like every other year."

"Wait?" my mother asked. "Wait while those things"—I had never seen her regard our family's work with such disdain, such suspicion—"drive you to do what, next?"

"They're my shoes."

The words came out without me deciding to speak them.

"What?" my mother asked.

"I sewed them," I said.

I couldn't tell her the rest, the awful scene with the debutante's father, the scissors, the pieces I saved for years.

"So before you let half the town know there's something wrong with what we do, what I've done," I said, "let me try something."

"What?" my mother asked, her voice rising as she threw a blanket across my back. "If you can't even cut them off, what else is there?"

Emil had shown up at the reservoir twice. Twice, he had pulled me back from the shoes' grasp. He knew something about the glimmer this year, about the odd magic tinting Briar Meadow. I could see it in the wear of his face. Whatever had come for me had left some trace on him.

I had to risk whatever he would think of me, whatever might come with him not believing me.

"I don't know," I said. "But I can think of someone who might."

Strasbourg, 1518

Weak around death.

It was a polite phrase Enneleyn used to use to explain why Lala and Tante and Alifair never came to executions. They did not gather for hangings or beheadings or lashings. They did not even attend when the sword itself was the spectacle; a nobleman's sentence would sometimes command a skilled executioner from across the Vogesen, bringing death with one graceful stroke of his blade.

It has always been difficult to see death as entertainment when the next on the stage could so easily be any of the three of them.

Now, watching them stand Alifair to hear his sentence, is the first time Lala and Tante have ever joined the waiting crowd.

Alifair does not look up. He does not lift his eyes to see the faces gathered in la Place Broglie. He keeps his gaze on the wooden slats at his feet.

The sight of his dirt-grayed shirt, his eyes ringed with sleeplessness, his face that shows he is plunged so deeply into resignation that he has no room for fear. It is all so awful that for a moment, Lala drifts away from it.

Her drifting away begins with thoughts of when she would

sneak up the ladder and into his bed. She would crawl under the blanket with him when it was cold.

Then one spring, when the ice wore off the trees and the branches were breaking into bloom, she kept climbing the ladder. She did it even when the weather grew too mild to feign a chill.

Sometimes, when the scent of blossoms in the air left them drunk, they pretended they were night courting, like the sons and daughters of wealthy burghers.

Amid these comes another memory, one that tears away the center of her heart.

Last year. The sweating sickness.

First it came for Tante.

"The bloody English sweat," Tante panted from her bed. "We have survived famine and ice and buboes and pox, but this will be the death of us, curse it all."

She ordered both Lala and Alifair out of the house, so they would not catch it. She ordered them to the flax farmer, who offered them his straw-covered barn until they proved well enough to enter the house.

They did not go.

Tante raged at them, covered in sweat, weak in her bed, and still they did not go.

Lala pleaded with God and Sara la Kali to save Tante. She fell to her knees before the crab apple tree, begging it to take her aunt's fever.

Alifair carried in water from currents upstream from the city walls, free from the lye and blood of the market and abattoir.

Tante accepted only a few sips, the pain of swallowing overtaking how thirsty she was.

Lala offered her feverfew and brown bread.

She would not take it.

She panted in her sleep. Sweat poured from her body, and Lala changed the sheets as often as she could dry them, doing what she could when they soaked through to the straw.

Alifair, by favor and what little money he had, obtained enough almonds to make a milk by steaming them in hot water. He strained it through cheesecloth to make it easier to swallow.

Tante took only a few sips. But Lala is still convinced the day she did was the day she tipped away from death and toward life.

It was also the day the sweating sickness came for Alifair.

It overtook him so quickly he could not get up the ladder, falling off the second rung. Lala caught him and put him on her bed, and he was already too weak to protest.

Tante proved as ruthless in her efforts for this boy as she had been in so much else. She did not accept his refusal of feverfew; she compelled him to drink. She procured, in ways Lala still could not guess, water from the spring of Saint Odilia and earth from the grave of Saint Aurelia.

She soaked halved lemons in hot water because he would not eat, would not take sauerkraut or garlic, and this was the only of the baxtale xajmata she could get into him. He needed every auspicious food he could swallow, as much as he needed their prayers to Sara la Kali.

Tante ordered Lala to bring whatever blankets they could find, to stay with him when the delirium came, to talk him through the open-eyed nightmares of the sweat.

"If he dies," Tante said, her eyes hard and not looking at Lala as they boiled water, "it is on your head."

Lala had turned, startled.

"I told you both to leave me," Tante said.

"You are my family," Lala said. "My blood."

"And I am all the mother you have," Tante said. "So you should have done as I ordered."

"And I suppose you want me to leave him now?" Lala whispered.

"If you're to be sick now, it's done. It was done the moment you both disobeyed me and remained here."

Lala went out of the house. She wrapped her arms around the crab apple tree and sobbed into its bark. She wished the woman in the black and yellow skirts were there in a way so desperate it became an ache in her body.

Now Lala hates this memory, tries to drive it away.

But it stays, fluttering around her like a moth. It brings her to the night she dried sweat from Alifair's body, soaking through all the sheets and rags they had. In his sleep, he laughed in a way that unnerved her in how much it sounded like crying. He drank water desperately, only to sweat it out within hours. In the dark, he shivered hard enough to tremble the straw mattress.

Lala held on to him, her eyes shut tight, her mouth against his head as she whispered into his hair.

I forbid you to die. I forbid it. I do not give you permission. You have my heart and you cannot take it with you.

After hours on her knees before God, and hours crying out to Sara la Kali, this had been all the prayer she had left in her.

The break of his fever the next morning, the deepening of his breathing, the way she was able to get salt-and-lemon-softened fiddleheads into him, seemed, at the time, as much of a miracle as Lala would ever hope for.

But now, watching him on the wooden stage that was built for the disaster of the great dance, that miracle has dimmed like an ember. She understands, now, that for a girl like herself to love a boy like Alifair would take as many miracles as there are fish in the sea and stars in the heavens.

In the unending moments of waiting for proud men to declare Alifair's fate, she grows dizzy. Her mind weaves and lands on an old story about an earl and a pope. She does not know if it is true, but the way the story goes is that the pope offered the earl a kingdom so remote that even the earl's finest horses and best knights could not bring him to it. The earl told the pope that the offer was the same as if he had said, "I give or sell you the moon. Now climb up and take it."

The boy who now stands, silently accepting his sentence, is as distant to her as the moon. Her kiss would never have made them both a world in which he could be hers. The heat between their fingertips, like ten small, identical stars, could not craft a Strasbourg in which they would both be allowed to live.

When they pronounce the method by which he will die, Lala pitches herself forward.

"Stop," Tante says, touching her shoulder.

But Lala pushes at the crowd in front of her.

Two sets of soft hands catch her arms.

Not soft because they are smooth; in truth, they are calloused and work hardened.

Soft, because of the lightness of their grip.

"You cannot help him now," Henne says, tears weakening her voice.

Geruscha has her other arm, and they pull her back.

But Lala will not take her eyes from the boy with the bound wrists and the downcast eyes.

All the canon priests' talk of mercy, all their posturing that they would show lenience if he made a full confession, it has all been a lie.

Lala cannot climb the steps to the wooden stage and take him. Her desperation cannot bring him closer any more than the sea can pull the moon down to her waters.

Emil

He shocked awake, sitting up in the dark room with sweat soaking the back of his shirt.

The dreams he'd startled out of stayed, a weight on his body. The sound of heels striking the ground. The smell of dust on hillsides, and horses within the city walls, and blood-stained stones.

A blur of the same black hair he and his grandfather had, the mix of curly and straight he always found in old photographs.

Then there was the pierce of a girl's scream, a woman's scream, a sound that unfolded like light separating into its colors. The fear, the protest, the taking of blame that should never have been hers. The rush of voices telling her she must take it, that all this fury belonged to her.

He still didn't get a good look at her face; the memory, passed down through blood, must have been too watered down. But he saw that hair, and the brown of her skin, a brown that might have gotten her mistaken for the daughter of a Turkish father and French mother. A brown that could be blamed on sun or lied away as Italian or even southern German, Black Forest.

The echo of that scream followed him. It was a ringing in his ears, a weight in his forehead, a stirring against the back of his neck.

He shook his head to clear it. The sound stayed with him. He closed his eyes, dug his nails into his palms, paced the floor. Nothing.

It was still with him early in the morning when he went out to the shed.

It was in all of them, truth and history written into their blood. And this was the piece that had come alive in Emil, setting fire to his dreams. Maybe it was because that was where it had started, hundreds of years of being forced out of one place, then the next, then the next, until it seemed like there was no air on earth someone would not object to them breathing.

Maybe it was because this was a time his mother and father had both studied, their fields intersecting in a span of years that included the dancing plague. What were they working on, Emil wondered, in the months before he was born? He wondered if the work of that moment, the thoughts swirling in this house, stirred up this particular corner of their family's history, enough that it would always be written a little brighter in Emil. Even if he didn't want it.

He tried to focus on the work in front of him, the small task of finding things he wanted to show Rosella Oliva. In the language of flames and colors, he had told her what he hadn't managed to say in years passing each other in the halls or at church. And the way she'd looked at him, the glow of the ion flames tinting her lips, he thought she'd heard him.

Maybe he could do it again. Maybe he could tell her that he remembered the gardenias she grew with her mother by showing her the crystals of copper chloride, jagged and blue green as a geode made from seawater. Maybe, by showing her different hydrates of cobalt chloride that ranged from blue to purple to pink, he could explain the gradual shift that had left him nervous and quiet around her.

Maybe he could even tell her about the awful moment of his family's history that was now pulling him backward, how it made him nervous enough that he didn't go after her last night, that he let her go home by herself.

In the rose-quartz pink of manganese chloride, he would tell her about the stone walls of Strasbourg and brutal heat of that Alsatian summer. He could tell her about the canal houses painted the powder blue of copper benzoate, the water and algae the colors of nickel chloride. He could show her the stained-glass-blue of copper sulfate crystals, because he could not tell her in words that this was his heart, jagged, and almost familiar, and made of something that felt far more threatening than beautiful.

But each time he blinked, she was there again.

Not Rosella.

His five-hundred-years-ago relative, her screams laced with fear and rage. She was there, and he recognized her by the brushstroke of her black hair and the brown of her hands.

I don't know what you're trying to tell me, he breathed into the clinging haze of his own dream.

He told her again, in case she could hear him across five centuries, across the moonless dusk that separated him from those who'd lived before him.

I don't know what you want me to know.

The feeling of a palm landed on his shoulder.

He turned around, looking for the hand and whoever it belonged to.

He found only the dark in the unlit half of the shed, and the sky, still pink between the door and the frame.

Heat breathed on his back. It cast a glow on his forearms.

Emil turned back around.

A stream of fire ran the length of the lab bench. It burned in every color he'd shown Rosella Oliva, all those flames tinted by ions. The blue green of copper. The marigold yellow of sodium. The purple of cesium and grass green of barium.

His hands wanted to move. But those colors locked him there.

This was what happened when he got near Rosella Oliva. This was everything that sparked and caught in the space between them. Between her, a girl whose last name held the lore of enchanted shoes, and him, whose family carried the history of a dancing plague, and the burden of blame for it.

His muscles flinched to life even while his eyes stayed on that trail of flames.

He went for the fire extinguisher (he could still hear Dr. Ellern's voice—*Turn the pin before you clamp down*) and swept a cloud across the lab bench.

He only distantly registered the last tips of the flames biting his sleeve.

"Emil."

He heard Rosella's voice in the same moment he felt her hitting his arm. It was more odd than frightening, her slapping at his wrist and forearm in a way that seemed startled, not angry.

It took him a minute to put it together with the pain of the fire singeing the hair on his left forearm. He realized his sleeve had caught only in the moment of her putting it out.

She looked at his arm, swearing under her breath. "We've got to get some ice on this."

He almost talked without thinking. *Cold water, not ice.* Another warning from Dr. Ellern. *Ice on a burn can leave frostbite.*

But he couldn't even talk. With her hands on him, he felt

the color of flames catching between them. It was brighter and sharper than the pain throbbing into his arm.

Whatever was lacing his dreams, whatever his relatives from five centuries ago wanted him to know, it led back to Rosella. He couldn't pin it down yet, but it was an instinct as clear and true as his mother's sense for when rain was coming.

He should have felt it the night Rosella kissed him, with that flash of red folded inside the glimmer, that vein of blood.

If he stayed near her, the space between them would turn to fire.

He pulled back so fast he almost dropped the extinguisher.

She blinked at him, eyes wide, but let him have the distance.

He looked back at the bench, breathing hard. Whatever heat was left moldered under a layer of sodium bicarbonate.

"It's us," Emil said, more to the ash-bitter air than to Rosella.

The truth he hadn't wanted to pick up and turn over in his hands now cut into him.

Both of those nights out by the reservoir, a fever had taken hold of Rosella, the same kind of possession as five hundred years ago.

She had danced, without wanting to. Something had compelled her to the edge of those rocks, and into the water.

"We can't do this," Emil said, feeling the hum of blood in his wrist.

She shook her head, like trying to shake her thoughts into place. "What?"

"This." Emil swallowed, still getting his breath back. "You and me. We can't be near each other."

"What are you talking about?"

"You're gonna get hurt. You already have."

"Me?" She looked at his arm.

He didn't look.

"It's us," he said, tracing paths between the nightmares that visited him as he slept and the ones she lived. "We're what's causing this."

"Causing what?"

His eyes skimmed over the sodium-dusted table, then the red of her shoes.

"Emil," Rosella said.

He flinched back to her. "I have to stay away from you."

"What?" she asked. "Why?"

He hesitated over the truth.

If anyone in this town, anyone outside his own family, would understand, it would be Rosella. The Olivas were the one family who didn't blink at the idea of baxtale xajmata, or at bringing food to their dead, or everything else that made most gadje glance at his family sideways.

The truth of his family's history felt like pins on his tongue, things he needed to spit out.

"Emil," Rosella said, his name turning harder on her tongue.

Emil took a long breath. "So back when my family lived in Strasbourg, there was a dancing plague."

"A *dancing plague*?"

"Yeah. It's exactly what it sounds like. People started dancing uncontrollably. Like they couldn't help it. And they kept dancing." He looked at the floor. "Even though it killed them."

"Dancing killed them?"

"Some of them, yeah. Heart attacks. Strokes. They literally danced themselves to death."

Saying the words felt like a draft on the back of his neck, like that unseen hand was nearing his shoulder blade again.

"When was this?" Rosella asked.

"Five hundred years ago."

She was blinking in threes now, like she was trying to resolve an image. "Why were they dancing?"

"There are a lot of theories. Ergot poisoning. Something in the water. But most likely?" He gave a resigned shrug. "Some kind of mass hysteria."

"And your ancestors," Rosella said slowly. "They were there?"

"Worse than there." Emil felt a tightness building in his jaw. "They were blamed for it."

The look on her face mirrored what he'd felt when his father told him. The sudden understanding. All the blood rushing to his forehead, like hanging upside down off a bed.

"What happened?" she asked.

He sighed in a way that was more bracing himself than exasperation, but it was a little of both, and he knew it. Rosella's family had skin brown enough that a little of him hoped maybe he wouldn't have to explain this. He wanted her to guess, to just know. Then he wouldn't have to say it out loud. This was all someone else's pain, five hundred years old, and yet somehow it brought back the shame of hearing his parents getting a call from his teachers.

Rosella watched him. She waited for him to talk.

"So in the first few years of the 1500s, anyone Romani was banned from France and Germany," he said. "It wasn't long before the independent cities did the same thing. I don't remember when it happened in Strasbourg. There are so many of these decrees sometimes I forget the dates."

"But where was everyone supposed to go?" Rosella asked.

"Great question, since a lot of other countries were making the same decrees," he said. "Some of my relatives assimilated. Some married gadje. My mom's family got by doing that for a long time. Some disappeared into cities. Any of them who couldn't pass knew that wherever they went, they could always be forced out. My relatives in Strasbourg"—he blew out a breath, feeling like he needed to clear out his lungs to finish saying all this—"well, they tried to pass."

He touched the sodium bicarbonate on the resin countertop, the dusting of white coming off on his fingertips.

"Unfortunately, people talk," he said. "And rumors that you're Romani get you blamed for things, especially in the 1500s."

"So what happened to them?" Rosella asked.

He shook his head, his jaw still held tight. "We don't know. After that summer they don't exist in city records. The best case scenario is they lost everything, their home, their business, all of it. They were driven out."

"That's the *best* case?" Rosella asked.

"Yes," he said. "Because the worst, and most likely, is that they were executed."

He winced under the memory of his own nightmares, that screaming that felt sharp as cut glass.

"Because they got blamed for the dancing plague," Rosella said. It seemed more like she was confirming than asking.

"Yes," Emil said.

"Because they were Romani," Rosella said, with enough resignation that this time he knew it wasn't a question. Her sigh fell like a slack balloon, as though the world disheartened her even if it didn't surprise her.

He looked at her, with her staring eyes dark enough that he couldn't pick out the points of black at the centers. Yes, she was a gadji, but she knew what it was to look how they looked in a town like Briar Meadow. And she could maybe guess what it was like to be his family five hundred years ago.

"Yes," Emil said. "Because they were Romani. And because they were unmarried women who made their own living. Because everyone thought they were witches. All of the above. Whenever something happens, people go looking for someone to blame."

She kept staring in a way he couldn't read. Disbelief? Horror? Deciding to stay really still until he just forgot she was there?

After everything he'd just said, the silence pricked at him.

Then her expression shifted, like a flame changing from one color to the next.

Strasbourg, 1518

Which four brothers live under only one hat?
(The legs of a table.)
Which mother and son can you see only after sundown?
(The night and the moon.)

All this is an awful, living version of the riddles Lala's father so loved.

Tante says that the harder they were to solve, the more joy Lala's father took in them. But what would he tell her now? How to save a boy who has made Lala's confession his own is the most impossible riddle, the most stubborn knot.

"Your favorite priest tried to speak for him, you know," Tante says. "And they brushed him away as if he were a troublesome child." She squeezes her eyes shut, giving a small shake of her head.

That shift in expression nearly drags Lala to the floor. She has always known Tante cared about Alifair. But the grief in her face now makes plain how much she loves him, as she would a brother or nephew.

Lala sinks onto a stool. "What has happened to this place?"

"Nothing that has not been happening for hundreds of years," Tante says, and the breaking in her voice makes it sound younger than Lala has ever heard it. "Those who dance just make it plain. Men tell their wives to be pure in the sight of God but then beat them and force them and show them less regard than their dogs. We lie sick in our beds while the wealthiest demand that the physicians see them first so that they don't bring our dirt across their thresholds."

Her voice grows bitter and cruel.

"Our roofs cave in while the councils debate if the cathedral needs another small fortune of gold." Tante tosses her hands, as though there is no helping it. "We endure cold and hunger while rich men take our tithes, swearing they're for the poor and for work of the Lord. Then they turn around and buy marble for their houses and silk for their mistresses." She releases a bitter laugh. "And they're the ones meant to commend us into heaven. Our spirits depend on baptism from *them*."

Lala cannot see tears in Tante's eyes, but she can hear them.

"And then they marvel when the bodies of their flock speak the truth their mouths cannot." Tante kicks at the frayed edge of a rush. "If the devil has hold of anyone, it's the men at their high posts, not those who dance."

Lala folds Tante's words and her rage into her body. How she wishes God would show Himself enough that the canons understood their part in all this, how their hearts have become as unyielding as the jewels on their fingers.

And now the wattle and daub speaks of Alifair's absence. Gall nuts swell and rot on the tree. The woad grows at hard angles like briar, as though it knows. The attic stays quiet. The straw goes undisturbed.

"This won't end." Lala doubles over, resting against her thighs. "They'll go looking for demons no matter who they've killed."

"Those who go looking for demons always find them," Tante says. "Even in angels."

Tante's words raise Lala upright.

They brighten and deepen, like the light and air turning woad dye from yellow green to blue.

The riddle comes to her, one that would be at home amid her father's garude lava.

How can a witch who is not a witch become one yet remain not one?

And with it, the answer.

If angels could be counted as demons, so could anyone.

So could she.

She has feared it for so long, never before considering how she might use it.

"Lala?" Tante asks as Lala moves toward the door.

"Rest," Lala says. "If you won't for you, then for your child."

"Where are you going?" Tante asks.

"Church," Lala says, letting Tante assume she will beg masses for Alifair's soul.

Lala runs to l'Église Saint-Pierre-le-Vieux.

She finds it empty save for Geruscha and Henne, on their knees before a transept altar.

Lala has no will in her to be exasperated.

At the sound of Lala's footsteps, Geruscha and Henne look up, casting her pained, watery glances before returning to their prayers.

The kind priest emerges from the shadows. Even from across the church she can see his grief in the stoop of his back.

"They have been praying for him since dawn," he says quietly enough that it will not echo. "And yesterday all before nightfall."

Lala glances back at their bowed heads.

Her friends have all made their retreat. Agnesona. Melisende. The merchants' daughters who once greeted her in the lane. They recoil from the taint of witchcraft. They see it on Lala like brambles caught in her hair. So why these two pray for Alifair as though he is their brother is as far a mystery to Lala as the path of the stars. She wants to take them by the shoulders and ask why they do not give up on her.

"Oh, Lavinia," the priest says, his eyes rimmed red from the salt of tears. "You live in a place that has fallen so deeply into madness, they think dancing is their greatest folly."

He says it with such apology, as though a gift he wished to give her has broken in his palms.

Lala draws him back into the shadows, so no one, not even Geruscha and Henne, will hear.

"I want to save him," she says. "And I think I might have a way to try, but I will need you in order to do it, even though you will never bless the means."

A light comes back to the priest's face. Not a smile. Nowhere near. But hope.

"Let us see about that," he says in a low voice, "shall we?"

So Lala speaks the words. She speaks them in the Lord's dwelling, expecting at any moment to either burst into flames or for the priest to order her to confession.

The priest only lifts his chin, considering, and then nods.

His nod feels as though it carries the thunder of angels.

He glances toward Geruscha and Henne. "Tell them," he says.

"No," Lala says.

"They will want to help you," the priest says, firmer this time.

She lowers her speech to a whisper. "I can't."

But Geruscha and Henne have already risen from their knees.

The priest motions between them, as though to say to Lala, *Well?*

Lala's voice feels choked with the memory of them appearing in the lane four years ago.

Their glances flit between each other, not settling. It is so quiet their breaths echo.

The silence wears down Lala first. Her tongue loosens with a bitter "Why do you care what happens to him? Why have you ever cared what happened to me, or him, or my aunt?"

She regrets it instantly.

She waits for the pain or anger in their faces.

"I love her," Henne says, so calmly that for a moment Lala does not know who she speaks of.

Then Geruscha lowers her gaze to her feet.

"As well you should," Lala says, trying not to sound impatient. "She is your friend, isn't she?" Geruscha and Henne have been the best of friends for years. It would be a great pity if there was no love between them.

"No," Henne says, her voice deeper, heavier now. "I *love* her."

Her emphasis on the word *love* is so great Lala feels the weight of it in her hands.

Now Geruscha's cheeks flush, so brightly it is visible even in the dim light of the church.

The meaning blooms in Lala.

Four years of understanding blooms in her.

The reason they placed Lala and her aunt as Romnia, and still offered her friendship so fervently.

The reason they have cared so deeply about Lala, and now about Alifair.

Lala and Alifair are not the only ones who have feared *Li livres de jostice et de plet*, who have lived with the threat of it like a knife at their backs.

If the friar knew, he would surely declare Geruscha and Henne to have violated *the natural law of God*.

Lala's eyes flash to the priest, and then back to Henne. Does she realize what she has said in front of him?

But the priest's face shows neither shock nor judgment.

Lala's heart feels heavy as a river stone.

How many have known about her and Tante, about Alifair, and loved them still? What friendship has her fear made her disregard?

It breaks Lala open.

She tells them her last desperate plan. It seems to spill from her lips all in one moment.

Henne and Geruscha agree before Lala has even gotten all the words out.

Then, there is everyone else.

Alifair has never made a spectacle of his kindness, so it falls to Lala to remember who has shown him gratitude. The brother and sister to whom he has given bread. The exhausted mother whose children he has kept entertained with stories of fairies from the Schwarzwald, so she can nurse her baby and steal a little rest. The homesick families comforted by songs from his Blockflöte.

Some, like Geruscha and Henne, say yes before Lala can finish her plea.

Others fear Lala, thinking she is a witch or worrying they will be thought one if seen with her. They withdraw into their doorways, clutching sprigs of angelica.

To them, she promises that, should they help, they will never set eyes on her again. She will never near their threshold as long as they and their children live.

That, it seems, is all they need to hear.

Strasbourg considers the burning of an innocent man to be a kind of show.

If there is to be any chance of saving him, Lala will have to give them a better one.

Rosella

On a first-grade field trip, Mrs. Woodlock told our class her version of Cinderella, the one that involved the stepsisters cutting off portions of their feet to fit the enchanted slipper. Five girls burst into tears, one after the other, and as they wailed Emil's mother looked over at him as though asking her son for some explanation of these tiny, fragile women who sat in front of her.

But when those girls cried, I laughed.

I didn't mean to. I didn't think the stepsisters' blood inside the glass slipper was funny. And I tried to press a hand over my mouth, the way I'd seen my mother do in church when the oldest members of the choir fell asleep.

My laughing would not stop. It flew out of me like wings.

Emil's eyes had flashed over to me, the hint of a surprised smile on his always-serious face, as though he thought I was fearless, and brazen.

But I had laughed because his mother's story didn't sound real. It sounded like something meant to be laughed at. The prince in the story sounded so boring—so beside the point, like the whole fairy tale could have happened without him—that to imagine the stepsisters giving up parts of their bodies for him seemed like a joke. A test. Like Emil's mother wanted to know how gullible we were.

When I laughed, some of the boys and two other girls did too.

But I was the only one the teacher told to sit on the bench during recess the next day.

Emil sat with me. He didn't say anything or cast me any kind of sympathetic look. He didn't look at me at all. I would have thought he was waiting for a bus, or about to read a book, but no buses ran on that side of the school, and he didn't have anything with him. He just sat with me, quiet, hands folded together like he was in a church pew.

When the teacher came over, wanting to object somehow, Emil just looked up at her. His face showed polite attention, but also dared her to find fault with him and me sitting in silence on opposite sides of a wooden bench.

That was the start of Emil and me, a gruesome fairy tale. He had been raised on them.

And now he had just told me another one, one even I couldn't laugh at.

An awful fairy tale that was worse for being true.

A small anger spun and grew in me.

"You knew," I said, more clarifying than accusing. "This whole time, you knew."

Emil opened his mouth, but hesitated.

I waited for my anger to wear down, like a rock tumbled through an ocean. But it just got slicker, harder to hold on to. It slipped from my hands and sank so deep I couldn't have brought it back up if I wanted to. I couldn't even see it anymore. I couldn't place the center of my rage. I just felt the weight of it, somewhere down in those depths.

I had spent this week wondering what in me was so dangerous, so thick with dark magic, that my family's own work turned against me. I had wondered what made me the one girl who transformed the shimmering spell of red shoes into something terrifying.

Now I caught the edge of it, that anger I couldn't place.

Realizing that Emil had held all this back, I saw every difference between his family and mine.

His parents were both professors, and my family was two generations away from the maquiladoras. My great-grandparents had worked shifts soldering circuit boards. At my age, my abuela had lost two of her fingertips in punch presses. She had been born in a village whose air and water was so thick with styrene that sometimes her sisters could not remember their own names. They whispered the chemical's name—*estireno*—with the dread of mentioning some fierce demon or vengeful saint. My great-grandfather would get headaches so bad he would bang his head on the wall. My great-aunt had died when she was nineteen, selling hairpins and chewing gum because she couldn't work fast enough for the factories.

I had worried that I had wrecked everything they had worked for, that I had disgraced all they had survived, with nothing but my own hands.

I never considered that maybe it wasn't just me, and my hands.

Because Emil hadn't told me.

He had seen me dancing along the rocks above the reservoir, and he hadn't told me. He had pulled me out of the water, and he hadn't told me.

"And you didn't think maybe this was something you should've mentioned earlier," I said, more statement than question.

"What if I had?" he asked. "What could you have done? It was five hundred years ago. What would telling you have done other than scare you?"

"I spent this whole time thinking you wouldn't believe me. But if you'd said something . . ." I faltered. I scrambled to find what I was saying again. "You didn't even need to tell me it was your family. You could have just told me this was something that happened."

"But it is my family." His voice rose again. "You wanted me to tell you like it was just facts out of a book? Guess what? I can't. Because five hundred years ago, my relatives lived this. Telling you meant telling you something about us, about me, about what's in my blood. Do you even get that?"

Our breathing went hard enough that I could hear both mine and his, a little off rhythm.

My anger now felt like something I was closing, like one of Emil's reactions burning itself out.

"You wanted us to stay away from each other?" I said. "Done."

Strasbourg, 1518

She waits until Tante Dorenia is asleep, then she opens the wooden trunk.

She lifts out a blue dress, deep as an autumn sky, and a clean shift. The underdress is plain, but so new it is nearly ivory. It looks as clouds against the blue.

Lala remembers dyeing the cloth, the batch coming out such a perfect shade that Tante could not bear to part with it. She told Lala she would wear it on her wedding day.

The feeling of a stone in Lala's stomach warns her that she may not live to see her wedding day, so she will wear this today, this perfect blue.

If Strasbourg demands a show, she must costume herself.

Next, she ties two pouches to her waist.

They weigh against her bare thighs, hidden by her skirt. In their depths, she hides a few things that will fit.

A small amount of money. A handful of dried sphagnum for the next time she bleeds. The tincture of safflower Tante gave her, so she may pretty her lips and cheeks should she need to charm a man. A pot of fine woad powder, blue as the deepest stretch of the Rhein. A jar of good iron gall ink.

If she survives this, she will find a way to make up the worth to her aunt.

Tante Dorenia's snore, a roaring, unsettling thing on the nights it has kept Lala from sleeping, now sounds of a music she will miss. Enneleyn used to say, without shame, that the prettiest women had the loudest snores. The thought of losing this one weighs deep in Lala's stomach.

She presses a light kiss onto her sleeping aunt's forehead, glossed with summer heat and the strain of her growing child. Tante smells of the garden, of all that Lala will miss. Of wild thyme and tansy, of yarrow and feverfew, of figs and cornelian cherries drying in the sun.

She kisses her palm and then rests it against her aunt's belly, to say goodbye to the cousin she will never meet.

She turns her back only once. She cannot bear to do it a second time.

On her way toward the city, she says goodbye to all these things that have watched her pass from little girl to reckless, heartbroken woman.

The blossoming woad, the yellow flowers of the plant that yield such blue dye.

The flax in bloom, the sky-colored petals making the field seem a mirror for the heavens.

The places that grew beneath her hands, and that grew her.

Emil

"A fire, Emil?" his mother asked.

Emil breathed out. "Please stop saying it like that. It sounds like you think I set it. Anyway, it's out. I got it all cleaned up this afternoon."

She set the first aid kit on the kitchen table. "What is going on with you?"

"Nothing. This season is just getting to me."

His mother eyed the floor. "I don't see a pair of red shoes on your feet."

He gave a tired laugh. "And yet."

Gerta rubbed her face against the table leg and then went for the hem of Emil's jeans.

Gerta, one of the few signs of Briar Meadow's falls that had stayed.

His mother gestured for his arm, with the kind of brusque insistence that left no room for objection.

She smoothed antibiotic jelly onto the side of his forearm. "It's so strange, isn't it?"

Emil tried not to suck air in through his teeth. "What is?"

"In Strasbourg," she said. "All those years ago."

Her eyes flashed between his face and his arm a couple of times, as though waiting for him to remember something. It came with an expression he knew well, one that said, *Don't you know this? I could have sworn I told you this.*

"I'm sorry," she said with a shake of her head. "I still forget sometimes you don't want to hear about these things."

He caught his mother's eye. "I want to hear about these things."

The words came out flat, but with enough weight that his mother's expression turned.

"Red shoes were supposed to help cure the dancing plague," she said. "And look at what they're doing now. Everyone in red shoes falling in love, driving faster, cooking with more salt and spice. What would the sixteenth-century church think of our little town?"

The words rattled around in Emil's head before settling.

"Wait," he said. "What?"

"Red shoes," his mother said. "The color was supposed to help cure the afflicted."

"Papa didn't say anything about that," Emil said.

"It's barely a footnote in the history," his mother said, taping gauze over his burn. "Shoes dyed red with carmine, or madder, and then blessed with holy water and balsam oil and the sign of the cross. It's a detail so small that most accounts leave it out entirely. But it's something, isn't it? The thought that a color could cure a fever sent by heaven or hell."

"Red shoes," Emil said. "Back then. This was a real thing?"

"Dozens, even hundreds of pairs." She set the last piece of tape. "The city ordered them made. Strasbourg's most powerful men paid for the leather and dye, the work of the city's craftsmen, and the travel of priests to Saverne to bless them. It's a strange fact in a strange corner of history, n'est-ce pas?"

Emil set his free hand against the edge of the table. He didn't realize until he did it that he was trying to steady himself, stop everything from moving.

Red shoes.

However much this was about him and Rosella, it was just as much about her family and his.

They were up against five centuries in more ways than she knew.

Why did we stop being friends? she'd asked him.

He'd let her think it was just that he couldn't take the teasing, the jokes about them being girlfriend and boyfriend. But it had never been about that, not really.

It was because her family's prayers to la Virgen de Guadalupe let her understand his grandmother's prayers to Sara la Kali. It was because their families both celebrated their dead as much as they mourned them. It was because the Olivas' familiarity with curanderas meant she understood him telling her about drabarimos, and the work of a drabarni.

It was because she always used the word *Romani*, instead of the slur most of their classmates turned it into.

Every time Rosella didn't reject something about Emil, it made it harder for him to reject it about himself.

He didn't fight to stay friends with her, because it would have meant fighting to keep some part of himself he knew he couldn't have.

That was the truth he didn't give her, because he didn't really know it until now: *Why did we stop being friends? Because you understood a part of me I had to pretend didn't exist.*

This time, he would tell her the truth she needed to know, that she wasn't just wearing red shoes her family had made.

She was wearing five hundred years of history.

Strasbourg had pinned its hope on red shoes to cure the dancing plague.

And now, five hundred years later, it was Rosella's family who'd made the red shoes enchanting Briar Meadow.

Rosella, the girl who knew him the way few gadje ever would. Rosella, the only girl he'd ever told the names of his family's vitsi, a girl who spoke the language of brown-skinned saints and food offered to the dead.

She was the girl the red shoes had come for, and that some thread of the dancing plague had come back for.

When he found her, in the tree-darkened shadows, he couldn't let that fever have her again.

He caught up with her. He set his hand on the waist of her dress and he held her. At first it was a try at keeping her still, so the fever wouldn't take her.

Instead, it took him with her.

Strasbourg, 1518

Blutgerichtsbarkeit.

Blood justice.

Ius gladii.

The right hand of the sword.

High justice.

Such virtuous words placed on men's whims for who lives and who dies.

Lala waits in the dim between lanes, folding herself into the shadow of the Tour du Bourreau. She sets her back teeth, hoping it will quiet the rhythm of her heart.

Spectators have gathered along the route, treating a burning as a diversion, a show little different from a tournament or a troupe of famed jongleurs. Merchants show off tunics embroidered with compasses. Grand seigneurs wear their ermine, and sleeves so wide that their servants must take care not to crush them. Hats form a sea of such varied color and shape that it seems fanfare fitting a coronation.

Blood court.

At least that name is halfway honest. Proceedings painted in blood.

Lala's rage is all that keeps her from withering with grief and fear. Its heat spurs her on.

She peers out, like a girl beneath trees, as though waiting for a royal procession in a forest. Patient as the sort of thief they consider all like her to be.

When the executioner and sergeants lead Alifair out, it is all she can do not to fall to the stone at her feet. He squints into the light, as though bewildered by the existence of the sun. The grime of stone grays not only his cheeks and clothes, but the rope on his wrists. His eyes look not frightened but hardened, and far-off, and she wonders how much of him is left.

She stills her breath.

She waits until they near where she hides, on their procession from the executioner's tower to the stake waiting for him at the Pont du Corbeau.

When they pass, she emerges, smooth as a darting fox.

She is small and quick enough to slip into the space before them, barring their path.

The sergeants draw back, as though she has appeared from the stone itself.

"You have stolen from me," she declares, not with grief, but with the cold voice of an affronted queen.

The crowd, gathered to watch a condemned man's progress to the place of his death, watches her.

The sergeants regard her as though she might be ill, or as though she might burst into dance. Not two lanes over, the afflicted continue with bleeding heels and paled eyes.

Alifair watches her as though he is desperately trying to comprehend her words, as though she has spoken in a language he does not know.

The executioner grunts in a way that shakes his wide shoulders. "Stay off, little girl. Give the men their room to work."

She stays in their path.

"I demand the return of my demon," she says.

The last word stings, having to call Alifair the word.

Forgive me, she breathes within her soul, looking at him. *I can find no other way.*

She turns to those watching, some in clothing dulled by work, some in the fine gowns and hose of the richest merchants.

"I demand return of all my demons," she tells the crowd.

Their eyes widen. They watch her as though she is possessed.

"Return them to me"—Lala imagines her eyes flaring as candle flame—"or the damnation of this town will be on your heads."

With this, the pausing crowd draws in a sharper breath, thrilling not just with fear, but with new gossip. They glance down the lanes, where the afflicted dancers throw their limbs.

The executioner grabs her and forces her through the street. "What do we say?" he asks the sergeants. "Shall we have two in a morning?"

They shove her forward so she cannot see Alifair. But she can feel his eyes on her back, the questions he cannot ask. *What in the name of heaven and earth are you doing? Why are you doing this?*

They lead them both toward the Pont du Corbeau. Maybe by the time they arrive there will be two stakes erected.

Along the way, she notices those whom she has asked for favors, those who either wish her gone from Strasbourg, or who wish life for Alifair.

As the sergeants prod her along, Lala casts her eyes on one, then another, then another, each time a cue. With each sharp turn of her head, each cut of her gaze, they drift into the streets. They toss their bodies about, moaning as though the devil himself has gone into them. They flail and spin. They jump and leap, sending finely gowned women screaming.

The sergeants stop hard. Though they are behind her, and she cannot see their faces, she can hear the choked pulling in of their next horrified breaths.

They watch the scene, more stricken in one moment than this city has ever seen. Each newly afflicted begins dancing, as though a mere look from Lala has made them do it.

Please, they all breathe, low as the drone of bees but clear enough to be heard.

Help us.

Keep our souls from her wickedness.

Their voices rise from small pleas to desperate shouts, each calling out their beseechings as they play the part of the dance claiming them.

The executioner gives Lala a hard shove.

But a sergeant calls out.

"Bring the friar," he shouts. "Now."

She hears his worry, how if he does not pass this obligation on to a holy man, he will be blamed for the failure. It has already happened once, the council and the physicians facing the embarrassment of having excluded the Church, and only making things worse.

Lala is what the sergeant expects of a Romani woman, what all the rulers decided she was when they forbade her and her aunt from their borders. To such men, she is nothing but sin and danger. And for all the times she has hated this, for all the times she has wished they would see the faith in her heart, in this one moment, she is thankful for their ignorance.

Rosella

ain and life sparked through the shoes. It lit up all those little tears in my muscle and made my ankles feel brittle as glass.

The red shoes bucked under me.

My body's instinct was to run, to hide in the dark cast by the trees' overlapping shadows. My parents were already so terrified of how these shoes held to my body, terrified of me. What would they do if they saw how the red shoes made me dance?

As the last gold in the sky cooled, the swirling heat of the red shoes rose up through my ankles. The delicate pain in each muscle brightened.

Once when I was little, my father told me that the moon was spiraling very slowly, an inch or so a year, away from the earth. When he found me crying in my room about it, crying millions of years in advance for our lost moon, he told me it was better that way. He told me that if, instead, the moon was spiraling toward the earth, it wasn't as though one day we'd be able to stand on our tallest ladders and touch it. Instead, our gravity would break it apart like a sugar cookie, all the glowing pieces strewn out across the sky.

Now I had a pained sympathy for that almost-moon. I was breaking apart under the force of the red shoes. They were my gravity, my earth, the part of me that made me move. They possessed my body so completely there was no fight left in me. I would scatter in pieces across the night.

The moment before the red shoes spun me deeper into the trees, he was there, as suddenly as a boy the dusk had made. He took hold of my waist and my shoulder and he held on to me.

This time, when the shoes took me, he went with me.

I held on to him, hard enough that we stayed with each other. The force of the shoes seemed like something he was drawing into him, something he was trying to take on.

I could have blamed it on the glimmer, how I pulled him deeper into the trees, a sliver-of-moon early evening that thickened the wood and ash smell of autumn. I could have pretended it was the same swirling magic that brought us the coywolves and light-bulb fireflies.

But the truth was that, in that moment, every memory I had of us lived in the heat between my body and his.

Setting ladybugs loose in his yard, little guards against the mites and whiteflies eating his mother's geraniums.

Hanging a glass hummingbird feeder outside his great-aunt's window in the weeks before she died, so she would see the bright flashes of their wings in the early hours before anyone was up and with her in her room.

Holding on our tongues the bright lilac candies his father swore by to prevent colds, how they looked like plums but tasted like lavender.

Fennel and caraway and plumajillo, the handfuls of scents that were his house meeting mine.

Fire in every color.

How, in his house, fairy tales were neither just the sparkle of fairy lights nor blood on glass slippers. They were beautiful and dangerous all at once, the glossed candy red of a poison apple.

We set our lips and hands against each other, and we were our age now, more careful than we were as children but also more reckless, with more of our lives at our backs. He paused his hand at the hem of my shirt until I nodded, my forehead against his. I kept my hand on his belt but didn't go further until he gave me the same *yes*.

When the red shoes tried to take me again, I drew him down into the leaves with me. I held him so close that even the fierce and relentless magic folded into their stitching could not find its way between us. They could not drag me out from under him.

I kept him on top of me, asking him with my whispers and my hands to hold me down as the red shoes tried to take me. I gave him my hands, and he held them against the ground, his palms to mine, fingers interlaced.

Shared between Emil and me, the red shoes' spell and power became something we could almost hold. Kept between our bodies, we owned it, and it shifted, becoming so small and dim compared to the light between our hands.

The shoes pulled at me, and the force buckled through my body. He kept on top of me, my arms locked across his back. For this moment, the frightening magic in the red shoes was ours. With our lips and our fingers, we spun it from curse to enchantment. Even this spell of velvet and beads could not rip us apart.

For those minutes, I was any other Briar Meadow girl in a pair of red shoes. Lovesick and brazen, with salt on my lips and fireweed honey on my tongue. My red shoes were mischief instead of wrath. They were defiance and flirtation emerging from a tissue paper–lined box. For this night, I shared the common enchantment of anyone wearing a pair of red Oliva shoes.

I could have told myself I didn't mean to hold on to Emil as hard as I did, that the intertwining of our limbs was all the fault of the red shoes, that slipping my fingers into his belt loop was more reaction than decision.

But I stayed, and he let me. And when I reached for the top button of his jeans, we were a blur of half questions, clumsy and nervous.

Do you . . .—and the answer, *Yes.*

Or, *Are you sure?* And the same answer, *Yes.*

And the hesitant, pausing laugh when we both realized neither of us had done this before, so neither of us knew how to lead.

The force of the shoes threw me again, and he held me tighter. His hand, first tentative as it grazed my thigh, now gripped it.

The shoes could possess me, but right now, I could decide what I did with the twirl and bucking of my own body.

He was on top of me, keeping me to this point on the ground.

I found his certainty in that nod, that *yes*. But with the will of the shoes moving me, I was the one driving this. I led him from underneath him.

Strasbourg, 1518

And so they bring the friar, who has been waiting with the stake at the Pont du Corbeau.

Or, they would, if every soul dancing for Alifair's life did not bar the way.

Their dance roils and shifts in lines. They gather into packs and then skitter out. They send the watching crowd scurrying in all directions. They block the quay so that startled onlookers cannot escape them.

Along the way are more who either wish to see Alifair free, or wish to see Lala gone from the city walls forever, or both. Lala sets her gaze upon them, and they writhe and scream and beg the good men who hold her to save them from her wickedness.

A few keep her eye a moment longer than they must. A young woman on the bridge winks in a way so small only Lala catches it. An old man near the quay inclines his head toward the sergeant, with a small smile of contempt, before throwing himself into an imitation of the dance.

A brother and sister toss themselves into the canal, pretending the dance has done it to them. They flail as though they are still dancing in the water as a few men scramble to fish them out.

Geruscha and Henne feign falling to the ground as though struck by a marsh light.

Their act is even better than they promised Lala. They could both be on a stage.

Aldessa, the flax farmer's cousin, sees them both, and a light comes into her eyes. A moment later, she imitates them, feigning tormented dancing.

"Bring someone!" the elder sergeant bellows. "Bring a priest, for God's sake! Any of them!"

The dancers impede the friar's progress. They block the canon priests. Lala can see their tall, proud heads bobbing to see past the afflicted.

How odd, that the only holy man who can find his way in, the only one the newly afflicted allow to pass, is the kindhearted priest of l'Église Saint-Pierre-le-Vieux.

"Here, old man," the executioner demands.

The elder sergeant grabs Lala by the hair and commands that she stop, but before he can snap her head back, Sewastian, the younger sergeant, eases his grip away.

"I'll handle her," Sewastian says. "It is you who should address the priest."

And so the older sergeant does.

"This woman has the devil in her," he says. "She afflicts simply by laying eyes upon those she passes."

The crowd parts before the priest. He gives an exaggerated lowering of his eyes and shaking of his head, as though it pains him to have lost one of his flock. He moves his lips and appears to be praying.

Lala wonders if it is all a performance or if he prays in earnest, perhaps that this will not conclude with Lala and Alifair swallowed by flame and him at the end of a rope.

The elder sergeant waves a hand, and Sewastian pushes Lala forward. He keeps his large palms on her shoulders, and Lala cannot tell if the rhythm she feels in his fingers is her fear or his.

She longs to look back at Alifair so badly it stings her eyes. But Sewastian holds her fast.

"Will her death free us?" the older sergeant asks, and though Lala cannot see his face, she hears the rage and worry in his voice, the way her unruly possession humiliates him in the very streets he has been charged to command.

The priest finishes his prayer, makes a sign of the cross, and lifts his head. "I must gaze into her soul." He walks forward, the hem of his robe lapping out with each slow step.

Far too slow for the executioner, who says, "Get on with it, old man. We'll burn her too."

The priest takes Lala's chin in his hand, and her heart bends in on itself for how much this feels like Tante, studying her forehead to discern the cause of a fever.

He makes a great show of looking in Lala's eyes.

Lala twists her longing for Tante into rage. She pretends to wither and writhe beneath the holy man's gaze. She hisses and throws her head side to side, as much as Sewastian's grip will let her.

Lala bares her teeth as though the priest's gaze singes her.

The priest draws away his hand.

"The devil is indeed in this child," he says, his voice sounding of such heaviness in his heart that Lala wonders if he should have been a player in morality tales. "But if you kill her, her legion will only find another soul to bewitch."

"Then what do we do with her?" The older sergeant's frustration clips each word.

The priest lifts his head to the sky in holy contemplation, and the executioner swears in impatience.

Each time the priest looks upon Lala, she writhes and shrieks, and Sewastian's thick fingers dig into her upper arms.

"We may turn to the Word of the Lord for our answers," the priest says, with weighted patience.

If fright weren't chilling Lala's blood, she would enjoy how well the priest is exasperating the other men.

"As recounted in the Gospel of Matthew, two men were stricken with demons," the priest says. "The demons withered beneath the observance of our Lord Jesus. And when He ordered them out, they begged to be cast out into a herd of pigs, who then rushed into a steep lake and died in the water."

"Get to the point." Sewastian tightens his grip on Lala. "What do we do with her?"

The priest pauses, an overdone affect of piety gilding his face. "Have you not listened, my son? You must drive her and all her legion into the countryside, as our Lord Jesus cast the demons into the pigs. With great prayer, perhaps Christ in his mercy will send them into a pack of wolves, and neither shall trouble us again."

He sets an eye on Lala, a reminder of what he told her in the cathedral.

Powerful men may count you as lowly as an animal, Lavinia, but the Lord counts men hating you as a sign of that which is holy within you.

"You must send her out into the countryside, never to pass through the city gate again." The priest returns his eyes to the two men. "Her and any demons who would follow her. Let them leave these good people and go with her."

Emil

The fever left them, like both of them had worn it out. It left them for long enough that they fell into a kind of sleep that was so dreamless it felt strange and soft, like the brush of her hair against his cheek.

After, it all seemed like it belonged in the same place as his dreams, this dark-haired girl among the amber trees. This girl he had mistaken for a woman from five hundred years ago, in a place where green oaks stayed in leaf even through hard winters. This girl, a dark silhouette against the fire-colored leaves, the red of her lips so bright it burned into him.

When he woke up, her cheek on his collarbone, her hair fanned over his shoulder, he looked for those same leaves. He looked for trees bright as sodium flames.

Instead, he blinked into daylight, and found a million rounds of flickering green.

The sun had bleached away the forms of the trees he'd grown up under.

What was left was not Briar Meadow's woods. It wasn't the road, or the houses beyond, or anything of the town he knew. All of it had blurred away. The night had brightened as fast as a match igniting.

Rosella stirred, the soft noise of waking at the back of her throat.

Both of them squinted into the daylight and those leaves that shivered like green wings.

His eyes adjusted.

The glare came less from the sky and more from around them, like they were in a room whose walls were light.

They followed that light, and the leaves around them went fuzzy at the edges. It happened like the colors of a painting running and then settling into something else. The trunks turned into city walls. The undergrowth hardened to the stone of the quays. The tallest tree became the cathedral spire.

It all held the same charge and apprehension as his dreams. And like his dreams, the haze of sleep both softened and sharpened the edges of things. It smoothed over the slope of canal bridges. It brightened the sun off the water. That single spire looked like a knife piercing the sky.

It all seemed so far from them, like they were watching from the Rhine. But he could not miss the shapes of dresses and tunics, and the smell of dust on the cobbled stones.

The familiarity flickered in his blood. It came with the same recognition as meeting a relative for the first time.

Strasbourg, centuries before he was born.

Emil made out the form of a crowd, a crush of figures mostly in skirts but some in men's clothes. They threw their arms toward the sky. They each spun to their own rhythm, none of them in time with another.

The understanding caught in his throat at the same time Rosella stopped a gasp in hers.

This was the dancing.

Dozens—hundreds?—of women and a few men casting themselves in time with music no one could hear.

On the quay, among the crush of the crowd, stood a woman—or a girl? She seemed no older than he and Rosella were. She stood in a deep blue dress, her black hair spilling down her back.

The sight of her rang in him so loudly he thought the cathedral bells had sounded the hour. He could map this woman's blood to his own. He could find traces of her features in old family photos and even in his own face.

He could match her scream to the shape of her mouth and throat and rib cage.

She stood just forward of a young man, his hands bound with heavy rope.

Emil placed them against what he knew of Strasbourg, the vague map that came from seeing his father's books a hundred times. He registered the reason for the crowd.

Both left him sick.

The young woman and the young man were being paraded along the canals.

They were being led from the Henckerturm, the Tour du Bourreau, the executioner's tower, to the Pont du Corbeau.

The route of public display before executions.

Men surrounded them. One holding the young woman still. Two on either side of the young man, one of them probably an executioner.

Executioner. A misnomer for a man whose job in medieval Strasbourg was not only to kill but to torment, torture, plague until the moment of death.

And one more man, a far shorter one, this one in priest's garb.

But why would he be here? Why would he not be waiting at the Pont du Corbeau to give them confession before their deaths?

Fear lit the young man's and the young woman's eyes.

But something else came with it.

A hard set to the young man's.

A defiance in the young woman's, a vicious will.

A look as though, if they were going to burn her and this young man, she was going to burn the city down with them.

Emil had no way to know, but in the next moment, the woman flinched in a way he swore was from feeling Emil's watch on her back.

She turned her gaze, as much as she could. For a second, he thought maybe she saw him.

Then the priest commanded her attention again.

The cathedral's high stained glass threw deep blue down to where they stood.

Emil looked down at Rosella's shoes, turned purple in the blue light.

Rosella didn't know what his mother had told him. The red shoes at Saverne. The dyed cloth crafted into dozens or hundreds of pairs. How they were meant to cure the fever.

How history had grabbed hold of her.

From the way she stared at the scene in front of them, her breath held still on her tongue, he thought she understood. The weight of his own rage seemed shared between their bodies, his grief over this girl and boy about to die, who had already died.

Emil wanted to set a dozen colors of fire to the bridge so everyone else would scatter in wonder and horror, and they would live.

But no one saw them except his relative. They were really here no more than he was in the history that played through his dreams.

There was no crossing the wide river of five hundred years between him and this boy and girl about to die. No altering what had already been.

All there was, was watching.

Strasbourg, 1518

The priest casts pronouncements with more certainty than Lala has ever heard from this humble man.

Any who follow her are the legion of the devil within her. If they are saints possessed, they will return when the demons have left them.

The canon priests' rage is bright as their jeweled rings.

But the dancers block them from reaching Lala and the sergeants.

They watch, but can do nothing.

"We do not make deals with the devil's children," the friar calls out.

"Burn her," a canon priest shouts, his head bobbing to see between the dancers.

Lala's heart pleats, folding in her bristling terror that they will kill her rather than bargain with demons.

The newest dancers move in a wave, their leaping bodies barring the way as they call out for the priest to help them, to free them from the devils within them.

The canon priests step back, hesitation and scorn in their eyes. Of course, they must think, those possessed by demons would insulate their demon queen. Of course her legion would not want the canon priests reaching her.

The chorus rises, sharp and sudden and miraculous as an appearance of the Virgin. More voices sound than Lala and Geruscha and Henne could have begged to join.

Make her leave us, they shout.

Do it, please.

Save us.

A few words come in voices Lala knows.

Melisende and Agnesona cast their arms to heaven, shrieking. They wail and dance with such fervor that their circlets and veils fall away, their red hair tumbling about their shoulders. Agnesona throws herself on the ground, writhing and turning.

Melisende, and Agnesona, and Lala. All three of them missing the girl who was their anchoring point, like the center jewel in a brooch.

The sisters turn themselves into a chaos of tormented limbs and pained voices.

Please, they beg, their words overlapping. *Cast her out and her demons with her. Please. Make them leave this city!*

The canons hold fearful sneers on their faces.

"Get on with it," one yells over the dancers' heads.

"Fulfill your office," another adds, "before she curses them all."

"Please," the kind priest says, glancing at Alifair, seeding so much desperation into his voice that Lala would believe him as an entertainer in a king's court. "Perhaps he can still be saved with prayer and confession. Perhaps we need not lose him."

It is a performance so beautiful Lala could kiss the ground at the priest's feet.

Lala's heart catches to see the skittishness in Alifair's face, the way he shudders at these voices because he does not realize she has bid them. She wants nothing but to kiss his eyelashes and brush his hair with her fingers. It is an ache as deep as the soreness between her hips each month.

But Lala hardens her voice, the way she imagines a sorceress in a fairy story would. "My demon prince will follow only me."

Confusion dims Alifair's features as he takes in the oddness of her speech.

"You need not follow, young man," the priest says, making a fine act of his pleading.

Lala tips her head down slowly, opening her eyes to Alifair, to try to tell him, *Trust me, you must trust me.*

His shoulders settle, and Lala breathes with the hope that he understands.

He draws toward her, leading with his chest, as though she is pulling him by the rib cage.

She takes hold of him, one hand at his back, the other at his collarbone as though she commands his heart.

She steals him, like tearing a pearl from a rich woman's throat, and the priest cries out his feigned grief.

Alifair tilts his head back at her touch, as though she bewitches him. His hair smells of the salt from his sweat and the rope that binds his wrists. But it smells also, still, of hazel and bay. The wind over fields of flax and woad.

"What have you done?" he whispers.

"We are aspen trees, you and I," she whispers back, her voice soft even as she keeps her face hard, to look as though she is issuing a command to her apprentice demon. "You cannot tear our fates apart, even to save me."

Alifair's smile is more like a breath, small and momentary, and it is broken by the hard interruption of shouting voices.

"Take her oath," a canon priest yells.

"Do it now," another shouts.

"Resist the demons within you," the kind priest begs Alifair, a last performance. "You need not go with her."

"Come off it," the executioner says, a tremble in his rough voice. Now even he believes that Lala may damn all in the city. "You heard them. Do something."

The priest gives his best look of defeat before raising his head.

"Be gone from us," he tells Lala. "You and all your legion."

Lala draws breath from the sergeants' fear, the executioner's fear, the fear of the gathered crowd, those caught between wanting to run and wanting to learn what will become of this scene.

"I will curse you all," she says, thinking of her heart turning to live embers. "Lay a hand on me or mine, and I will curse you all even in my death."

The priest grabs her hand, pulling her away from Alifair. He casts sad eyes to Alifair, the look of a grieving shepherd.

He sets Lala's hand on the Bible.

"Swear on our Lord's Word that you will be gone from us," the priest says, "or may His wrath cast you into the sea of darkness."

Lala hisses and writhes as though the touch of the book burns her.

The priest holds her hand fast. "Swear you will not harm another of these souls."

She tosses her head, whipping her hair into her face.

"Enter the city gates again," the executioner says—even now he must have his word—"and flames will be the last sight you ever know."

"Give the oath," the priest says, "or your hand will stay upon this holy book until the Lord's return."

Lala glares up at him.

"I swear it," she says through gritted teeth. "And I swear it on pain of a thousand devils." She spits the words at the crowd around her. "I will take my legion with me and I will keep them from this wretched place."

The crowd gasps at the words.

The priest remains steady. It is a shimmering moment, one that will probably make him a canon should he want the office.

"Then by God and by His saints and angels," the priest says, "I hereby banish you, the demon living within our Lavinia, the demon who torments our Alifair, and all yours who here afflict."

Rosella

The girl in the blue dress looked so much like Emil that I knew, even before I saw the recognition in his face. They belonged to each other in a way that crossed five hundred years.

She had hair more like his or mine than the oil-shined coifs of women in the crowd, and she wore it loose instead of braided or covered. The heat and her own sweat had fluffed it, what my hair used to look like by noon before I started carrying a brush like Piper taught me to. She had skin and eyes so close to Emil's that they looked like colors she had passed down to him.

She was already beautiful, even through the far lens of all those centuries. On top of a cream underdress she had on a dress as deep blue as an autumn sky, a color she wore as well as if she'd been born in it.

But the defiance in her eyes could have singed the hems of her captors' sleeves. And it gave her a raw gleam; I couldn't look at her long without feeling the sting of that brightness.

It had frightened the proud men enough that they loosened their hold.

Then, with a last look between her and Emil, with the act of her seeing him, truly seeing him, all of it vanished. The bridges and the water and the towering cathedral spire whirled around us, as though we were dancing again.

It spun down into a single still point, and we were back in the dark trees, back in a town and time we knew as well as our own bodies.

"She didn't die," Emil said, his hands on my upper arms like he was trying to keep me warm. "They didn't die," he said, breathing the words more than saying them.

"They didn't die," I said, half confirmation, half echo.

I wanted Emil to find his next breath in that space, the possibility that this girl, and the boy she had loved enough to take with her, had survived.

The cloud cover between the trees was iris-petal blue. The season was sloping down toward winter, toward bright snow and silver icicles. It was always that moment, between one season and the next, when we let that year's glimmer go. It would fade, and everything would settle.

Briar Meadow stirred around us, flickering with the moment of this season's strange magic leaving us.

We knew, by now, that we had to let go of any magic that got caught in the boughs of our trees. We had watched crescent moons that burned as bright as full ones dim again, like candle wicks catching and then settling. We had waited for grandfathers to stop consulting crows on the morning weather report, and the crows to stop answering back. We saw mothers and daughters who'd spent nights on roofs trying to count every star climb down and back into upstairs windows.

Briar Meadow had spent years learning to let go. If you tried to hold on to something past its season, it turned on you. Coywolf pups bit. A reservoir that had been warm enough to swim in froze over. Fireflies caught in jars blew the glass apart with their heat.

I thought of Aubrey in her butter-yellow coat; she would leave her sister's pair of red shoes at the edge of her front yard as she interlaced her fingers with Graham's. I thought of Sylvie, in her pewter-gray A-line, setting her pair at the end of her family's brick-paved driveway. A woman who'd rediscovered her love for bread would leave hers on an outside windowsill. Another who'd started feeding peanut brittle to the raccoons she'd once feared would carefully place hers in the park's rose beds. A boy would whisper *thank you* to a cardinal-bright pair before letting them go; on his feet now would be a pair of ballet flats he'd never dared to wear out before this year, those red shoes giving him the nerve.

We would give up the red shoes, like we gave up everything else, and the glimmer would leave us.

I looked at Emil, his hands still on my upper arms, his face still wearing the distraction of five centuries ago.

If I'd had to live in these red shoes, if I'd had to let them almost dance me to death so Emil could see what we'd seen, so he could know, it was enough. It was worth them taking me into their fever.

Now it was time to let them go.

But when I reached to take them off, they held to me.

Mud stains dulled the bittersweet-berry fabric. The lace of dried salt patterned the satin. But they still sealed to me.

The air around us grew an edge, the sharp lemon-pith smell of magic overstaying its welcome. It sounded less like the wings of a hummingbird and more like electricity through overhead lines.

I tried again to rip them away.

This time, my own touch felt like the point of a hundred knives.

Strasbourg, 1518

The priest holds her a second longer, to show he does not fear her, and then releases her.

She cries out with relief, holding her hand as though it might wither before her.

A few who were part of the act make a show of returning to their senses, as though they do not know how they came to stand where they are. They stumble, dazed, returning from a trance. Their families, either in true fear or in their own performances, weep to have them return. They take their faces in their hands and thank God the demons have left them.

The priest nods to the sergeants, his holy work done.

A single glance is all Lala can risk to offer him her last gratitude.

The sergeants take hold of her and Alifair, driving them toward the city gate.

With each step, a crowd gathers behind them, shouting at their backs, rushing them toward the edge of the city. They shout that they will drive the demons out, on pain of the angels. They rush and overtake even the sergeants, who vanish into their numbers as though swallowed.

Lala hisses and shrieks back at them, as though resisting their justice. They will find it all the sweeter for being harder won.

Lala and Alifair keep their speed to stop from being pushed or thrown to the ground. Alifair follows her as if in a dream, a boy taken by an enchantment.

The crowd shoves them to the city gate, the sergeants nodding permission to the guards. They send Lala and Alifair stumbling through.

The crowd stops at the gate, shouting their insults that would drive them into the countryside.

Demon.

Whore

Devil's wife.

Witch.

Zigeuner.

What would have wounded her days before now breathes fortitude into her, like wind spinning rain into a storm.

She has set lies before them, and they have taken up every one.

So much that the crowd does not dare pass the gate.

Lala and Alifair leave behind them the cathedral spire, with its rose window and blush-stone.

They leave behind the Pfalz, and the mint with its gold coins.

They turn their backs on the cannon foundries, and the barrels of grain loaded onto boats and taken from a city that needs them but cannot pay for them.

With each step, they place greater distance between themselves and the magistrate, and the councils, and all others who can see nothing for the glint of the sun off their own gold.

They leave this city of such weight, built on such weak ground that wood and iron had to be driven into the earth just to hold it up.

Then Lala hears the grinding of footsteps, a smaller

crowd, behind them. They follow to the gasps and whispers of the greater crowd, a few of their names called, a scattered chorus of horrified cries. *Dear God, no*, or, *Come back, please*, or a crumbling sob.

Still, these few stream away from the greater crowd. They do not rush or storm. They follow in purposeful strides, a rhythm Lala can hear without turning.

Lala draws close enough to Alifair to reach his wrists. She pulls at the rope binding him, staying near enough for her body to shield her hands. A witch, powerful enough to curse with no more than a look, should be able to bid the rope unwind with less than a breath or a word. Those following her, those who have let her go, cannot see her working at the knot.

They will both need their hands free to fight, though she has little idea what they will fight with. Especially when she must pretend she needs no further weapon than the demons she commands.

She works the knot loose. Alifair knows well enough to keep his hands before him, so the crowd at their backs will not catch what she has done.

She keeps her hands back from clasping his and tending to the raw, reddened skin encircling each wrist.

There will be time for pressing witch hazel and lavender to his skin only if they live to this evening.

Lala holds her throat tight, understanding that any crowd that follows could mean to kill them the moment they are too far for the priest to witness.

She holds the rope in her hands. She keeps it. It will be the one weapon they have.

Emil

It was in the second of Rosella almost crumpling to her knees that he understood. He registered what he should have considered days ago.

The red shoes weren't just a sign of a fever trying to take her.

That fever lived in the red shoes themselves.

Rosella looked at him, her breath held in her throat.

"This is never going to end," she said, the words barely audible.

The guilt landed on him, like that feeling of a palm on his shoulder.

Maybe, if he and Rosella had never met, none of it would have happened. The bitter ashes of his dreams turning to live embers. A pair of red shoes becoming as deadly as they were beautiful.

Maybe it had to be both of them, him and Rosella sparking against each other like the iron and flint his five-hundred-years-ago relatives would have held in their hands.

There was Rosella, the daughter of a family who crafted red shoes famous with the suggestion of magic. Red shoes that came with the hint of something scandalous that only made Briar Meadow love them more, and that the men who ruled sixteenth-century Alsace would have hated.

There was a scrap of history Rosella didn't know, and that Emil had just learned—the red shoes meant to cure la fièvre de la danse.

And there was Emil, descended from a girl who made herself into a witch to save the boy she loved. For just long enough to survive, she had transformed herself into the brazen demon everyone thought her to be.

Together, these things flared and lit, like raw sodium in water.

Commended back into the hands of the devil for the blessing and good of the people, who now live free from the demons who once plagued them.

Since his father had told him those words, Emil had repeated them over and over in his head.

Of course Strasbourg assumed his five-centuries-ago relative was telling the truth when she confessed, with such venom in her voice. Of course they wouldn't consider that she might have done it to save a man's life, and her own.

She had taken what everyone else had put on her, and she had made it hers. They had held a knife to her back, and she had twisted it from their hands without them even noticing.

Rosella's eyes fell to the ground. "I thought . . ." She trailed off.

Emil held on to her. She returned his grip, keeping herself standing.

He knew what she thought. He saw it in the pain in her face, her fear over how that fever still wasn't letting her go.

Probably, she thought she'd been pulled into this for no reason except that this year's glimmer had touched every pair of red shoes her family made. She probably thought this only went as far as figuring out something about his family, about la fièvre de la danse, about a city held in some frightening plague five hundred years ago.

But this was just as much about her as it was about the Olivas, the same as how it had been as much about him as about his family.

It had to be.

Emil had never quite turned his back on his family's history. He never could. But he'd stopped looking right at it. It became a set of stars just off the side of his vision. And going that long without looking straight at it had made it little more to him than a cautionary tale. It was a warning of everything people were capable of, all the reasons his grandfather had told him to keep his heart open but his hands ready.

He'd thought that if he ever looked back, he'd get stuck there. But the past had come for him anyway, because there were things it wanted him to know.

And there was something it wanted Rosella to know, something he would never be able to get at because it didn't belong to him.

She had to, because it was hers.

Emil said Rosella's name in a way sure enough that it brought her eyes back to him.

"Everything that happened to my family, I stayed as far away from it as I possibly could," he said. "I didn't want to look at it, at any of it, because I was afraid of it. I never would've admitted that to my dad, not in a million years, but that's what it was. I was afraid of it."

He caught her elbows in his palms, keeping her up.

He held her gaze. "So what are you afraid of?"

This time, when her expression shifted, it was all the flame colors at once.

Strasbourg, 1518

"Do not look back," Alifair whispers to her, knowing any gaze will provoke them. It will make those who follow see them as prey all the more.

Lala knows no other way to frighten them off than to give them the spectacle they wish.

She screams and runs off the road, dancing this way and that, never in a straight line, not even for a few steps.

Alifair follows deep in his feigned trance.

Lala treads over rocks and weeds, throwing out her arms as though demons might tear open her flesh. She puts all her soul into the dance, and hopes it will be enough to scare away their pursuers.

It is not until they are into the trees, out of view of the city gate, that Alifair sets a hand on her arm.

"Lala," he says.

The name alone startles her. He has never called her that within anyone else's hearing. Tante Dorenia taught him well not to.

She falls still, quiet enough to feel the watching eyes behind them.

A small crowd stands, not with the look of wanting to catch and kill. More with a blinking patience.

Lala recognizes a few faces.

There are the brother and sister for whom Alifair bought bread.

And Aldessa, the flax farmer's spinster of a cousin.

The two maid friends who have lived together as long as Lala has been alive, neither of them married.

A few men who hunt together in winter.

A group of women who share a household, claiming to be sisters, but who look as little alike as black willow and birch.

Emich and Roland, two apprentices whose masters once beat them for being found lying together, considered a mercy compared to the loss of an arm each as *Li livres de jostice et de plet* would have called for.

Two old men and their wives, all of them white- and silver-haired. But neither husband stands with his wife. It is the men who stand near each other, and the women with each other, in a way that makes Lala wonder if the wives have spent more nights in the same bed than with their husbands.

There is Geruscha, with a tiny, hopeful smile on her face.

Henne stands alongside her, clasping her hand.

Lala looks to Alifair, but his face shows the same incomprehension she feels.

"What are you all doing?" Lala asks them. "Why have you come?"

Their bodies part, and Tante Dorenia emerges, proud as a queen. By the way she holds herself, the slight shape of her belly shows.

The sight of Tante, among all these who hold a common thread within their hearts, nearly undoes Lala's own.

"Did you not hear your own words?" Tante's smirk is as small and bright as a sickle moon. "We are your legion of demons."

Rosella

With every feeling that the shoes were cutting into me, with every sense that the glass beads were needles piercing my skin, I remembered that night when I was five. I remembered watching outside the workroom door as that man insisted my abuelo hand over his work for nothing. I remembered my abuela defying him with her best pair of scissors.

I'll save you the bother of carrying them home.

For years, I had run as far from that night as Briar Meadow would let me. I had decided, in that moment, that I would never land there, that I would never let my family be there again, having to wreck what we loved just so it would not be stolen. And with every time I decorated bake sale tables with Graham, I had taken that vow deeper inside me. With every time I dressed like Sylvie, in dove-gray sweaters and black pants as neat as licorice candy, I repeated it. I would never let men like that make me destroy the work of my hands, because, instead, I would learn to pass alongside their daughters.

I had been so sure I could learn the rules that made girls like Piper. I had been so caught up in those rules that I never considered I might one day have to take a pair of scissors in my hands and break them.

And I had worn my fear on my body in shades of red.

But these shoes, the shoes my grandfather had made with his hands, I had stitched back together with my own. They held the history of where we'd come from, villages with air so bad my grandmother said Santa Muerte had to wear a gas mask to get close enough to claim the dead.

They held the work of our hands.

They were as red as our blood.

Words formed in my mouth, sharp and sweet. They were mine, but had the sheen of being a gift I was accepting onto my tongue.

And as I did, the memory of something Emil said flared in my brain.

Something he'd told me in the light of small, petal-colored flames. About being on a bridge with his own grandfather, both of them watching the mirrored triangle of current behind a buoy. How it looked like it was moving even when it was staying still.

That was the thing about staying still, he'd told me, about holding your ground. When there was a current coming at you, if you managed to stay where you were, you left a wake.

The power Strasbourg had over his family was not only in the secrets they made them keep, but in making them think they had to keep so many secrets to begin with. It came in making that girl believe she herself was a living secret, something to be kept in the dark.

Then that girl, that woman in the blue dress, had taken hold of everything a whole city had said about her. She had grasped their whispers and suspicions. She had taken it all in her hands, and used it.

They had declared her a witch, and she'd stayed still, accepted the word, none of them realizing she was sharpening it between her teeth.

I looked at Emil, this boy who'd just told me how hiding from his own family's history had gotten him nowhere.

I let go of him.

And I danced.

I threw myself between trees, spinning and whirling. I threw my arms toward the moon.

The motion sent pain through my ankles. It made my heart feel hard as a root.

But I danced.

Emil had taught me that sometimes the only way to leave a wake was to stay still. And in these red shoes, staying still meant this. To stand my ground, I had to do the thing I feared.

I moved fast as the wind through the trees' amber. I spun toward the light of the nearest road. I put my own fever into the red shoes. I moved fast enough to turn the red shoes to a blur of color, the glass beads a handful of flung pomegranate seeds.

I danced out of the woods and alongside the road. I danced past houses and mailboxes, past cars slowing to see the odd girl flitting along the soft shoulder.

With every turn, I brought my body farther into the light of the glimmer and the moon, the streetlamps and the spill of amber from windows. I caught silhouettes in those squares of light, but I didn't stop.

So much of our town was out tonight, waiting for the glimmer to fade. Waiting like they had every year, for the spiders to stop weaving webs of silk so fast our town looked draped in lace shawls. Or for the stars to lose the pink tint they'd had for weeks.

I danced past them all. My family's priest. The mayor and her wife and their children. Teachers I'd had in grade school.

My own mother and father, with their always Band-Aided hands.

I danced past the houses of girls I knew.

Aubrey and Graham, in their neat rows of similar constructions that always seemed newly painted.

Sylvie, in her family's looming, crumbling Victorian.

Piper, in jeans and a moth-white sweater, the moon bleaching her hair almost as pale as she watched from the end of her tree-shadowed driveway.

With each twirl, I declared myself an Oliva girl, with my brush-brown body and my fingers made beautiful by the calluses of needlework. I was an Oliva daughter, whose great-grandparents had lost pieces of their fingers to the maquiladoras, and lived to make lives of their own by hand.

I was an Oliva, our history written in blood and thread and the glint of glass beads.

I had learned, from my own fearless abuela, to take what I feared, and use it.

I had learned, from a girl with rage-lit eyes and a blue dress, to grasp the blade the world held to me, and hold it myself.

With each twirl, I felt the shape of my own forming words, how they mirrored the ones I'd heard as a little girl, listening at the workroom door. I tasted my abuela's defiance, the metallic glint of it, her willingness to destroy part of herself so no one could take it. *I'll save you the bother of carrying them home.*

My story was not a fairy tale of a cruel-hearted girl whose shoes danced her to death, or a kindhearted one who threw her red shoes into the river. This was not a story about a wicked queen made to wear iron heels, or a lovely, golden-haired girl in slippers of glass.

This had been about a fever, a nightmare, a dance made into a curse.

It was about women turning their own fears into their sharpest blades.

When my own voice came, it was so brazen and laughing I didn't recognize it. It sounded like a higher, filmier version of how I remembered my abuela's voice, what my grandmother might have sounded like at my age.

I knew it was my own voice only by the feeling of it breaking out of my throat.

"I'll save you the trouble of making me dance," I said into the night air, to the glimmer, to the red shoes on my feet, to a fever that had come back after five hundred years.

With those words came the unsteady sense that the ground was breaking apart underneath me. Like my reckless dance had enough force to crack sidewalk and pavement and cold-packed dirt.

But when I looked down, it wasn't the ground breaking apart.

It was the red shoes, tearing along their sewn-together seams. They split open across the red cloth, as though the shoes were being sliced to pieces again while still on my feet. As though my abuela's scissors were dancing with me, unseen and flitting alongside each of my steps.

The shoes were tearing back into the confetti my abuela had cut years ago.

I drove my feet into the ground, dancing in time with the memory of my grandmother's scissors, flashing silver.

I'll save you the trouble.

I'll dance myself.

I danced, my words their own blades. They slipped into the seams. They slid between the red cloth and my skin.

I'll save you the trouble.

I'll make myself dance.

And I danced the red shoes to pieces.

Strasbourg, 1518

All in Strasbourg must imagine them leaving to plague some other town, or vanishing into the mountains or forest. They walk deeper into the countryside, the rumor of their possession scaring away thieves. When they must walk at night, they dance and shriek as though they are afflicted, and none draw near.

Though she did not know it, Lala has kept good company in her fear of *Li livres de jostice et de plet*. So has Alifair, who is far from the only soul in Strasbourg whose being and heart do not match the name he was once christened with.

There are so many who live or love in ways they have had to hide.

There are others with them who carry different weights in their hearts. A girl and boy in love who would be made to marry others. A man who does not wish to marry at all. A woman who has learned blacksmithing at the side of her brothers and father, but would not be allowed to practice the trade.

They all follow not only Lala but Alifair, this boy whose kindness has been a lamp to them. They follow Tante Dorenia, who even with child walks in a way that leads.

Tante Dorenia, who Lala can now call *Bibio* out loud. She can call her *Aunt* in the language her mother and father would have given her little pieces of, like bits of bread and honey.

They find greens and wild horseradish in the woods, blackberries and acorns, mushrooms that Lala brushes dirt from and that Bibio Dorenia inspects. They sleep outside in the summer warmth, though already Lala thinks of autumn, especially for her bibio's child. Some of them have family in the villages and plains, who might let them sleep in attics or barns. Some have allies in Strasbourg, who bring belongings from their abandoned homes; when these go missing, it is further counted as witchcraft or sorcery.

"We will make our living selling rare things," Bibio Dorenia tells them all as her belly grows and the season deepens. "Beautiful dyes like our woad. Violet champignons from beneath the pine trees. Baskets woven of unboiled branches. Marchpane jewels." She nods to the boy who was a baker's apprentice. "Liqueurs we make ourselves. Delicate fruits like golden plums." She smiles at Geruscha, who has always had a hand for the more temperamental trees. "We will make ourselves a town that seems crafted so much of magic it will sound as a dream to any who speak of it."

They thrill to her as though she is an enchantress spinning a story.

When Lala was a little girl, her bibio used to tell her of an ancient people, die Phönizier, known for their skill in navigating by the stars and for tinting glass. From rock and sea snail shells, they made dye as violet as the twilight sky, and no one dared attack their ships, for they were the only ones who knew how to craft purple rich enough for a king.

Lala does not know if it is true. But she must believe it now, when her bibio tells the story again. They will be a place of purple, an outpost of the rare, so others will think twice before harming them.

They are still looking for where they will stop for autumn when her bibio wakes Lala and Alifair early, and leads them to a meadow fringed with aspen trees.

"You both like them so much, why not?" Bibio Dorenia spreads her hands toward the winking green leaves.

Lala looks around, fearing hunters or guards rushing from the woods. "This is a lord's pasturage."

"It is." Her bibio casts a proud look over the meadow. "He rather likes the idea of having a fairyland on his estate. That, and the things we will make, will be our greatest power."

"So we're to be figures in his menagerie," Alifair says, sounding more worried than indignant.

"Perhaps we would be," her bibio says. "If our keeper was not the greatest peacock of all."

Alifair shakes his head, uncomprehending.

Bibio Dorenia lifts her eyebrows at them both. "He is a lord in affrèrement with his best knight."

Alifair's wry laugh sounds as a whisper, a breath through the trees.

Bibio Dorenia presses her lips together into a small smile. "Un pain, un vin, et une bourse."

One bread, one wine, and one purse.

Affrèrement. The bond of brotherhood that allows two men to live together under blessing of the law. Lala has heard the word, but it has always seemed a myth to her.

Perhaps it is because it is a luxury conferred more upon lords than journeymen.

"It is, of course," Bibio Dorenia says with exaggerated piety, "a spiritual bond, no more." Then she breaks into that smile again. "He will let us live here for first chance to buy the finest of anything we grow or make."

Lala shakes her head, marveling. How has she done it? How has a Romni with no husband and a growing belly waltzed into the graces of a lord in the woods and pastures of the Black Forest?

With the question comes the answer.

The same way Bibio Dorenia made herself into dyer of the most coveted ink and blue in Strasbourg, at an age little older than Lala is now. The same way she guarded Lala in a country that forbade their very blood.

She has a will and a heart as shining and deep as iron gall ink.

Emil

In his dreams, the air smelled of salt and cloth, of stone and the water skimming by the quays.

But instead of la fièvre, instead of the screaming, there was the quiet beneath the aspen trees. There was the boy from the Pont du Corbeau, the one with lighter hair. He wore a clean tunic and shirt, his wrists free from the rope Emil had last seen on him.

Not a boy. A man, Emil realized with a longer look.

Then there was the girl, the woman, Emil's relative. Her features looked softened at the edges, as though the centuries were a veil between them.

She wore that same blue dress, but with her night-black hair crowned with flowers that let off their smell of fruit and sugar.

He could barely take the impact of her, this woman who lived five hundred years before him, whose soul was its own lantern.

In his dream, she kissed him on the temple, and her touch was both chill and heat, the way stars burned hot but existed in the cold of the sky.

He took the weight of her blessing, and she walked into the aspen trees, her skirt trailing across the undergrowth.

The man waiting for her offered his hand. She took it, the light of her warming at his touch.

Emil couldn't hear what they were saying as they faded into the trees. All he could catch were the bright laughs and low voices of a girl and a boy walking home together.

He woke up to the feeling that he wasn't alone in being awake. He followed it downstairs, to where his father had a half dozen books open on the kitchen table. His usual method, where Emil's mother instead kept neat stacks of tabbed pages.

Emil flicked the burner on under the kettle, knowing his father never turned down caffeine, no matter the hour.

"What are you doing up?" his father asked without looking away from the page.

The answer to that question felt like it had a hundred corners. It had all the edges and points of the stellate shapes Luke built on weekends.

But Emil could start here.

"That blue cloth you were talking about," Emil said, taking cups down from the cabinet. "What were you trying to tell me?"

Now his father looked up.

"The blue cloth you showed me the picture of," Emil said.

"I know what you mean," his father said.

"So what were you gonna tell me about it?"

His father cast his eyes back toward the book in front of him, and Emil worried that he'd shrug, say *it's not important.*

His father took a breath in, pausing before speaking, like Emil had seen him do in lecture halls when he'd visited campus.

"You know." His father took off his readers. "The things our ancestors did in the sixteenth century would probably be of particular interest to you."

Emil sat down across from his father. "Why's that?"

"What they did," his father said. "Dyeing blue with woad. Making ink from oak apples and rust. It's all chemistry. The right composition gives you the right color." He folded his glasses, a sign that he would talk for a while. "You'd like it."

It was the first door opening.

Der Streuobstwiese, 1518

The news arrives with the first breath of autumn.

The dancing plague has faded from Strasbourg. Word comes along with pilfered items brought by those who have not denounced them, who still aid them in secret.

The fever has passed like a storm, and it slowly becomes a thing that anyone outside of Alsace will not know as rumor or fact, truth or morality tale.

There is talk that the afflicted were taken to Saverne, another attempt, and this time given wooden crosses, which made them fall before the image of Saint Vitus and recover their senses. Others say the cure was holy water and balsam oil, and the avoidance of all drums and tambourines. Many insist it was pairs of red shoes that banished the sickness, while others say the red shoes were given only to those cured, as a sign of their healing.

All will have their versions, meant to explain, as one would of fireflies in winter, or lightning appearing in a cloudless night.

Lala lifts her face toward the hillsides, the soft air on her cheek.

The light itself has grown less white and more golden, almost amber. In summer, the color of wildflowers is washed pale by the brightness, but now the shades deepen. The blues and pinks become rich as rivers and berries.

Traveled men used to say they could see the cathedral spire from across the Rhein, from as far as the Black Forest. They could spot it more easily than half the castles in Alsace.

Lala cannot see it now. Not from here.

But she shuts her eyes and sends on the wind her prayer for all la fièvre de la danse took. Especially one girl, remembered to Lala as her friend, remembered to so many others as the Lily of Strasbourg.

Autumn deepens, and her bibio's command does not diminish with the growth of her belly. She assigns the work of fetching water, fishing, gathering fruit or nuts or firewood. She instructs the craftsmen to teach those with strong backs and ready hands. They build houses, first from sticks and straw, and then wattle and daub, bracing for the coming November. She looks on as they construct the frameworks of timber, filling in the spaces with woven twigs, daubing with mud that dries into hard walls.

It is the beginning of their meadow orchard. It will become a place where their lord's rich friends will buy ink or dyed cloth. Moon pears or carved wooden beads. Perfume of roses, orange blossom, pine. Bread with petals baked in.

But tonight they pause their building. Tonight, the two bakers' apprentices go back and forth from an oven built with stones and lined with clay. The cheesemaker's widow and the woman Lala once assumed was her sister milk cows they have stolen back from their farm. The boy and girl who ran away together debate what can stand in for animal's blood in a recipe—crushed plums? Wild figs? The milk of mushrooms dyed purple with violets?

It is one of the last warm evenings of the season. The yellow has started at the edges of the aspen leaves, penning in the green at the center. Thanks to Geruscha's hand, the moon pears grow heavy on the wild trees, the first of the rare fruits their meadow orchard will boast.

Tonight, Lala has the smell of lavender and rosemary on her skin. Tonight, Aldessa binds herbs into a fat bouquet and tells Alifair to bathe with it, shooing him away from his work on the land.

Here, the world opens, like a bud loosening under rain and sun. Here, Lala will wear cloth she embroiders herself with clovers and roses, the sun and the moon, all the things the world forbade her. And maybe, one day, the delicate cloth of a dikhle covering her head.

Tonight, Bibio Dorenia helps Lala into her blue dress, the one always meant for her wedding day, the one she wore when she left the city walls. Lala has since embroidered the edges, and the layers of her underskirt lap at her feet, like water on a shore.

Her bibio finishes lacing the bodice.

"Thank you," Lala says, giving such weight to the words, she hopes her aunt will understand.

Thank you for blessing something you would be judged for allowing. Thank you for leaving your home and making another, twice, for me.

Bibio Dorenia nods in a way that makes Lala imagine she understands. She weaves a chaplet of meadow roses into Lala's hair, the scent of nectar drifting down over her like the lightest snow.

Geruscha ties a cluster of wild lilies together with rosemary.

"For memory and fidelity," Geruscha says, her voice bright as the stars. Lala accepts all Geruscha's bubbling superstitions, including this morning, when she insisted Lala swallow a rose hip for lifelong happiness.

Geruscha finishes the knot and offers Lala the bouquet.

"Wait," her bibio says before Geruscha can hand the bouquet to Lala.

Her bibio adds a few sprigs of wood betony and angelica, the purple and bluish flowers that so many thought would ward off witches.

With that sickle moon of a smile, her bibio gives the bouquet back.

The older women scatter mint and marjoram to be trod underfoot throughout the night. In with the baskets of flower petals are bits of bright paper, a gift of the manor lord.

Each time Lala turns her head, the wild roses release a little more of their perfume. It is thick and sweet in the air by the time she faces Alifair, who looks glow-eyed in a way that could be love or could be the other men getting drink into him for his nerves.

In his best shirt and tunic, he looks more man than boy. There are no oak leaves in his hair. Dust does not frost his forehead. Locks of his hair, still wet from the river, fall before his eyes.

They stand by the light of an applewood fire, another gift from the lord of the land. Josse, the declared priest (declared by Bibio Dorenia), calls them man and wife, and the cheer and stamp of the gathered brings the smell of mint into the air. It is so strong Lala feels bewitched by it.

"You look like the fairies my mother told me about in stories," Alifair whispers, so skillfully no one notices him speaking to her.

Her eyes flash to his.

It is the first time he has offered anything about his growing up, about the family he has lost, without her asking.

She holds this piece of him, freely given, close, like a locket tucked between her breasts. It makes a flush rise in her face.

She wonders if it is visible beneath the way Bibio Dorenia has rouged her cheeks and lips with her tincture of safflower.

The women help in tying red cloth to join their wrists, a symbol of Alifair becoming her husband.

She kisses him, brazen as a star moving from its place in the spheres. It is only in the soft touch of his hand under her chin, holding her in their kiss, that she realizes he has wanted this as much as she has. It is only at the taste of his mouth, the bite of the rosemary and mint he holds between his back teeth, that, for this moment, she forgets all that has come before.

She forgets there is any brighter color in the world than his mouth on hers.

Rosella

I found my father hunched over a pair of butterscotch-gold shoes, finishing a seam.

I wondered how long it would be before he made another pair of red ones.

My mother would pull out a jar of beads that looked like garnets tomorrow; she had always been the same kind of defiant as my abuela.

But my father was a little more careful. My mother would have been the one to let the forest cats and the dandelion fluff stay forever, and he would have been the one to remind her they had to let them go.

He would make shoes as blue as the five-petaled periwinkles spreading alongside our house every spring. And ones as ember bright as the marigolds drying along our windowsills. He would make pairs the same blue-touched green as wet sage.

But maybe not red, not until he knew for sure that the breath of this fall had left Briar Meadow.

I sat next to my father and threaded a needle I knew he couldn't see without his strongest reading glasses.

He didn't look up, so at first I wondered if he'd seen me.

Then he handed me a pair of gold drawstrings, giving me the task of guiding them through the casings.

The faint pleating at the corners of his eyes was better than a smile.

In my hands, my Oliva hands, these drawstrings felt like cords of light.

My parents probably worried when I left the house later that night. But they didn't stop me.

Piper and Sylvie were already at the reservoir, watching the sky (Aubrey and Graham were likely kissing behind some tree, but I couldn't see them). Emil's friends were debating something, as usual, gesturing with their hands as though shaping models from the air in front of them. But I didn't see him with them.

I walked carefully, nebula bursts of bruising crossing my ankles and heels. I folded my arms against the cold and watched the sky over the reservoir.

The glimmer looked like a layer of sheer, sequined fabric over the moon. It was fading as slowly as a glow bracelet dimming, but we always swore we could see it, the slight dulling of that light an hour at a time.

When the wind took a swirl of leaves, I couldn't help wondering if it was sweeping away the last pieces of my red shoes.

The heat of someone else next to me was my first indication that Emil was there.

I almost asked about his arm, the taped-on gauze showing at the edge of his sleeve.

Then I found his eyes in the dark.

Even with as little light as the moon and the glimmer gave us, something about him looked sharper, more awake. More resolved, like an old photo that had finished developing in solution.

I uncrossed my arms, my hand finding his.

A blue spark and a slight shock flitted between my fingers and his.

We both jumped back, laughing at the same time when we realized it was static. Not a trail of ion-dyed flame. Not some dangerous magic that lived in the space between his family's history and mine. Just our hands meeting in dry, charged air.

Probably, we would settle around each other.

Probably, but maybe not yet.

So for now, we stood next to each other, watching the sky.

Der Streuobstwiese, 1518

The scent of wild roses is still in their hair and clothes when Geruscha wakes them both.

Lala sits up, startled by wondering if a sergeant is at the door of this still-drying wattle and daub.

Then she smells the rosemary and lavender and remembers where they are. Der Streuobstwiese. The meadow orchard that is now their home.

She slides her palm onto Alifair's shirt. He turns over with a soft moan and sits up. The moon through the oiled paper of the window shows the place on his neck where Lala kissed him hard enough to leave a mark.

Geruscha crouches. "It is your cousin," she says, and then runs off at the order of an older woman.

"My what?" Lala asks, before snapping into recognition.

Alifair lights the single tallow candle. The light gilds his shoulders as he puts on his boots.

Emich and Roland are following Aldessa's orders, fetching whatever she asks. Josse prepares water for the blessing.

The birth is more groaning than screaming, her bibio seeming frustrated and put out by the length of the whole matter.

"This child clearly wishes to be born," she says weakly, "so why not get on with it?"

Henne rubs oil on her belly. Alifair offers to play his Blockflöte to distract her, a new one, crudely and quickly made from maple wood.

Bibio Dorenia summons Alifair close.

"If you play that blessed thing now," she whispers, "I will snap it in two."

Lala gives him a look back to tell him that, for his sake, he is best to leave this part to the women.

With that, he is off to gather water and wood alongside the other men.

Bibio Dorenia begins screaming, and Henne goes out to tell everyone to open chests, untie knots, shoot an arrow into the air, to bless the last moments of the birth.

Bibio Dorenia squeezes Lala's hand so hard Lala fears it will snap off.

And then, just when Lala thinks her fingers will break, he is there, her cousin, his face new and red as a berry. The first small sapling off their gathering of aspens.

He will grow up among wild pears and wood betony. He will know the many forms love takes.

Josse blesses him with the water, and then Henne does the same, with salt and a dot of honey on his forehead. Bibio Dorenia, Lala knows, will not let go of him until he is baptized, and maybe not even then. She will keep a piece of iron near her bed to protect them both.

"And what will you name him?" Lala asks, dabbing sweat from her bibio's forehead and hair.

Bibio Dorenia traces her finger over the baby's small hand. It is the first time Lala can remember seeing her bibio's wonder as plain and glimmering as a child's.

"I thought I would name him for your priest who cast us out of the city." She gives Lala a teasing smile.

Lala tries to call up the man's Christian name, and flushes with the shame of how she cannot.

Bibio Dorenia laughs.

"Emil," she says as she bends to her son's small hand and kisses it. "His name is Emil."

Strasbourg, 2018
Author's Note

Yesterday, I flipped through a British issue of *Harper's Bazaar* that had been left behind in a lobby and found a spread commemorating the seventieth anniversary of Moira Shearer dancing in the film *The Red Shoes*. The pages showed Misty Copeland, Isabella Boylston, and Tiler Peck wearing breathtaking gowns and brilliant red shoes, and talking about how vividly the film captures devotion to dance.

Sometimes your obsession with a story follows you even as you're following it.

Hans Christian Andersen's "The Red Shoes" has enthralled me for as long as it has horrified me. As a young dancer, the idea of becoming possessed with dancing both frightened and thrilled me. It stayed with me, the thought that a woman's body, and the color she puts on it, could be so powerful and so dangerous.

I knew the cautionary tale the original fairy story was meant to be, a warning to selfish and vain girls.

But I also recognized it as a warning that women—our bodies, our will, the colors we wear and the colors we are—have unimaginable power. Red shoes, I slowly understood, were not only a symbol of the forbidden. Red shoes signified the bright fire of being a girl, a woman, who is unafraid of her own body and what it wants.

If Andersen's "The Red Shoes" has ever entranced you the way it has me, you'll probably recognize the references to the original story and its typically stated provenance in the pages of this novel. But long before I wrote a word of this book, I wondered if Andersen might have drawn inspiration from a strange corner of Alsatian history, a fever that plagued the city of Strasbourg in 1518.

Five centuries later, I'm in Strasbourg, where the glint of the canals and the warmth in the air almost lets me imagine this city in the summer of 1518. Because at the moment, my obsession is red shoes not only as a fairy tale but as a point where fairy tale and history intersect. A Hans Christian Andersen story about a girl whose red shoes dance her to death, and the unbelievable but true account of a dancing plague that happened in this city five hundred years ago.

The dancing plague of 1518 is far from the only one in historical record. It's not even the only one that happened in Alsace. But it was one of the largest, affecting hundreds, and, thanks to both contemporaneous accounts and the invention of the printing press, one of the best documented. This novel is a work of fiction, drawing on the accounts of several dancing plagues in the region during the Middle Ages. But the occurrence in Strasbourg in 1518 always was, and remains, the central inspiration for the story, and the guiding framework for its historical reference points.

I came to Strasbourg for three reasons: to research the parts of the book I hadn't yet written, to fact-check the ones I had, and to learn what today's Strasbourgeois think of *la fièvre de la danse*.

The answer to the last one turns out to be *not much*. Several people I've met had no idea what I was talking about. Some looked on in fascination at the French articles I pulled up on my phone. Others thought I was talking about "dancing fever," the kind more fit for disco movies, and wondered if I was old enough to have seen any. (This was, I will admit, likely due to the shortcomings of my fledgling French.)

In the days I've been here, I have breathed in rhythm with this landscape. I have walked its forests. I have stood beneath what remains of Strasbourg's first astronomical clock. I have been shamed out of the same church that shuns Lala from its pews (as modern of a city as Strasbourg is, it has, as every city does, those who would rather not see a girl of color and her trans husband beneath its sacred stone arches). I have grown dizzy under the spire of its enormous cathedral, and I have climbed to the top of it, so high that I could see far-off mountains in one direction and distant forest in another.

And I have found the generous spirit of those who want to share the history of this place. Some have helped me access information about medieval Strasbourg that had previously seemed impossible to find. A few not only knew about *la fièvre de la danse*, but have dedicated significant scholarly energy to the varied sources that tell its story.

Before I changed where the first affected woman began to dance, from city lane to country road, I had to know what the historical record said about her (sadly, very little; even her name is recorded differently depending on the chronicler). Before I centralized the locations of the great dance Strasbourg officials put on to try to cure the fever, I had to learn about the Marktplatz and guildhalls they filled with dancers. Before I went after the recorded detail of the red shoes at Saverne, I had to find out how sure historians were that it was true.

The answer is both maddening and realistic in its ambiguity: We don't know. We may know that impossibly large hail fell on a particular day in a particular year, but we don't know how important the color red truly was in the story of *la fièvre de la danse*, just as we don't know for sure what caused the fever itself. The detail of the red shoes became part of historical record within the same century, so it's possible that the color red played as strong a role as chroniclers suggest. It's also possible that some mentions are exaggerated, fabricated, or drawn more from rumor than fact. And if red shoes were in fact given at Saverne, the reason why such a cure was put forth is lost to the last five centuries.

But I still followed that bright-dyed thread. I followed the path of historical records that note these red shoes. I still wondered if perhaps Hans Christian Andersen had, at the back of his mind, a little piece of history that mentions red shoes, and an Alsatian city gripped by dancing as though it was a plague.

Those possibilities remain the blazing heart of my story. And held within that same heart, at the center of this book, is my own heart as a queer Latina woman, with all that means today, and all it would have meant five hundred years ago.

As far as historical record states, Romani people were not blamed for the dancing plague. Neither were queer or trans Strasbourgeois, as far as we know. And as much as historical record states, there were no witchcraft trials associated with *la fièvre de la danse*. But none of these is whole-cloth invention. The persecution and expulsions of Romani communities referenced in the story, the barring of Romani people from whole cities and kingdoms, are tragically real. Brutal laws punished LGBTQ+ identity. And the historical period in which the dancing plague occurred saw thousands if not tens of thousands executed on charges of witchcraft.

History, no matter who writes it, cannot hide the blood on its hands.

But neither can it hide those who lived it.

People of color existed in medieval Europe. As did the LGBTQ+ community, though their conception of their own identities would likely have been far different from today. *Affrèrement*, the supposedly platonic pledge in which two men joined their lives, was well acknowledged in medieval France.

Girls like me were here five hundred years ago. So were boys like the one alongside me right now.

Much has changed in five hundred years. And so much has held. Both the good in the human heart, and the vicious insistence on finding someone to blame.

Tomorrow, I will fly back to a country that so often blames my communities for that which they do not like, and that so often hates us for what we are. I love it, my country, even as I sometimes fear it. I go back to it knowing a little more about women who walked this earth before me. I carry their history home with me, on my fingertips that have brushed cathedral stone, on the soles of my shoes that have walked these narrow, cobbled lanes, in my heart that is growing a spark into a story and that led me across an ocean to follow it.

Though no one knows exactly on which street *la fièvre de la danse* began, I'm writing this from a patch of cobbled stone likely not far from where that first woman started to dance, and not far from where the city's most powerful men would have decided Lala and Alifair's fate. I live in a very different time, in a very different world from the two of them.

But I'm walking this ground, a girl of color alongside the trans boy she loves.

So this is where I leave you, dear reader, five hundred years after *la fièvre de la danse,* five centuries after Lala and Alifair would have left these city gates for the last time. It's probably appropriate that we part here, among this city's living and its ghosts.

Thank you for following me deep into a fairy tale that has long frightened and enthralled me, and a moment in history that grabbed hold of me and wouldn't let me go. I leave you on these cobbled lanes, with my own pair of red shoes on my feet, and my heart full of gratitude for every one of you who came with me this far.

Acknowledgments

"So I have this idea for a 'Red Shoes' reimagining about the 1518 dancing plague." Those words were all it took for my agent, Taylor Martindale Kean, to be fearlessly behind this novel before I even wrote it.

I have Taylor and many others to thank for this book's existence. Here I'll name a few:

Full Circle Literary, for making a wonderful home for authors.

My editor, Kat Brzozowski, for believing in this book and for refining it in ways only she could.

Jean Feiwel, for having me as part of the Feiwel & Friends family.

Brittany Pearlman, for her tireless work and encouraging spirit.

Rich Deas, for his phenomenal art direction at MacKids; Liz Dresner, for giving this story an absolutely stunning cover; Cat Finnie and Mike Burroughs, for such gorgeous cover elements.

Everyone at Feiwel & Friends and Macmillan Children's Publishing Group: Jon Yaged, Kim Waymer, Allison Verost, Liz Szabla, Angus Killick, Molly Brouillette, Melinda Ackell, Kerianne Okie Steinberg, Teresa Ferraiolo, Kathryn Little, Julia Gardiner, Lauren Scobell, Ashley Woodfolk, Alexei Esikoff, Mariel Dawson, Romanie Rout, Mindy Rosenkrantz, Emily

Settle, Amanda Barillas, Morgan Dubin, Morgan Rath, Madison Furr, Mary Van Akin, and Jessica White; Katie Halata, Lucy Del Priore, Kristen Luby, Melissa Croce, and Cierra Bland of Macmillan Library; and the many more who turn stories into books and get them to readers.

Taryn Fagerness and the Taryn Fagerness Agency, for helping my stories travel the world.

The writers who helped me refine this book: Robin Talley, who lent me every medieval history reference she had on hand and talked me through how she does research. Tehlor Kay Mejia, who waded through an early draft. Michelle Ruiz Keil, who helped me focus in on this story's themes.

Thank you to Robin LaFevers for helping me work through the sexism, morality, and, ultimately, the transcendent feminism within the original story of "The Red Shoes."

Thank you to Jessica Reidy, for her editing and guidance with bringing out Lala's and Emil's Romanipen and strengthening their emotional journeys. Thank you to Parrish Turner, for helping me enrich Alifair's story and illuminate his life as a transgender young man in sixteenth-century Alsace.

There were many scholars and researchers whose work helped me understand the history and context of that summer in 1518: John Waller, who answered questions about the Holy Roman Empire. Kélina Gotman, whose scholarly work proved an invaluable source. Cecile Dupeux of the Musée de l'Œuvre Notre-Dame, who was generously willing to talk to me despite my very middling French and who helped me access the text of firsthand sources, and the Musée staff, who kindly helped me find my way. The City of Strasbourg, in particular those who run and maintain its spectacular museums; so much of this book would be inaccurate or absent without your help.

My mother, for keeping up my faith in happy endings, and my father, whose reaction when I told him about this book's topic was similar to William Shawn's reaction to John McPhee wanting to write about oranges.

My husband, for hunting down oak apples with me, for putting up with *la fièvre de la danse* I fell under while researching this book, and for being my traveling companion, and sometimes translator, in the museums, libraries, and landscapes of the Bas-Rhin and the Schwarzwald.

Readers, for seeing both the brutal truth and the hope held within fairy tales. Thank you.